DEADLY GAME

BY

R B CONROY

CCB Publishing
British Columbia, Canada

Deadly Game

Copyright ©2010 by R B Conroy
ISBN-13   978-1-926918-17-4
First Edition

Library and Archives Canada Cataloguing in Publication
Conroy, R B, 1944-
Deadly game / written by R B Conroy.
ISBN 978-1-926918-17-4
I. Title.
PS3603.O57D43 2010   813'.6   C2010-906050-4

Original cover art design by Jinger Heaston: www.jingraphix.org
Author photo by Julie DuBois: www.sunrisephoto.com

Publisher: CCB Publishing
             British Columbia, Canada
             www.ccbpublishing.com

Acknowledgements

Writing a novel takes time, patience, perseverance, and a little help along the way. A heartfelt thanks to all my friends and family for their support and encouragement. You have had a tremendous effect on my desire and motivation to write—your support means everything to me.

My sincere gratitude to my publisher Paul Rabinovitch, who is a bright light in the difficult world of book publishing. He is honest, precise, always on time and a joy to work with. Much appreciation to my talented friend, Jay Overmeyer, for his laser editing. The man can find a needle in a haystack. And last, but certainly not least, with love to my wife Cheryl for her unwavering devotion to my work. Without her guiding hand throughout this project, this book, as well as my other novels, would never have been written.

Dedication

In memory of Stan Fox—a caring person,
a dear friend and sorely missed.

Chapter 1

Branch closings, budget cuts, and staff reductions—it had been another long day for Alex Crane. Exhausted, he spun around to catch a glimpse of the setting sun through the ceiling high windows behind his desk. He soaked up the tranquil scene for a few moments and then looked below at the Soldiers' and Sailors' Monument in the center of downtown Indianapolis. He watched as a city worker in a green uniform stabbed at tiny pieces of litter and dropped them in a canvas bag—preparing "the circle"—as the locals liked to call it, for another day. An annoying beep from his direct phone line interrupted this relaxing end-of-day ritual. He reached back and lifted the receiver just in front of the fifth and final ring.

"Hello."

"Alex?"

"Yes, dear?"

"Did you forget?"

Alex rubbed his forehead. "Why…uh no. Dinner with the Everett's tonight." He breathed a quiet sigh of relief as he remembered the dinner date with their neighbors.

There was a pause on the other end of the line, a long, exasperating pause which screamed at Alex, *I know you didn't remember, but I'm not going to say anything.* "We're picking them up at eight; it is now seven thirty and you have a twenty-five minute commute."

"It's past rush hour; I-65 should be running pretty well. I should be home in fifteen or twenty."

"Hope so," Nicky sighed. "Hmmm….there it is again."

"There's what again?"

"That car."

"Come again?"

"That car with dark windows, it just drove by again for the third time."

"Lots of cars have tinted windows and there are a couple of houses for sale near us. Probably lookers."

"Guess so."

"Gotta run babe, bye."

"Bye."

Anxious to leave, Alex slid his last file into the center desk drawer, typed some morning instructions for his secretary and exited the room.

Dinner with the Everett's was important; arriving home late again would not be well received by his very punctual wife. When Nicky said eight, she meant eight. It was a big deal for her to be late and Alex knew it. He hoped traffic would be light on Interstate 65. Parts of the road had been under repair for over a year so bottlenecks, even at this time of day, were common.

"Hello Will." Alex smiled warmly at the security guard who was standing with his ample backside pushed against the open elevator door.

"How's the big boss man tonight?"

"Just fine, thank you."

"With all these late hours, your wife's gonna think you're havin' an affair or somethin'." The stout man's belly shook from laughter.

"She knows better, Will. Besides, with you here watching me, how could I get away with anything?"

"You're right; I probably would have to tell her. That Nicky is one sweet lady," the good humored sentinel snickered.

Will was part of the security agreement Alex negotiated with his bank's board two years ago after an extortion attempt against one of his senior officers. Still chuckling, the guard stepped out of the entryway, laying his hand against the inside of the door.

"I pushed the main floor Mr. Crane. At this time of day you probably gonna ride all twenty-two without stoppin'."

"Probably so, Will. See you tomorrow."

"Sure thing, boss."

The door closed; the elevator jerked to a start, shuddered briefly and then gained speed on its way to the bottom. As Will predicted, Alex reached ground level without stopping. He waited anxiously for the accordion-like door to rattle open. When he stepped out of the tiny cubicle and started to walk through the quiet corridor toward the parking garage, he saw someone hovering in the shadows near the elevators. The dark figure suddenly moved toward him.

Alex glanced at the security station–it was empty. The guard must have stepped out for a moment. Alone, and without security, Alex suddenly felt very vulnerable. Fists clenched, he prepared to confront the approaching figure. Alex didn't carry a weapon or mace; such things were unnecessary in the usually secure building in the center of downtown Indianapolis. A pointed object was protruding from the man's right hand as Alex braced for the coming assault. Suddenly, the night sensor on the security lights kicked-on, illuminating the lobby area. He instantly recognized the man with folded papers in his hand; he breathed a huge sigh of relief.

"Strom! I didn't expect you to be here at this time of the evening. You had me back on my heels for a minute there."

"Well…uh forgive me Alex, I didn't mean to alarm you. But Barnes told me you often worked late and I was at a United Way meeting at the Hyatt, so I thought I would run over and see if I could catch you before you left. When I entered the lobby and saw the elevator start from the top floor, I knew it must be you so I found a spot on that bench over there and waited for you to come down."

Strom Winslow was a big, imposing man with thick gray hair and bushy eyebrows. He had a large, round face and a broad flat nose. His wide mouth seemed to curve into a smile with the smallest of efforts. Strom was the owner of the largest beer distributor in the Indianapolis area and also on the board of the Midwest Consolidated Bank, making him, in effect, one of Alex's bosses.

Alex composed himself and wiped his sweaty hands dry with a handkerchief before vigorously shaking Strom's outstretched hand. "Well I'm glad you came over my friend, it's always good to see you." He looked intently at Strom, begging an explanation for his unsettling appearance.

Strom continued, "Alex, the reason I'm here is that I think there is something we need to talk about and I thought it important that I talk with you tonight, before the board meeting in the morning."

Alex knew what was coming. Still coping with the Fannie Mae and Freddie Mac banking crisis of a year earlier, their losses in the bond market the past year had been enormous. To complicate matters further, the individual mortgages that made up the huge bonds were still going sour at an alarming rate and needed to be replaced. It had reached the point where the Midwest loan originators could no longer make new mortgage loans to their customers fast enough to replace the bad ones inside the bonds. The situation was still worsening and the bottom line was suffering. So far, the board had stopped short of blaming Alex, choosing instead to assign responsibility to greedy bond managers and an over-stimulated mortgage market. But something told Alex that this assessment was about to change.

"I only have a few minutes, Strom. Nicky and I have a dinner date this evening and I'm already running late." Alex wanted Strom, prone to rambling, to get right to the subject.

"Sure, Alex, I'll keep it short. It seems that Barnes O'Brien, and some of the other board members, are concerned. Our bottom line is not what it should be and our stock holders have been getting kind of nervous lately. They're starting to ask questions. Blaming subprime mortgages and an overheated market isn't getting it anymore."

"Uh…huh, so now it's "let's blame the president". Is that what you're trying to say, Strom?" It was Alex's style to get right to the point. He knew more about the banking business than his collective board put together. He didn't like them making judgments on such matters, especially when such analysis disagreed with his.

Strom didn't appear to be surprised by Alex's sharp response. "Well, not entirely Alex. The board appreciates all you've done over the years for Midwest; it's just...uh they don't like your stance on the bailout money. They...."

Alex interrupted, "Are you saying they don't want me to pay back the twenty-five billion?"

"Chairman Barnes feels we could use the money; our losses are still growing."

"That's blood money, Strom! There are all kinds of strings attached to it. Besides, I can borrow the money cheaper on the open market right now. I thought I explained that to everyone at the last meeting. I thought everyone was on board with the payback."

"They were at first, but they feel you may be jumping the gun. Like I said, our bottom line doesn't look that good and we are continuing to get pressure from our stockholders. Barnes, and the board, feels we need to take another look at the situation."

Alex shook his head, "Barnes and the board or just Barnes?"

"Dunno."

Alex could feel himself becoming agitated. After a long day at the office and running late for dinner, this was the last thing he wanted to discuss. But Strom had always been a loyal ally in his fights with the board and he had made a special effort to come and warn him before the morning meeting.

He took a deep breath, "Listen Strom, I appreciate you coming over here this evening, I really do. But we can work out of this thing without Government help. We never should have accepted that bailout money—the Government so innocently calls TARP—in the first place. We need to pay it back!" Alex shook his head, "TARP—it sounds like something you throw over your boat or the back of your truck."

"Borrowing is tough now Alex, I'm not sure you can get the money we need on the open market and this money is already in the bank."

Alex grimaced, "The Government makes everything sound so easy with their bottomless pockets. And you're right Strom, borrowing is getting a little tougher, but we can still survive. I can still borrow the money. Our commercial paper is holding its own, and our mortgage delinquencies are better than they were a few months ago. We are on our way to working our way out of this crisis. We'll have a few bad quarters and then we'll be back on track. The worst thing we can do is stay in bed with the Feds. They will own us! They're already telling us what rates to charge, who we can and can't lend to and what programs we can offer. It won't be long before we're like every other Government agency—broke and totally dependent on Uncle Sam. It will basically be the end of Midwest Consolidated as we know it."

The old man looked directly at Alex without speaking. Then he shook his head and smiled, "I knew you'd say that, Alex." He laid his big hands on Alex's shoulders. "I'm with ya, pal. I don't want those clowns anywhere near our bank. I was just testing you a little. You can count on me."

"Thanks Strom, I'm going to need all the help I can get at that meeting tomorrow."

The big man's hands fell to his side. "I've been

lobbying some of the weaker board members to see it our way." He shot Alex a hard stare. "But if they hold tough, it could get ugly. You know Barnes, he never saw a Government program he didn't like and he can play plenty rough when he has to."

"I know Barnes can be a real pit bull at times, but that money has been nothing but a monkey on our back. We need to get rid of it so I can manage this bank the way I want to."

Alex smiled reassuringly. "We'll fight the good fight and let the chips fall where they may." He lifted his hand high and shared a hand clasp with his loyal friend. "See you in the morning Strom."

"Okay my friend, and don't forget your flack jacket. You're going to need it!" Strom hurried through the front door; Alex turned and resumed his walk to the parking garage. Once inside the garage, he picked up the pace and ran toward his car. The only sound in the expansive garage was his car keys and loose change jingling in his pocket.

He slid his keys from his front pocket and unlocked the car door. He dropped into the bucket seat, started the engine and hurried out of the nearly empty garage. Alex had spoken to Strom with great confidence, but deep inside he was worried. It had only been in the past few years that his salary and compensation package had risen to the level of other banking consortiums the size of Midwest. He and Nicky had recently built a new house in the exclusive Zionsville area near Indianapolis and were just starting to enjoy the good life. With so much at stake, he knew his decision to pay back the bailout money could put his job in jeopardy. Chairman Barnes had threatened as much. Alex rued the day he asked the successful attorney to be on his board—he had been a thorn in Alex's side ever since. Charming, when need be, and a natural politician, Barnes always seemed to find a way to sway the board's vote in his favor on big decisions. The previous fall he worked behind the scenes to convince the board to accept the bailout money over Alex's very strong objections. And once again, it appeared as though the board was leaning his way on the payback. Alex was also concerned that Barnes, now his Chairman, might use this crisis to move Midwest toward a possible change in management, one that he was certain would not include him. "We need to be more flexible and open-minded", he so often stated during heated debates with Alex. The bank's stock, which had been as high as twenty-nine, was now trading at just under three dollars a share. This would be a terrible time for the bank to buy Alex out; it would be a financial disaster for him and his family. He had to find a way to sway the board to come around to his way of thinking.

Chapter 2

"You were kind of preoccupied at dinner tonight, honey. You weren't yourself," Nicky said probing her husband.

"I was hoping no one would notice." Alex gave a quick honk to the Everett's as they stood by the front door of their house waving good-bye. He smiled meekly at his attractive wife. She looked stunning in her black pantsuit and silk blouse. A delicate diamond necklace hung around her bare neckline and was accentuated by two small diamond earrings. Her dark brown hair was pushed back on the sides revealing her classically beautiful face. And more importantly to Alex, beneath that lovely exterior, was an equally lovely person. Kind and caring, she was a dedicated wife and mother. Alex loved her more than anything in the world.

"Don't worry honey, you covered yourself well. I'm sure the Everett's didn't notice a thing."

"Hope not."

Nicky pressed her reluctant husband, "Did something happen at work today?"

"Well…uh yes it did. I didn't have time to tell you earlier; we were in such a rush to get to dinner."

"Yes, you were late again."

Alex gave Nicky an exasperated look. "Sorry, but Strom Winslow came over to see me just after I left the office this evening. He caught me in the lobby of the building."

"Hmmm….he probably wanted to talk to you about the bailout money."

Alex shook his head, "You're amazing."

Nicky gave him one of her cute little grins. "Things aren't that complicated, dear. Uncle Sam gave you twenty-five billion dollars and the board wants you to keep it. You want to give it back and they don't like it one little bit."

Alex slowed almost to a stop; his headlights reflected off the empty guard station at the entrance to their neighborhood. He accelerated through the tight opening and turned right.

"Want to go with me tomorrow? You could probably solve this problem in oh….ten minutes or less."

"No way! All those rich old men would scare me to death."

"Right now, they kind of scare me too," Alex smiled.

The turn signal flashed as he turned into their driveway. Alex slowed as they passed under the still rising garage door and came to a stop. He looked in his mirror, headlights flashed by. He watched a dark sedan drifted slowly past their house. Alex pressed the opener and the big door slowly rattled shut.

Nicky's hand fell tenderly on her husband's arm. "Alex, let's go north. Let's move full time to the lake. You don't need this job. With your background, you could get a good position in South Bend or Fort Wayne. You could work a few more years and then retire and enjoy the lake and those grandkids."

Alex grimaced, "I thought you liked it here. We've finally arrived. We live in a two million dollar house and you drive an Escalade, for cryin' out loud!"

"I know, it's fine here but we both love the lake, and we've been here twenty years. That's long enough."

Alex looked away toward his cluttered work bench at the back of the garage, "I….uh don't know. Most of my retirement is in the form of stock options. Right now, our stock is under three dollars a share. My retirement is in the tank right now. And I just can't see myself running away from this fight. It's just not the way I do things."

Nicky's hand slid off his arm. "I'm not sure your bank's stock is going to get much better for awhile. But it really doesn't matter. We have plenty of equity in this house. Even if we sell below market, we have other holdings. We could get by. Just think about it, dear, that's all I ask."

"I will honey, I promise." He leaned over and gave her a quick peck on the cheek.

"Hope you enjoyed that, it's about all you'll be getting for awhile," she joked as she slid out the passenger side.

Alex playfully sang '*I can't get no satisfaction,*' as he climbed out of his seat and hurried around the front of the car.

"You're hopeless," she laughed as they came together by the back door and fell into each other's arms, hugging and laughing.

Alex sang on, "*I try and I try and I try. I just can't get no…*"

A giggling Nicky interrupted, "Okay! Okay! How about a quick shower and then we'll take it from there?"

Alex pulled her very close and spoke softly, "How about a shower together?"

"We tried that when we first got married and never made it out of the bathroom."

"I know."

The two playful lovers quickly entered the house and hurried upstairs for their late night rendezvous.

Chapter 3

"Pardon me Mr. Crane; Mr. Winslow is here to see you."

"Okay Erica, send him in. And could you bring us both a cup of coffee? Strom likes his black."

"I'll be right back with the coffee sir."

Born and raised on a dairy farm in North Central Indiana, Alex Crane's father was a stern, but loving, taskmaster. He had taught Alex the value of hard work at a very young age. His mother was out-going and friendly and taught Alex the value of relationships and getting along with others. Strong and fleet of foot, Alex was also one of the best athletes to ever come out of North Central Indiana. He earned all-state honors in both basketball and football at Oak Hill High School. After graduating from high school, he went on to be a star athlete at Butler University in Indianapolis, majoring in finance and graduating with honors. After a stint in the Navy, he found a job as a loan officer at a tiny bank in Sweetser, Indiana. Using his father's work ethic and his mother's charm, he moved from Sweetser to a larger bank in Marion, Indiana and then eventually climbed the ladder to become the President of Midwest Consolidated Bank, one of the largest banking conglomerates in the country. Smart and aggressive, the former star athlete developed into a tough and determined in-fighter in the rough and tumble world of twenty-first century banking.

There was a quick knock, the office door swung open. "Come in Strom, have a seat." Alex waved at the empty leather chairs fronting his large oak desk.

"Thanks Alex. Got any coffee 'round this place?"

"Erica will be right in." Alex nervously shuffled some papers on his desk as the large man lumbered over and collapsed into the chair like a big bag of potatoes.

"Damn, if I gain any more weight you're gonna have to put some bigger chairs in here."

Alex chuckled, "You could always stand up."

Strom managed a guttural laugh.

The always efficient Erica hurried in and set a cup of coffee in front of Strom and on Alex's coaster, which featured a still somewhat discernible picture of Tony Hinkle, the legendary Butler basketball coach.

"What did you think of the meeting?" Alex asked.

"There was plenty of blood spilled in there today—I've never seen Barnes so determined. I thought you were very forceful and persuasive in your arguments, but I still think it's a toss-up."

"Do you think it would do any good for you to talk to any of the board members again privately, maybe Cliff and Lisa? With you and me and those two, we could swing this thing our way."

Strom's brows narrowed, he leaned forward and looked directly at Alex. "I feel confident about Cliff and I'm hoping Lisa is in our camp also. She's a little harder to read, but I'm optimistic. The others are all hopeless; they're caving into the pressure from Barnes and our stockholders." Strom shook his head.

Alex fidgeted with his watch, something he always did when he was anxious. He stood and began pacing back and forth behind his desk.

"They're not caving because of pressure from Barnes. Those selfish old fools are just looking out for themselves. They know that keeping the money could be bad for us in the long run, but they also know it might help prop up our stock in the short run. Then they can sell out to the first merger offer that comes along, take their millions and play golf every day at Crooked Stick."

"I think you're right, Alex, I just didn't want to say it. But they're not bad men—remember they're all in their late sixties or seventies and they're seeing their investments erode away because of this subprime fiasco. They want to try and salvage what they can and go on with their lives. What the hell Alex, they don't have ten or twenty years to wait for things to turn around."

Alex dropped into his chair, rubbed his face with both hands and glanced over at his faithful cohort. "You're right, Strom. I could fight this until I'm blue in the face but its not going to make a bit of difference. In the end, just like in almost every other business dealing I've had in my thirty years in banking, it all boils down to money. They're worried about their money."

"I agree, except for Barnes and I think it's political with him. He wants that Ambassadorship to Ireland in the worst way. He needs this bank to look as good as possible for the midterm elections and the Presidential, which is just a little more than two years from now. If Midwest has problems, it will reflect poorly on Barnes. He doesn't want that.

"You're right—he mentions that ambassadorship frequently. But no matter, Lisa is the key and she can be hard to figure. Let me think about this. The board says they want an answer by the twenty-third. That's more than a week from now so we have a little time."

Strom propped his elbows on the desk, his eyes clouded over; he reached over and gently squeezed Alex's forearm. "This decision you're making could have dire ramifications. Everything we've been doing for the past twenty years has suddenly been turned upside down. You have great courage, Alex; sometimes I wish you didn't have so much. If you don't soften your stance, I'm afraid this thing could take you and Nicky away from us. If that happened, I would be heart-broken."

Alex patted Strom's huge hand, "Thanks Strom, you're a good and loyal friend, but Barnes railroaded me once on this money situation. He's not going to do it again. And, I'm not going anywhere—at least not for awhile."

"Keep your head down and your left arm straight out there today," Strom ordered.

"Will do," Alex replied.

Strom struggled to lift his big torso from the deep chair and hurriedly left the office. Alex stood and watched as the door fell shut. He quickly cleared his desk and snapped the speaker phone back on. "Clear my schedule Erica, I'm out for the afternoon."

"I know Alex, it's Wednesday. Your schedule is already clear."

"Thanks Erica, you're the best. And by the way, what's the high for today?"

"The paper said 90 this morning."

"Hmmm....another hot August day. See you tomorrow."

"Bye."

Alex slipped into his private restroom, changed into his golfing clothes and quickly ducked out the side entrance of his office.

. . . .

Alex's pulse quickened as he struggled up the hill toward the first tee at Crooked Stick, an exclusive country club in Carmel, Indiana, a near north suburb of Indianapolis. He looked forward, with great anticipation, to his weekly game of golf. Nearing the tee, he knew that he was in for some serious ribbing from his golfing buddies for showing up late. The three of them were already pacing on the tee and taking occasional short, quick practice swings as they awaited his arrival. Jake, owner of a local computer store, was the first to see Alex approaching the tee.

"Evening, Alex," Jake joked, leaning down to tee up his ball.

"Good afternoon everyone. Sorry I'm late."

"Late? Hell, we're all tickled pink," Dr. Will Everett barked. "This is the first time we've teed off before 1:15 this month."

Alex grinned and shook his head, "That's BS Doc, and you know it."

"Okay fellas, take it easy on him. He probably had to run an errand for Nicky or something," attorney Joe shouted.

The other players howled in delight. This was the ultimate insult among golfers—to insinuate that an order from one's wife was the reason for being late.

"You're all hopeless," Alex shot back. "But at least your money's good, so let's hit it."

"Throw your bag on my cart, we're riding together," Jake ordered.

Alex dropped his bag on the back of his old friend's cart, tightened the strap, and carefully lifted his prize Taylor-made driver from the bag. He yanked off the head cover and tossed it in the little metal basket behind the seat.

"Twenty a hole and double for birds," Doc announced. The wager had been the same for years, but someone always had to announce it just to be sure they were all on the same page. And, as usual, all of the men nodded in the affirmative.

"Good," Doc replied, "Joe and I will play you two sandbaggers."

"Like taking candy from a baby," Alex joked as he and Jake enjoyed a high-five.

"Couldn't have said it better, pard," Jake laughed.

Doc leaned over and ripped some grass from the ground and gently tossed it in the air. "The wind's right at us and it's a two hundred yard carry over deep rough to that damned fairway," he complained.

"You're the one who always wants to play Crooked Stick, Doc, there are other courses around here, ya know," Jake barked.

Doc addressed the ball and prepared to hit his drive. The group suddenly fell quiet as he slowly lifted his club and swung hard at the ball. There was a sharp metallic clicking sound as his driver blasted into the ball.

"Great drive, Doc!" Joe shouted. "Looks like another big day for the good guys."

The other men hit their drives with all of them successfully reaching the distant fairway. They jumped aboard their carts and sped down the asphalt pathway toward their next shot.

"Tough day at the office?" Jake asked. Golf tees and loose change bounced in the cart's console as they drove along the bumpy path.

"Yeah, seems like they're all tough lately. The board doesn't want me to pay back the bailout money and I'm determined to do it."

Jake shook his head. "The Government is throwing money around like it grows on trees. That stimulus bill is huge. It's kind of scary, but I'll take it, I guess."

"Oh yeah?"

"Yeah, we've been chosen to help install broadband throughout Marion County. It's a huge project and should make us well for the year. It's not really needed. We're replacing an existing system, but what the hay? If they got an extra hundred mil to throw around, we'll take it."

"Nice deal. You install the unneeded broadband and take your money and run. It's different with the TARP money, it's more long term. They get inside your organization and soon they're running every facet of your business. It's not long before they're telling you when you can go to the bathroom."   The brakes squeaked as the cart jerked to a stop.

"You're up, short knocker," Jake joked.

"What are we Jake? About 130?"

Jake leaned over the side of the cart and looked down. "This sprinkler head right here says 136. Looks like a wedge."

Suddenly, Joe Patterson shouted from across the

fairway at the two men. "I was there yesterday Alex, it's about 165. Hit a seven!"

"Thanks Joe," he shouted back at his opponent. Alex watched as Joe and Doc, their shoulders shaking in laughter, continued toward their balls.

"Seven my foot," Alex said quietly. He reached into his bag and lifted out his pitching wedge. "If I hit a seven iron from here, I'll fly the green by thirty yards."

"Those ass-holes will do anything for twenty bucks," Jake laughed.

Alex made a couple of practice swings, took his final stance, held still over the ball, lifted the club up slowly and took a nice steady swing. A large divot flew into the air as the ball smacked off the clubface and shot toward the green, bouncing twice and then rolling down an incline to within ten feet of the hole.

"Great shot, partner!" Jake exclaimed.

He and Alex chuckled, they turned and watched Joe and Doc both hit their shots into a greenside bunker. The two shook their heads as they angrily slammed their clubs in their bags and jumped back in the cart.

Suddenly, the smile disappeared from Alex's face. "I worry about my grandkids Jake. With all this massive spending taking place in Washington, we're going to leave them with a bankrupt country that's supported by a bankrupt Government."

"Yeah, I know Alex. I worry about my grandkids a lot too."

They arrived at Jake's ball. "You're up, long knocker."

Jake hopped out of the cart, yanked his gap wedge from the bag. He took a couple quick swings and knocked the ball up on the green about twenty feet above the hole.

Jake paused and looked at Alex, "I'm glad you're making a stand at the bank Alex. We need more people to do that."

"Thanks Jake, but I've got a big problem."

"What's that?"

"We just had our monthly board meeting and they seem to be leaning toward keeping the bailout."

"Hmmm….that's not good," Jake lamented as he hopped in the cart. "Better update your resume."

Alex shook his head as he accelerated up a steep hill toward the green. Jake was a seasoned business man, and very savvy in the ways of the business world. He knew that if Alex didn't keep the money and the bank struggled, he would be the one the bank blamed. With the economy so weak, and with the passage of the massive health care legislation, there would be further strains on the business community. It could be years before the economy returned anywhere close to prior levels. Alex would be in a very precarious situation.

Alex yanked his putter from the bag and watched his opponents blast from the bunker—both shots landing well short of the pin.

"Was that bet forty a hole?" Jake shouted.

"We said twenty," Joe retorted.

Doc two putted for a bogey but the feisty Joe canned a thirty footer for a par.

"We need this one, Jake," Alex reminded.

Jake walked around the green gazing at his twenty-footer from every possible angle. The others waited patiently, leaning on their putters, observing the familiar dance. After what seemed an eternity, Jake approached his ball and made two excruciatingly slow practice swings and then finally addressed the ball. After another lengthy pause, with his head shooting back and forth from hole to ball innumerable times, he finally stroked the ball; it slid by and came to a halt some six inches past the hole. He strolled forward and made his tap in for a par.

"Damn!" Jake extorted as he bent over to remove his ball from the hole. "It's up to you, Alex. Knock it in."

"Looks like a double-breaker to me," Doc chided Alex as he quickly lined up his ten-footer.

As Alex lined up the putt, he thought of the changing situation at the bank and the heartfelt pleas from Nicky to cash it all in and move to their beloved lake home. It made him realize just how fleeting life's circumstances could be. Moving was a million miles from his mind just a few weeks ago. Alex took a deep breath and softly stroked the ball down the hill toward the hole and then threw his arms in the air in disgust.

"Thought you had it," Joe mused as he watched the ball dip down in the hole and then pop out. "Too bad, bucko."

Although disappointed by the near miss, Alex smiled warmly at his golfing comrades. He paused by his bag and looked carefully at each of them, something he almost never did. They were a motley crew. Doc looked rather distinguished with his small round glasses pushed to the end of his long, aquiline nose. He whistled quietly as he meticulously slid the cover over his shiny putter.

The pudgy Joe, his arms covered with thick black hair and the obligatory cigar sticking out from between his slightly stained teeth, grunted an insult at his opponents as he jammed the pin in the hole.

Finally, he glimpsed at his fast approaching friend, Jake. Tall and nattily dressed, his bright white Ben

Hogan hat accentuated his forest green outfit. Jake glanced toward his friend and smiled warmly.

A feeling of melancholy swept over Alex, he knew that he would see these old friends only occasionally if he and Nicky moved to the lake. Their relationships meant a lot to him. He knew that no matter what his score would be this day, that it would be a good day with his friends. "Nice putt, my friend," he said to Joe.

"Well…uh thanks Alex," a surprised Joe replied. "Back at ya, I thought yours was in too." Alex felt two affectionate pats to his shoulder from the usually combative Joe.

"All square!" Doc chanted. The carts groaned up the steep hill toward the second tee.

"Not for long!" Jake challenged.

Chapter 4

"Good morning!"

Startled, Alex wheeled around from a rear file cabinet to find the squatty Barnes O'Brien hovering over the front of the desk. As he had done so many times in the past, the brash man had taken the liberty of entering Alex's office without announcing himself to Erica.

"Oh…uh good morning, Barnes, good to see you." Alex quickly stood, the two men shook hands.

"Hope I didn't alarm you. The door was open so I just came in."

"Certainly not, Barnes, I was expecting you. And how are things at O'Brien and Son?"

"We're makin' money." A tight grin broke out on Barnes's round face. Originally from the Boston area, Barnes O'Brien had moved to Indianapolis some twenty years earlier at the urging of his wife, Dora, an Indiana native. He immediately opened a law firm, hanging his shingle on a fourth story office in the Market Tower Building. A gifted trial lawyer and brilliant before a jury, he soon acquired a reputation as a gritty, and sometimes ruthless, adversary in the courtroom. Aggressive and smart, he eventually acquired offices in several major cities in the Midwest, including Chicago, St. Louis and Detroit. And like most attorneys, he donated generously to the Democratic Party. Rumor had it that he was in line for an Ambassadorship to Ireland. Barnes's son, Shawn, joined the firm two years ago after graduating from Indiana University School of Law. A dedicated family man, Barnes was thrilled when his only son took a position in his firm. Plus, the addition of Shawn gave him more freedom to pursue his political ambitions.

"How's Shawn?" Alex liked Shawn, a congenial and friendly young man—he was nothing like his opportunistic father.

"That kid of mine really knows his stuff." Somewhat sensitive to the lackluster reputation his son was garnering in legal circles around town, Barnes never missed an opportunity to sing his son's praises. Alex understood and appreciated his commitment to his son.

"He seems like a bright young man."

"He kicked Bob Brown's ass the other day—got a huge settlement for our client in that asbestos case."

Alex smiled broadly, "Hmmm, that's good. Brown's a good lawyer. It's no easy task to win one from him."

Actually, Bob Brown had been a wonderful liability attorney at one time, but after years of hard drinking and a couple of debilitating strokes, he was a sad case—often treating the jury to lengthy nonsensical diatribes in the courtroom, while using his wadded, yellowish handkerchief to swipe away streams of drool falling from the corner of mouth. The well-known litigator had become, more or less, a joke around town.

"The kid's getting there, sure enough is," Barnes lifted his chin proudly.

Alex nodded.

After savoring his somewhat over zealous comments about his son for a moment, a sober look fell over Barnes face. "That's enough about the boy. We have much more serious matters on our plate."

"Yes, and...."

Barnes interrupted, "Alex, we've beat this TARP issue to death, so there's no need for us to rehash all of the tedious details. Why don't we just get to the bottom line?" He paused briefly and looked directly at Alex.

"Yes...yes I agree Barnes, I...."

Not wanting Alex to set the agenda, Barnes interrupted again. "This bond market is not going to rebound completely for some years. The traders are still cautious and yields on mortgage-backed bonds are still failing at an alarming rate. And when our commercial paper starts going bad, as we all know it will, we could be in serious trouble. I can...."

Slightly agitated, Alex took his turn at interrupting. "Our commercial portfolio is doing fine Barnes. Except for a few small ma and pa deals, we have no major problems with any of our commercial loans. We have underwritten these loans very conservatively over the years, only working with the best managed and most solvent businesses. I'm not saying we'll never take a loss, but overall, our commercial paper is some of the best in the business—no doubt about it."

The aggressive Barnes shot up from the desk. "That's bullshit, Alex! The way this market is heading we could experience tens of millions in commercial losses. This market is going to continue to deteriorate and local businesses will start to fail. Combine that with our bond problem and we're headed for a disaster. And whether you like it or not, we're going to need the deep pockets of the Federal Government to stay afloat. If you don't see that, you're fooling yourself!"

Red crept up Alex's face, "Not so, Barnes! We are in trouble today because we got too deep into the Freddie and Fannie stuff, and *you* led the charge, my friend. That's why we're in this mess!"

The hardened trial lawyer, used to emotional confrontations, smiled coolly at the fuming Alex. "The board proposed to get more aggressive in the secondary market last year and you said yes."

"Yes, I did, Barnes, but only after the board agreed not to do subprime mortgages. I was adamant about it, but somehow those requirements were changed while Nicky and I were vacationing in Europe."

He paused, his eyes fastened on Barnes. "I just discovered from our auditors that we have been doing subprime mortgages for over a year. I feel like I have been duped. Somehow, the motion to loosen our guidelines was never mentioned in the minutes of that emergency meeting."

"Are you accusing me of purposely omitting something from the minutes? That's a very serious accusation, Alex."

"You were Secretary of the Board at the time. Show me in those minutes where subprime mortgages are mentioned." Alex was now staring bullets at the hardened lawyer.

Undaunted, Barnes gritted his teeth and continued, "While you were off vacationing, First Financial Securities informed me that we were having problems delivering the required number of Freddie securities to our institutional investors. Our investors were screaming, so I asked Strom, Chairman at the time, to call the emergency meeting. During the meeting, I made a motion that we explore ways to acquire more mortgages so we could adequately fund the bonds. I left the decision on how to do this to the originating department of our subsidiaries. They made they call."

Alex leaned up and began pacing behind his desk. "You what? You left it up to the subsidiaries and their originators?"

"Why certainly, they're our front line for making loans."

"They work on commission, Barnes! They're going to make any loan they can get their hands on, subprime or whatever. Why in the hell wasn't I told of this decision?"

"It's in the minutes of that meeting."

"The hell it is! I've combed over and over those minutes. The only reference in the minutes is a comment by you that our investors were getting nervous and that we had to be more aggressive in our originating offices. That is a hell of a long way from allowing street originators to make policy!" Alex turned and glared at his paunchy adversary. Alex seldom swore, the use of profanity several times underscored his contempt for Barnes.

"Strom said he called you and brought you up to date."

"Barnes, you know that Strom knows very little about the secondary market. You had him call me because you knew he didn't understand the implications of the actions you had convinced him and the board to take. He doesn't know a subprime mortgage from a car loan."

Alex walked to the front of the desk, "But you do

Barnes, you know the difference. You also knew that when the green light was given to our originators, they would jump on the chance to make subprime loans. Their commissions would sky rocket. And you also knew that by wording the minutes they way you did, that I wouldn't know of it until literally hundreds of millions of bad mortgages had been made and then pooled together into bonds. It's a disgrace Barnes, and you know it. Your actions may have single-handedly put Midwest in financial jeopardy."

Barnes stoic exterior couldn't hide his anger. The right side of his broad mouth curled up in a smile, "You were informed of the meeting and I thought surely *you* would understand the nature of things—you are a very bright man. We had obligations to fill. Vito was getting nervous. We couldn't wait."

Eyes wide, Alex continued, "Now I see." He looked away from Barnes. "It's all clear now. It's so damn clear and I've been such a fool."

"What are you talking about?"

"It's all about the money. Once again, it's all about the stinking money! You and Vito and money! Isn't it convenient that you and Vito have offices in all seven of our major markets?"

Barnes stood straight and puffed his chest. "Hell, that's only good business Alex. We need to have local securities dealers, the regulations are different in every state, and you know that.

Alex's eyes narrowed. "I can't imagine the amount of money that you and Vito have made over the past several months. It has to be in the tens of millions."

"You knew First Financial was one of the dealers we used to package our loans. That was no secret," Barnes said cautiously.

"Yes I did, but I didn't know they had opened offices in all of our major cities. The St. Louis manager told me about it the other day; it didn't smell right then and it still doesn't."

Alex shook his head disgustedly. Alex took great pride on always staying on top of things; it was humiliating to admit how Barnes had manipulated him. "I feel like such a fool," he murmured.

"There's no law against First Financial opening an office in another city. And as far as that board meeting goes, the minutes clearly direct a change in policy. If those minutes were challenged, you wouldn't have a leg to stand on. There has been no wrong doing here, Alex."

"Oh I'm sure a man with your great legal mind has thought this through. I would be a fool to challenge the legalities of this situation, but what you have done is despicable. You have put this institution in financial jeopardy for your own selfish greed and political ambitions."

Barnes pushed his narrow rimmed glasses up on his nose and tilted his head. "We weren't the only one that was struggling, there were hundreds of other banking institutions that took that bailout money to help cover their losses."

"Maybe so, but I'm still running this bank and you and Vito have done enough damage. The money will be paid back if I have any say in it."

Seething, Barnes forced a smile and turned to leave. "The bottom line is that we can't afford to pay back that money. It won't happen because I have the votes to stop you. You better jump on board, Alex, before it's too late."

Alex was stunned by the 'I have the votes' comment.'
He stood motionless as Barnes exited the room, leaving
him alone with his thoughts. As usual, what had started
out as a way for Alex to force Barnes into a corner had
turned out to be a win for the crafty lawyer.

"He's done it again," he whispered. He pushed a line
on his desk phone.

"Erica."

"Yes?"

"Get me Strom on the phone, right away."

"Right away."

Alex pushed his chair back, leaned down and opened
his lower right desk drawer. He pulled out a file contain-
ing the minutes of the past several board meetings. He
hurriedly dropped it on his desk and began scanning the
contents.   A short time later, Erica's speed dial light
began flashing.

"Yes."

"Strom is on line three."

"Thank you." Alex impatiently jabbed the button.
"Hello, Strom."

"Yes, Alex, and to what do I owe the pleasure of this
call?"

"Barnes just left and we had a little heart to heart."

"And how is Barnes?"

"His usual charming self."

There was a nervous chuckle on the other end.

"Strom, I'll make this short and sweet. He just told
me that he definitely has the votes to approve keeping
the bailout money. Is that your understanding?" An
accomplished multi-tasker, Alex continued to read
through the minutes.

There was a pause, "Why no. It is true that old Seth Boardman and Jack Mathews are firmly on board with Barnes. But I really feel I have convinced Cliff Williams and Lisa Carl to vote our way."

"Hmmm…it must be Lisa." Alex lifted a copy of one of the minutes for a closer look. "Barnes wouldn't show his hand unless he was certain he had the votes."

"That's for sure. Maybe it is Lisa."

Alex flipped the page of the minutes. "I may be onto something here Strom. At the board meeting on June 15th, Lisa seconded Barnes motion to accept the money. It's not much, but it is an interesting second."

"That's for sure."

"Have you polled the members lately?"

"Yes, I polled them at the last meeting, and I…"

Alex interrupted, "Was that just before Barnes and I got there?"

"Yes….yes, I polled the members just before you and Barnes arrived. When I asked them, in confidence, who was leaning toward voting in favor, Seth and Jack raised their hands and Cliff shook his head in the negative. Lisa was texting someone on her cell phone and didn't reply. Now that I think back, she may not have even heard my question."

"Uh…huh, she didn't answer so you assumed she was not in favor."

"Yes exactly."

"Very interesting, it looks like Lisa may be the deciding vote and Barnes thinks she's in his camp."

"Probably so, he's good friends with her husband, Ed Carl. But on the other hand, she has voted your way many times. I think she has the hots for you."

"Looks like she might have the hots for Barnes right

now."

"Maybe so."

"I'll be in touch, Strom. In the meantime, please don't talk to anyone about this. I think we may have a problem here."

"Okay, you know where to reach me."

Chapter 5

The vibrating sensation ran down his leg, he slid his BlackBerry from its holster. He turned onto the long, winding drive that led to his lavish, three-story home in the exclusive Carmel, Indiana area. He looked at the name on the illuminated screen and answered, "It's kinda late Barnes, this better be good."

"Sorry about that, Vito, but I need to talk to you."

"Sounds important, what's up?" Vito pulled his sleek BMW into his four car garage, right next to his vintage 1962 red Corvette. Vito Taglioni was a muscular man in his mid-forties who worked out daily at a local gym. His black curly hair dangled over his forehead and a long scar drifted down the side of his broad, pocked face to the end of his thin dark mustache. He attributed the scar to a gang fight on the mean streets of Chicago as a youth, but others in the know put the blame for the scar squarely on the shoulders of his third wife. In a jealous rage, she yanked a butcher knife from a kitchen drawer and slashed her unfaithful husband across the face. Whatever the cause, it gave the ruggedly handsome man a somewhat fearsome appearance.

Vito had moved to Indianapolis fifteen years earlier after a less than stellar career in the bond markets in

Chicago. Fired from his position as bond manager at Manufacturer's Hanover for double dipping on commissions, he had come to Indianapolis looking for a new beginning. He borrowed some money from an old friend and opened a small investment firm, naming it First Financial Securities. Using his charm and good looks, he was able to make the right connections in Indianapolis and his firm began to flourish. One of those connections was Barnes O'Neill. With the help of Barnes and others, he was now one of the biggest securities dealers in the Midwest.

Barnes cleared his throat, "I just had dinner at the club."

"Good for you. I just played poker for three hours at the club. Congratulations!"

"Cut the bull, Vito—this is important."

"Okay, okay what is it?"

"Anybody around?"

"No, I'm sitting alone in my garage and the opener light just went off, so it's darker than hell in here. I might kill myself just getting to the back door."

"Listen up. I met with Alex this afternoon and he's been snooping around. He's starting to figure out how we slipped this subprime deal past him."

"Hmmm....I'm surprised a man as smart as Alex hadn't figured it out sooner."

"Like I told you when we planned this, Vito, Alex only receives an annual review of the branches. He gets all the financials on a daily basis, but there was no way for him to detect, by looking at the numbers, what kind of mortgages were being made. He only knew that business was good and Midwest had decided to be more aggressive. He had no reason to be suspicious."

Vito coughed nervously, "What about the policy changes you made when he was of town? Is he on to that?"

"Yes, he grilled me about it this afternoon. He's madder than hell."

Vito sat up in his seat. "Now listen to me, Barnes. You said this was an iron clad deal. You said you had it all figured out—I don't like what I'm hearin'!"

"It's under control, Vito—just calm down! We've just got to go over a few things, that's all."

"Like what?"

"Be sure all your filings with the Securities and Exchange Commission for branch approvals are complete and up-to-date. Contact all your branch managers and tell them to avoid calls from Alex's office or his accounting firm. He might try to dig deeper. If you notice anything out of the ordinary, call me right away."

Vito squirmed, "You're makin' me nervous, Barnes, and I want to know what's up."

Vito's interior light came on, illuminating the garage as he crawled out of his car and made his way to the back door in the darkened garage. The hood felt cool on his hands as he felt his way around the vintage Corvette, eventually finding the doorknob to the back door. He stepped inside, his phone pushed to his ear.

"Just do what I say Vito."

"Okay, okay I'll have Claudia check all of our branch filings in the morning and I'll call the managers."

"Don't forget."

"I won't."

There was a click on the other end of the line. Vito stood staring at his cell phone for a moment and then walked nervously across his large kitchen into the family room. He glanced down the hall toward the master suite. His wife always left their bedroom door ajar. The room was dark. She fell asleep quickly after reading each evening; he could hear gentle snoring sounds coming from the room. He hurried back to the kitchen; perspiration was beading up on his forehead. He removed a handkerchief from his pant pocket and dabbed his brow dry. He pushed the speed dial on his BlackBerry and began pacing in front of the large island in the middle of the kitchen.

"Vito?"

"Yeah."

"Everything okay? It's eleven-thirty."

"I know, I know. Did I wake you?"

"No, you're lucky. I was up watching a rerun of a Pacer's games from last season and they're getting their butts kicked."

"You and those Pacers."

"Just a minute."

Vito could hear the click of a light switch, some rustling around and then the snap of a cigarette lighter. There was a pause and then a deep exhale. "Okay, I'm ready, go ahead."

"That's a bad habit, you need to quit."

"Mind your own business."

Vito laughed nervously, "Barnes just called and said Alex may be turning up the heat. Barnes says he's not happy."

"About what?"

"The subprime mortgages Midwest has been originating as a result of that meeting last summer."

"Oh that meeting when Alex was in Europe. I thought Alex was brought up to speed about that."

"I guess not."

"Hmm…I'll bet he is mad."

"Alex is one tenacious son-of-a-bitch. He's not going to take this lying down."

"What can I do about it, Vito?"

Vito opened a cabinet door and pulled out a bottle of Seagram's. He splashed the brownish liquid into a small glass and dumped it in his mouth.

"Well…un nothing I guess, I just thought you might know something."

"Well I don't. You're on your own on this one, buddy."

"Do me a favor will ya?"

"I'll try."

"Let me know if you hear anything."

"Oh no!" There was a deep exhale, the ashtray rattled.

"What's the matter?" Vito asked.

"The Pacers lost by fifteen."

"You're hopeless,"

"Goodnight Vito."

"Goodnight."

Chapter 6

Louie slapped frantically at the screaming radio. He cursed the loud, obnoxious sound that he heard every morning, but it was the only sound that was loud enough to wake him. It was the third slapping and the one that usually got him going. He peeked over the covers and looked around the room, as if somebody might be watching him. Then he yanked his blankets back, exposing his rotund torso to the empty room. Rolling to the edge of the bed, he ran his hands through the thinning gray strands on his balding skull, yawned loudly and pushed his arms to the ceiling.

After what seemed an eternity of just sitting and staring into space, he stumbled into the bathroom, passing gas along the way. Once inside the small room, he turned the water on to just the right temperature, slipped off his baggy pajamas, tossed them onto the nearby hamper and stepped into the shower. A guttural rendition of the old favorite "When Irish Eyes Are Smiling," soon filled the air. Italian by descent, his mom was part Irish and taught him the song as a boy and he loved it. No other song ever came to his mind in the shower.

After several minutes of butchering his mom's

favorite tune, he quickly punched the shower off, pushed the plastic shower curtain back and groped frantically for any sign of a towel on the nearby rack. Coming up empty, his arms collapsed around his shivering, naked body as he hurried over and snatched the only remaining bath towel from the linen closet. He wiped himself dry, draped the towel around his paunchy midsection and prepared to shave.

He grimaced as he looked at himself in the medicine cabinet mirror and pushed his thinning gray hair off his forehead. He snatched his old Norelco from its corroded charger on the counter and began pushing it around his cherub face, missing several spots in the poorly lighted room. He would shave off the little colonies of hair he missed later in his office with an old razor he kept in his desk just for that very reason.

After shaving, he slipped into his boxer shorts, lifted a crinkled blue dress shirt from the small bedroom closet, pushed up the collar, grabbed the obligatory red tie from the tie rack, created a crooked half Windsor knot and pulled it tight. Next, he lifted yesterday's gray slacks from a nearby door knob and pulled them on. He slipped on a pair of stretch socks and his brown loafers and hurried to the kitchen.

Outside, he could hear the rush hour traffic rumbling past. He shot a glance at his watch. It was a little after 7:30 and with a twenty minute commute to work, he had little time to spare. This usually meant a strawberry pop tart, his breakfast of choice each day. Louie, a creature of habit, liked to keep things as simple as possible.

A moment later, with pop tart in hand, he rushed to his carport and jumped into his 1998 red Ford pick-up.

After backing carefully onto the always busy West Armitage Street, he headed east toward the nearby Kennedy Expressway. The old Ford jerked as he pressed hard on the accelerator. His destination was Midwest Consolidated Bank, on the corner of Harlem and West Fullerton in the Elmwood Park district on Chicago's West Side. Only a ten minute drive in low traffic, in the morning rush hour it became twenty or twenty-five.

This had been Louis "Louie" Campano's daily ritual for over forty years. He took over Campano Federal Savings Bank back in 1979 from his retiring father. His father had opened the office in 1929 with a five hundred dollar loan from a friend. Through hard work and diligence, Louie's father had built up the assets to more than two hundred million when he turned it over to his son. Louie, very popular in the predominantly Italian community, had increased the size of the savings bank to nearly five hundred million dollars when his board decided in 2000, much to his objection, to sell the bank to Midwest Consolidated. Still single, the job at the bank was Louie's life—a life that had become much more difficult since the merger with Midwest.

The large metal sign ahead read 'Reserved for President," as the dusty truck jerked to a stop. Louie looked in the rear view mirror, removed his glasses and pawed away some pesky eye-puck before exiting his modest vehicle. He then hurried into the back door of the bank and ducked down the back hall.

The main lobby of the bank was a beehive of activity, with a small army of tellers gabbing with one another as they carefully counted their cash allotments for the day. In the many offices near the teller area, loan officers were busy reviewing files and discussing complicated issues with the secretaries before the doors opened at eight o'clock.

Louie glanced at the busy scene and then ducked into his dimly lit office near the back door. His secretary, Ava, always turned on the light on his desk when she arrived at 7:00 sharp. Later, she would return and lay hand-written notes on his desk concerning his day's activities. The worn leather chair creaked as Louie's large frame fell in it. He reached forward for the notes and began reading them. Soon a scowl appeared on his face. "Bad day," he murmured to himself, as the always dependable Ava, stepped in his office.

"Good morning, Mr. Campano."

"What's good about it?" the usually congenial president groused.

"I know, Louie—Jack Montrose." A trusted confidant for over thirty years, Ava could get away with calling her boss Louie after her initial salutation in the morning. Louie didn't mind—she was a great employee and a true friend and she never addressed him that way outside his office.

"More file maintenance I guess."

Ava shook her head.

Jack Montrose, an old friend of Barnes, had taken over as the main bank's controller a few months after the merger was completed in 2000. Louie had lobbied to keep his local controller, Paul Rizzo, a trusted associate for over forty years, as his controller in Elmwood Park. But for some unknown reason, Rizzo suddenly resigned two weeks later. It was one of the first indicators for Louie about the nature of bank take-overs. All the promises of 'working together' and 'mutual respect' were soon forgotten as Midwest began to sink its talons deeper into the bowels of his beloved bank.

Now, it was ten years later, and Louie had very little say about the day to day operations of his bank, except in the area of employee relations and small personal loans. It was demoralizing and frustrating and he hated it. And to make matters worse, Jack Montrose had been on a campaign of "routine" file maintenance on all of his accounts for the past several weeks.

Not well schooled in accounting principals, Louie had very little idea what was going on. He and his father had taken on the role of being mainly public relations people—the bank's faces in the city. Neither of them knew much about the nuts and bolts part of the business; they had always left that up to their controller, Rizzo. Recently, over lunch, Rizzo had warned Louie that the file maintenance Montrose was doing seemed out of the ordinary to him, but Louie thought it was just sour grapes on the part of Rizzo. Like so many times before, today's visit by Montrose was unexpected. And, as the note indicated, had not been announced to Louie and his staff until after the close of business the day before.

"I guess there is a lot of new accounting stuff coming down the pike these days," Ava reassured.

"Seems like it," Louie replied. "Wonder why we always get Montrose?" The other managers tell me that they rarely see Jack."

Ava smiled at her perplexed boss, "Don't know, Louie—maybe he just likes us."

"Maybe so." Louie shuffled through Ava's notes. "Well….uh who's first on my appointment schedule today?"

"The United Way Chairman is coming in at 8:30. He

wants us to commit a little more per employee this year, says they're having trouble meeting their goal."

"Another important meeting," Louie murmured.

"What was that?"

"Oh nothing. What else is on the agenda?"

"HR wants to meet with you at 10. The tellers are complaining about the increase in their health insurance premium. They say it's more than their raise."

Louie shook his head, "Tell them to call Indy. Is that it?"

"You have a two o'clock with Butch Ferinni, says he wants to put a pool in his backyard. Says he tired of 'sweating his ass off all summer.'"

"Hope they don't find any bodies when the dig up his backyard."

"Louie!" Ava scolded. "Butch loves you!"

"I know," Louie smiled warmly at his old friend. "Thanks, Ava."

"For what, Louie?"

"Oh, just about everything I guess—setting my schedule each day, opening my office in the morning, trying to put a nice spin on everything. You're a wonderful friend; you make my life here tolerable."

The face of the modest secretary turned instantly red.

"Why don't you take Friday off? You've been putting in a lot of hours lately."

A huge smile exploded on Ava's face. She clasped her hands together, her thin body wiggled in excitement. "Oh thank you! My sister is coming in from Milwaukee, that would be perfect! What a nice surprise, thank you so much Louie!"

"Thank *you*, Ava."

As an excited Ava exited the room, Louie's office line lit up. "Yes, what is it?"

"Mr. Montrose just arrived and would like to go over a few things with you in the board room."

"Be right there."

Chapter 7

"Strom?"

"Yes."

"It's Alex."

"Hi Alex."

"Can you meet me on the circle for lunch in a few?"

"Yeah, sure Alex. Usual place?"

"Yeah."

"I'll be there."

"Thanks."

Alex hit Erica's line.

"Yes Mr. Crane?"

"Would you call Blue and Gates and see if Ted can meet Strom and me for lunch at the Circle Deli?"

"Certainly, sir."

. . . .

Alex walked briskly down Meridian Street toward the thirty story Soldiers' and Sailors' Monument. He turned left off Meridian onto the circle drive that bordered the monument and headed for his impromptu luncheon with Strom and his bank's attorney, Ted Blue.

Several passers-by nodded as he made his way down

the busy sidewalk to the Circle Deli. Alex loved Indianapolis; it was big enough to provide many of the cultural advantages so often identified with the big cities while still maintaining its small town charm. As he maneuvered along the wide sidewalk, he felt a tap on his shoulder.

"Hey, big guy."

Alex turned to see his stylishly dressed attorney, Ted Blue, who was just a step behind.

"Hi, Ted. Did Erica get ahold of you?"

"Yeah, I was here at the Title Company finishing up a mortgage closing, so it worked out great. But there is only one thing."

"What's that?"

"The meeting is over lunch so I can't bill you."

"When did that ever stop you?" Alex grinned at his old high school friend. Ted was a full partner in the largest and most successful law firm in Indianapolis. Graduating with honors from the IU School of Law, he was one of the most sought after legal minds in town. Alex felt fortunate to have him as his lead counsel at Midwest. A man of integrity, he trusted his old friend completely and loved his aggressive, take no prisoners, style.

The two men walked a short distance and then left the busy sidewalk and entered the Circle Deli. The restaurant's friendly greeter, Monica, smiled warmly.

"Hello, Mr. Crane."

"Good morning Monica, and how are you?"

"Just fine. Thank you, Mr. Crane. Mr. Winslow is already here and he's sitting at your favorite table."

"Oh great."

"Follow me."

"Lead the way."

The men fell in behind Monica as she wove her way through the crowded restaurant. Several of the businessmen and women in the room nodded at the well known men. As they approached the table, Strom was busy reading the menu and didn't notice them.

"Hello Strom."

Strom looked up from the menu, "Oh, hi, Alex." The two shared a vigorous handshake. The ritual duplicated itself with Ted.

"You're early, Strom. You're getting fast in your old age," Ted quipped.

"Old age! Want to arm wrestle smart-ass?" Strom retorted. A broad grin broke out on his wrinkled face.

"I wouldn't do it, Ted. You were a punter in high school. Strom was an all-state tackle."

"I'll pass." Ted smiled at a grinning Strom.

Alex lifted his menu. "What's good today?"

"They have ham and Swiss with a cup of minestrone on special," Strom offered.

"Sounds good to me," Alex replied.

"Me too," Ted said as both men tossed their menus on the table.

Just seconds later, the smiling waitress approached them. "Oh boy, my three favorite dirty old men are here today," she joked as she banged three sweaty glasses of water on the table.

"Hey! We're not *all* old, Libby!" a smiling Alex exclaimed.

"You're old to me, Mr. Crane." she retorted.

The powerful men laughed out loud; they loved being brought down to size and the feisty Libby never disappointed.

"What'll it be, fellas? I ain't got all day!" The cheeky waitress kept the needle in.

"We'll have three of those ham and Swiss specials," Alex said. "And give me the check please."

"Will do, Mr. Crane. Just water to drink?"

"I'll have an ice tea," Ted said.

"Thank you, fellas." The waitress finished her notes and hurried off.

Alex's expression changed quickly after the fun exchange with Libby. He looked directly at the other men. "I'm a little pressed for time so I'll get right to the point. Gentlemen, I think we may have a problem brewing at Midwest."

Their smiles faded, the men listened intently.

"You're both aware that I want to pay back the TARP money to the Feds in its entirety."

The men nodded.

"Strom and I have already had a few lengthy conversations about this recently so let me bring you up to speed Ted. If you have any questions or comments, please feel free to jump in at any time."

Ted nodded again.

"I don't think it's a secret to anyone that I was opposed to accepting these funds last fall."

"Yes, that was kind of Barnes's baby," Strom offered.

"It certainly was Strom, and Barnes doesn't want to pay the money back. He seems hell bent on stopping me; he's more determined than I've ever seen him. I'm not sure what's driving him."

"He has a dog in this fight for certain, Alex. He owns quite a bit of Midwest stock as I'm sure all of the board members do. I don't agree with Barnes, but maybe he sees his investment being threatened and he thinks that keeping the bailout money will help. It could be as simple as that," Ted said matter-of-factly.

Alex scribbled nervously on his napkin. "You're right, Ted. Barnes and several of the board members are getting older and their retirements are an issue, but I don't think Barnes is that worried about his Midwest stock. He has huge holdings and is a very wealthy man. It's more than that with him—he's on a mission. I've never seen him so determined. And as of late, I have discovered some things that concern me."

"Such as?" Ted queried.

"Well, you know our friend, Vito Taglioni, over at First Financial Services?"

"Yes, yes, I know, Vito. Who doesn't?"

"Well, First Financial handles all our big bond deals here in Indy. The other day, I discovered, quite inadvertently, that Vito has opened satellite offices for First Financial in all the cities where Midwest has offices."

Ted's eyebrows rose slightly. "Well, he certainly has the right to open an office wherever he likes as long as he gets all the red tape right."

Alex felt exasperated. "That's not all, Ted. Barnes has opened offices in all the same cities and he and Vito have been making a fortune for the past year peddling those bonds. Something smells fishy and I don't like it."

"I'm sorry, Alex. But Vito has every right to open a storefront in any city he chooses," Ted replied.

Agitated, Alex scribbled more aggressively. "Isn't that a conflict of interest or something with Barnes?"

"Not unless he handles your account himself—which I'm certain that he doesn't. Otherwise, the man has a right to make a living."

"A very good living!" Alex squirmed in his seat.

"No law against that."

Alex pushed on. "Remember when Nicky and I went to Europe last year?"

"Yes."

"Well, in my absence Barnes asked Strom to call an emergency meeting of the board."

Ted replied, "As a board member, Barnes has every right to do that, even though it seems inappropriate with you out of town. Did he document the meeting so you would know what took place?"

Alex grimaced. "He documented it alright, Ted. Barnes is no dummy. But what he did in essence, without making it appear so in the minutes, was open the flood gates on subprime mortgages, something he knew I was vehemently against. The result was that he and Vito got rich and now Midwest has millions of dollars worth of bonds going belly-up every day."

Ted leaned back against the shiny cushion on the booth. "Did the board approve the action?"

"Yes....yes they did; but they didn't know his objective. He did a masterful job of masking his intentions. He merely made a motion to leave the decision on how to acquire more mortgages up to the local managers in each town and the board approved."

"And?"

"And....those managers and their originators are on commission, Ted! You can't leave underwriting decisions up to them! They love subprime—any warm body can qualify for a subprime mortgage. The board gave them the green light and they started making mortgages to anyone who walked in the door! Barnes knew it would be a disaster for the bank, but he also knew that he and

Vito could make a fortune in the meantime. And all this happened while I was out of town." Alex shook his head in disbelief.

"Inappropriate maybe, but certainly not against regulations. Ignorance is no excuse under the law. Your board should have known better than to approve such a potentially problematic policy, especially with you not at the meeting."

Strom's face flushed with embarrassment. He felt the sting of the attorney's insinuations.

The usually measured Alex leaned forward and rested his elbows on the table top. "Damn it, Ted! Something stinks here and you know it! With Barnes's political ambitions and close connection to the current administration in Washington, who knows what he's up to? Midwest did over six hundred million in mortgages out of our Chicago branch alone last year—a billion six total in all offices. And for some reason our controller, Jack Montrose, has been running up to the Chicago branch every other week lately. Something is not right here, Ted." Slightly embarrassed by his uncharacteristic outburst, Alex glanced around the room.

"Hmmm…..Montrose. Wasn't he Barnes's hand-picked man?" Ted queried.

"Yes, Barnes highly recommended him when Stackhouse retired—said he was the smartest CPA in town. We interviewed several people and Jack held up well during the interviews, so with Barnes's blessing, I hired him."

Ted leaned forward, rubbing his hands together. "Why does Montrose say he is going to Chicago?"

"He says Louie Compano and his father made a mess of things. He claims the files are a disaster and many of the entries on the computer are incomplete and coded improperly and they are requiring a ton of file maintenance."

"How big is Jack's staff?"

"He has ten accountants under him."

"But he always goes himself?"

Alex's eyes narrowed, "Yes. He said that it's such a mess up there that he has to go personally. He doesn't feel he could trust it to one of the younger accountants."

"Aren't they all CPA's?"

Alex nodded.

"Hmmm…well, it's probably fine, Alex, but I would keep an eye on that Chicago situation. You might want to poke around a little bit—maybe talk to Compano and see what he knows. But we all know Louie is not an organized person. His shop *could* be in a mess. It's probably just what Montrose suggests."

Alex was taken aback by his good friend's lukewarm support of his suspicions. He sat up, his face flushed red. "Damn it, Ted! You're on retainer here, but you act like some attorney I just bumped into in the men's room a few minutes ago. Something smells to high heaven here. I don't give a hoot what the regulations say! And when I tell my over-paid, hotshot attorney about it, I shouldn't have to sit here and endure endless references on how everything appears to be normal. I'm starting to wonder what I'm paying you for!"

Eyes wide, Ted twisted nervously in his seat. "Sorry Alex, I'm just trying to look at both sides." He paused as if in deep thought and then continued, "Greed can be an ugly thing, Alex, and you're right, these boys have been surprisingly active the past couple of years. I am going to request the necessary documentation on all of Vito's branch applications just to be sure they're up to snuff. Those approvals happened awfully fast. At the same time, I'll request random photo copies of several of their mortgage files to be sure they are following the guidelines set by the local managers. Something tells me that these guidelines have never been put into writing. Also, I want a full accounting of all transactions by both First Financial and O'Brien and Son that involved Midwest, including the complete money trail. I want to know who got paid for doing what and when. In the meantime, if you don't mind, I will ask your outside auditors, Dulin and Dulin, to do an audit on Louie's office. Particularly in regard to all the file maintenance Montrose has been doing lately. If we find a rat in the woodshed, I'll move in at a moment's notice; I promise you that."

Alex leaned back, sighed and shook his head. "It's about time you came to life, I was beginning to wonder. Maybe I'll leave you on retainer for a little while after all."

Ted shook his head, "On retainer for a while my ass! I'm the best attorney in town and you know it."

A calmer Alex grinned.

The ice rattled as Strom lifted his water glass toward the center of the table. "We have some real challenges in front of us, fellas. Let's all work together and get to the bottom of this thing."

The men touched glasses and smiled warmly at one another. The conversation soon shifted to more personal topics. All sense of divisiveness quickly vaporized as the close friends reminisced about silly pranks on the golf course and other special times together.

"Grubs up!" The smell of minestrone filled the air as the brusque waitress arrived and banged the long plates on the table. "Enjoy fellas, and please don't slobber on yourselves." Libby grinned as the men roared their approval.

Chapter 8

The Boston College fight song resonated through the sunlit lounge at Meridian Hills Country Club.

"Another Scotch, Willie."

"Sure thing. Mr. O'Brien, if you promise to turn that thing off. I'm a Notre Dame fan."

Barnes coughed up a hoarse laugh as he lifted his cell phone from his vest pocket, and hurriedly scanned the screen.

"Yes Vito, what is it?'

The familiar voice blared from the phone. "What the hell is Alex up to? He's got me real nervous all of a sudden."

"What are you talking about?"

"Blue and Gates sent me a memo today. Said they want copies of all my branch applications for the past three years. They also asked for copies of all my transactions with Midwest Consolidated over the same period. This stuff is making me real nervous Barnes."

Barnes yanked the soggy cigar from between his teeth and snuffed it out in a nearby ashtray. "He can't request information on your branches—he's not your attorney. He works for Midwest." Barnes coughed and waved the drifting cigar smoke away from his face.

"You're wrong about that one. I called my attorney, Shawn O'Brien. Know him? He says that according to new regulations passed by congress last May and I quote, 'Any and all agencies providing for profit services to a federally chartered lending institution shall provide to such institution, upon request, any and all information pertaining to said transactions. Failure to do so will be punishable by blah, blah, blah,"

"Hmmm…..they're always changing those damned regulations." Barnes downed the Scotch and banged it on the bar.

"What if he finds out about….?"

Barnes quickly interrupted, "He won't. They're just checking on the mortgage backed securities and bonds we've been selling. Alex is embarrassed that so much happened under his watch, so he's checking everything out." Barnes could hear street noises on the other end of the line. "Are you downtown Vito?"

"Yeah."

"Well, then close your damned window. It's hard to hear you over all the traffic noise."

"Okay, okay."

"That's better. Now listen to me Vito, don't call Shawn any more about this. I know you usually work with him, but we better leave him out of things at this point. Just call me if you have any questions."

"Okay Barnes, but I'm nervous about those branch applications. All seven were approved in less than a week. It usually takes months or even years just to get a hearing and then you have to beg, borrow, and steal to get an approval. President Moretti's pal at the SEC did a hell of a job ramming them through. To get seven branch applications approved that quickly never happens unless you have inside help. And Blue is a frickin' expert on such matters. If he figures out what we've been up to, he'll dig deeper into our relationship with Moretti and then we'll really be in deep shit."

"Moretti can handle Blue."

Barnes slid off the bar stool, walked over and looked out the large window fronting the golf course. He was now safely out of earshot of Willie and several tables of poker players that dotted the elegant lounge.

"Listen Vito, let's just hold tight and see what develops here. This new administration likes to play Chicago style politics; they can get plenty rough if necessary. Alex will be taking on the whole Federal Government if he pushes too hard. He'll snoop around for awhile and try to make us uncomfortable, but I don't think he will press too hard right now. I'm sure he suspects that we have ties to the Moretti camp, but when push comes to shove, he'll back off."

"Let's hope so, Barnes. We wouldn't look good in prison stripes!"

"Calm down, Vito. Montrose knows what he's doing. I gotta run, I have a 1:30 tee time. Keep in touch, Vito, and let me know anything and everything you hear." He turned and hurried toward the members' locker room at Meridian Hills Country Club.

"Okay, but I'm warnin' you, Barnes, if...."

Barnes stopped quickly and pulled the phone tight to his ear. He interrupted his tempestuous friend, "Now you listen to me, Vito. You were nothing but a small time operator with a bad paper trail out of Chicago when I met you. Now you're a rich man. If we hadn't helped Moretti with those donations, you'd still be living in a one bedroom condo in downtown Indy. Don't you ever threaten me again! Do you understand?"

Always intimated by Barnes, Vito was silent.

Barnes clicked his phone shut without saying good-bye and hurried into the locker room to change for his golf game with Bill Worthem, a frequent golfing companion and the head of the Democratic Party in Marion County.

Barnes threatening outburst toward Vito was not uncommon. A product of an Irish ghetto in the heart of the mean streets of Boston, he could play plenty rough when necessary. Brilliant as a child, he never had much of an affinity for the books, choosing instead to join an Irish gang at age fourteen. Fearless, and always aching for a fight, he soon became the gang's leader. He remained leader until he was arrested on an assault and battery charge at age eighteen. The charge was the result of a brutal beating by Barnes and two other boys of a rival Irish gang member over a turf war on the Southside. His fellow gang members were eventually convicted on felony charges and sentenced to two years for assault and battery with intent to inflict bodily injury.

But lucky for Barnes, his father stepped in. Barnes' father ran a popular meat market in downtown Boston and was well connected politically. He provided young Barnes with a good attorney, and after a brief hearing, he was able to get his sentence reduced to just six months. The judge in the case, smitten by the boy's charm and good looks, had asked for the boy's school records before final sentencing. Shocked by his 144 IQ and almost perfect SAT's, the judge made an unusual ruling. The court ordered Barnes to either enroll in college and get a four year degree or go to jail. His father, wary of his son's bad behavior, gladly enrolled him in Boston College for the fall semester. Aware of the many horror stories circulating around town about the Massachusetts's penal system, Barnes took the deal offered by the judge and was soon a pre-law student at Boston College.

Sporting several scars, both physical and emotional, from his days as a gang-banger, the young Barnes immediately took to the more secure and civil environment at the ancient university. He was able to use his leadership skills honed on the mean streets of Boston to become president of his class both his junior and senior years.

After graduating cum laude in 1972, his application to attend the prestigious Harvard Law School was soon approved. In his senior year, he was elected Head of the Harvard Law Review and graduated with honors in 1974. After graduation, he was immediately hired by one of the most esteemed law firms in Boston, where he practiced law until he, and his wife Ellen, decided to move to her hometown of Indianapolis in 1989.

By all accounts, Barnes was considered to be one of the finest trial lawyers in both Boston and Indianapolis. The feisty litigator never forgot his days on the tough streets of Boston and was not opposed to using bullying tactics when he felt necessary. He would often confide to his wife Ellen that "courtroom battles were easy. If you win, nobody comes after you later with a stick and club. And if you lose, you don't have to drag your battered body to the nearest emergency room for treatment."

While at Harvard he became heavily involved in the Young Democrats organization. He carried his political ideologies, spawned in the ultra-liberal Boston area, into his law career. He served brief stints as a prosecuting attorney in both Boston and Indianapolis. He gave generously to the Democratic Party and hoped to someday be appointed ambassador to his beloved home country of Ireland. With a new liberal President from Illinois just elected to office and the current Ambassador to Ireland about to retire, his chances seemed better than ever to fulfill his dream.

Vito Taglioni, a childhood friend of President Moretti, had initially introduced Barnes to President Moretti a few years earlier at a fund raiser in Indianapolis. The two hit it off almost immediately. It wasn't long before the then candidate, Moretti, and Barnes were speaking openly of the possibility of an Ambassadorship to Ireland. Just recently, Barnes had received a personal, hand-written note from the President reassuring him that he had not forgotten their discussions. He also thanked him for his "most impressive" support during the campaign. Barnes was elated, showing the note to anyone and everyone who would look at it. With his passions excited and his goal very much in sight, the determined Barnes was not going to allow anyone to stand in his way of becoming Ambassador to Ireland.

. . . .

Beads of perspiration glistened on Vito's forehead. He shoved his BlackBerry into its waist holster and gripped hard on the wheel. The dressing down by the ill-tempered Barnes had upset him, but with the pending audit by Blue and Gates, he had to be on the best of terms with Barnes. Having Barnes displeased with him, if only briefly, only served to heighten his anxieties.

Tough and macho looking on the outside, Vito, in many ways, was still just an insecure kid from Chicago.

Vito glanced up at the large sign on the front of his office building as he swung into the parking lot. It read *First Financial Securities,* with an inscription below reading, *Trust Is Our Middle Name.*

Parking in his reserved spot, Vito hurried inside. He hoped he could make it to his office near the front of the building without being stopped by one of his secretaries or young associates. With everything that was coming down, he needed the respite of his cluttered office to make a few very timely phone calls.

As he hurried toward his office, the large open area was buzzing with activity. The big board, stationed high above the room on the east wall, was the center of attention for many of the coatless brokers as they looked skyward from their small desks to see if there had been any changes since they looked at the board just a few minutes earlier. Other brokers talked animatedly on the phone with prospective buyers and sellers, hoping to land that one big deal that could move them from their small condos in downtown Indy to the more exclusive enclaves of Carmel and Zionsville on the north side. With the recent blow-up of the bond market and the impending new regulations by the feds, time was running out for these wannabe dealers as they sought their fortunes in the fast-paced world of securities dealing.

Vito's hopes of clear sailing to his office were interrupted at the last second by a shout from his office manager, Cliff Stone.

"Oh, Vito."

"The anxious owner stopped by the door to his

office and turned to face the fast-approaching manager, "Yes Cliff?"

"Got a minute? Something has come-up."

"Can it wait? I have some important calls to make."

The young man grimaced, "I don't think so boss. I think we better talk now."

Vito paused and took a deep breath, "Great, now what?" he mumbled. "Come on in."

The two men entered Vito's very messy office. Piles of green file folders were stacked on the guest chairs, on both corners of his desk and on top of the file cabinets on the back wall. The total lack of organization in his office would be a total embarrassment for most businessmen, but it didn't seem to bother Vito. He lifted a few of the files from the chair in front of his desk and asked his manager to sit down.

"What is it, Cliff?"

Cliff quickly took a seat as Vito dropped the files on his desk and nestled into his large leather chair.

"I'm here about the Blue and Gates request for the branch filings boss."

"Yes…yes, what about them?"

"We can't find Chicago."

Anything but Chicago, Vito thought. Eyes wide, he shot up in his seat and shouted, "You can't find what? What the hell are you talking about?"

Cliff spoke quickly, "It's gone, its not there. We've looked everywhere."

"You've looked everywhere?"

"Yes, it's not here. I'm telling you boss, it's not here."

Vito shook his head in disbelief, "We've done more than 600 million out of that office this year my boy! A legal firm is asking to audit our files from that office and we can't find the branch applications we sent to the SEC! Is that what you're telling me?"

Cliff sunk down in his chair. "I'm afraid so."

Vito stood and began pacing back and forth behind his desk. "Alex Crane is on a mission to discredit me and we can't produce the most basic of information. Why, it has to be here. I remember signing the request form."

Not looking at his boss, Stone opened the file in his hand. "Yes…yes you did. It's right here."

He lifted the form from the file and handed it to Vito. "But that's all we have. There are no market studies, no empirical data on population trends, industrial capacity, and so forth."

"Can't we do that now and backdate everything?"

"I asked Jason, in our accounting department, about doing just that and he said it would take weeks to gather that kind of information, especially since it pertains to conditions that existed more that a year and a half ago. And Alex wants copies of the applications in a few days."

Vito stopped in front of his chair. "Did you ask Jason to explain just how the hell this happened?"

"Well…uh yes, sort of. Jason said that…."

Vito interrupted. "Sort of!"

"Well…uh, yes I did."

"Damn it, Cliff—spit it out!"

"Uh…he said that Chicago was one of the last branches to be approved. Our SEC connection had approved the other applications sight-unseen. Jason was certain that the SEC wasn't even looking at the files that we sent them. And with so many things on his plate at the time, Jason never got around to sending in the documentation for branch approval for Chicago. We received an approval form via e-mail that included the branch number. You signed it and Jason put it in the file."

Vito shook his head, "We have no way out of this. We have no paper trail showing attempts to process the information for the file! We have no e-mail records showing that we had sent the requested information to the SEC. This is unbelievable."

"I have an idea, boss."

Vito stopped his ranting and looked hopefully at his young assistant. "Go on."

"Well, the way I look at it, the SEC has just as much to lose as we do. They are going to have to explain how they gave a branch approval for a large securities dealer without receiving the necessary documentation. It usually takes months and years to get branch approval. It all smacks of political cronyism, which could reflect very badly on the Chairman of the SEC and eventually on the President. If this leaks out, the media would have a field day."

Vito coughed nervously. "Good point. Go ahead."

"I would suggest that we stall Alex as long as we can—just tell him we are trying to obtain some necessary documentation from the SEC and they are not cooperating. That will buy us a little time. Then, in the meantime, we could have Jason contact our man at the SEC and explain our predicament and ask him if he has any ideas on how we can deal with this problem. Something tells me he will come up with a solution."

Vito spoke quietly, almost to himself. "Alex will be very suspicious; he knows how these things work. But it's far better to have him wondering why we're stalling than to have him know the truth. It could be, that at the end of the day, nothing will happen. Alex may threaten us, but it's highly unlikely that a banker from Indianapolis will try and take on the Federal Government."

Vito leaned over and punched a button on his office phone and lifted the receiver to his ear.

"Yes, Mr. Taglioni?"

"Claudia, get Jason Howard in here right away!"

"Yes sir."

"Good thinking, Cliff. We'll just throw the ball into the SEC's court and let Crane fight with them. What the hell—the Government has more to lose than we do."

Cliff got up from his chair as the door to the office swung open and Jason Howard, Vice-President and Controller, walked hastily over to Vito's desk. His hand was shaking as he reached toward Cliff for a shake, "Afternoon, Cliff."

"Good afternoon, Jason."

After a quick shake, Jason lifted his hand toward Vito. "Hello Mr. Taglioni. I didn't know your were back in the office." He quickly withdrew his hand when Vito, sporting an ugly scowl, refused the gesture.

"What the hell were you thinking, Howard? What stupid-ass kind of tortured logic led us to this? Explain yourself man! Explain yourself!"

Vito knew the basic premise of Jason's failure to document the file; Cliff had just explained it to him. But his insecurities really consumed him at times like this and he became an ugly bully. He wanted very much to humiliate Jason in front of Cliff for two reasons: one, he knew that Cliff would tell others in the office about his tirade and it would put the fear of God in them and two, he wanted to absolve himself from any responsibility.

Vito knew that he was a weak president, very seldom in the 'shop', as he called it. He knew very little about the day to day operations of his firm, leaving all management decisions to Jason and Cliff. He chose instead to spend much of his time gambling at Crooked Stick Country Club and frequenting local gentlemen's clubs, such as the Gold Club and Club Venus. Sins of the flesh were commanding more and more of Vito's time lately, leaving little time or energy for the hands-on management of First Financial. He was lashing out at Jason to send a message to anybody who might challenge his authority. It was a quality that even Vito despised about himself, but he was too self-absorbed and cowardly to change.

"I'm truly sorry, Vito. It's just that the SEC wasn't putting any pressure on us at all. It was obvious the required documentation wasn't a priority for them, and with all that was going on around here, I didn't get the file completed."

Drops of saliva flew as an angry Vito continued to berate and demean the terrified young man. "You idiot! Do you realize what you have done? This thing goes clear up to the President of the United States!"

Jason's legs pushed harder against the desk, and beads of sweat glistened on his forehead. "Maybe...uh Cliff and I can come up with some way out of this mess."

"Cliff and I, Cliff and I," Vito spoke with a childlike refrain, mimicking his young controller. He suddenly jumped up and leaned forward; his face was only inches away for the terrified young man. He spoke in a low groaning whisper. Cliff stood motionless next to Jason, eyes wide with anticipation. "If we weren't so busy, I'd fire your ass right now and let you go out and find another job that paid you two hundred grand a year, but I can't. I hate to say it, but I need your worthless ass right now."

Jason stood quietly, legs shaking.

Vito stepped back, "Fortunately for you, Cliff has come up with a plan that might work and I want you two to get to work on it right away."

Jason spun toward Cliff looking slightly confused. His eyes begged more information. Cliff smiled and shook his head in the affirmative at his good friend. "We're going to put the ball in the Commission's court. I can explain it to you in my office." He shot a glance toward Vito for approval to leave.

The malevolent boss shook his head. "Even though we have a plan, this thing is a hell of a long way from over and it's going to raise all kind of red flags with the Midwest attorneys. I want a report everyday on how things are going. If I'm not here, call or text me on my BlackBerry. I want this thing fixed! Now, get the hell out of here—both of you!"

Cliff turned and gently laid his hand on Jason's shoulder. His friend and fellow officer's dress shirt was soaked with perspiration. The two young men turned and walked slowly from Vito's office, quietly clicking the door shut.

Shaken by his cruel treatment of his young associate, Vito walked over to his office window and lifted the curtain back and stared aimlessly at the busy street scene below. A very conflicted man by nature, his eyes started to glaze over; a tear appeared in the corner of his eye and then rolled slowly down his cheek. "You rotten bastard." he whispered.

Chapter 9

"Bye honey, I've got bridge tonight."

Alex felt a quick peck on his cheek as he entered the kitchen. Nicky snatched her purse off a nearby bar stool and hurried toward the garage.

"Who's your partner tonight?"

"Jeannie, Sharon's on vacation."

"Oh boy, see ya at midnight."

Nicky paused by the door, "I know, she's a talker. There's lunch meat in the refrig if you're hungry and I've got things pretty well around for the weekend. You just need to pack your stuff and don't forget your new swimming trunks." She flashed a quick grin. "Sorry to leave you alone."

"That's alright dear, don't worry. A golf tournament is on TV tonight and Phil Mickelsen is leading, so take your time, let Jeannie feel her oats." He smiled broadly.

"Men!" she replied and then disappeared into the garage.

Alex could hear the garage door rattle shut as he snatched a thick glass from the small cabinet above the refrigerator. A few seconds later, narrow cubes from the ice-maker jingled into the glass. He grabbed the bottle of vodka from the nearby counter and began pouring.

He stopped pouring at half full and opened a small bottle of tonic water and filled the remainder of the glass. He dropped a chunk of lime in the glass, loosened his tie, hurried over to the family room and plopped into his favorite leather recliner. Yanking hard on the handle, his feet soon went horizontal. He reached for the nearby remote and settled in for a night of good TV. The PGA coverage would be starting in five minutes. With the remote in hand, he glanced at the shelving to the left of his TV. There was a recent picture of his son, Jarod, and his family, smiling and waving as they exited the boat after a day of tubing at the lake. His two grandkids, Katie and Eli, were eleven and seven respectively. He loved his family deeply and was glad that he was able to give them an exciting lake home to visit. The children couldn't wait to go "up to the lake" to visit Grandma and Grandpa. He shuddered when he thought about the pending problems with Barnes and the board—problems that could threaten the very lifestyle to which he and his family had become accustomed. His iPhone chimed; he slid it from the holder and checked the screen before answering. He didn't recognize the number and there was no other identifying information.

"Hello?"

"Uh….hello Alex, sorry for calling you at home— It's Josh Dulin here. I hope I'm not interrupting anything."

"Oh no, that fine, Josh. Always nice to talk with you—what's up?"

"Well, Ted Blue called yesterday and said that you wanted a surprise audit on your Chicago office as soon as possible. He said that you were concerned about the inordinate amount of attention that office had been given by your controller, Jack Montrose.

"Yes, yes, Ted and I discussed the activity at the Chicago office and I did want the audit right away. I explained that to your secretary when she called to verify the request."

Alex was waiting for the hammer to fall. Josh Dulin was an extremely reserved man; he would not call Alex at his home in the evening if he didn't have something very important to say.

Josh cleared his throat, "You're my biggest account Alex, so I wanted to take this one myself. I cleared my schedule yesterday and drove up to the Chicago office first thing this morning."

"Good."

"When I arrived, I received an unexpected greeting."

"From Louie?"

"No, Jack Montrose was there."

"I know, he's working on new software for the computers in the loan department on the other side of the building. I didn't think it would be a problem."

"Well, today at least, he wasn't working in the loan department. He was back in the savings area. It was a little uncomfortable trying to set up shop. Out of professional courtesy, neither Jack nor I volunteered any information to the other. It was a little tense in there. He was very interested in what I was doing."

"Go on."

"Finally, his curiosity got the best of him. He walked over to where I was working in the corner of the room and said, "You're kind of out of rotation, aren't you?""

"Jack knows when you schedule your audits, so he would be aware that this visit was off schedule. What did you say to him?" Alex mused.

"I told him such surprise audits were pretty routine, no reason for concern."

"Did he buy that?"

"Not really, he once again asked me what my visit was about and I gave him a standard non-answer answer. He continued to watch me the rest of the day. His obsession with me may have caused him to make a huge mistake."

"Go on."

"Well, I was doing some preliminary runs on the computer when Montrose came over by our work station, for the third time in less than an hour, to get a cup of water from the cooler. He set a couple files on the table next to me and turned toward the cooler. I took advantage of the opportunity to glance at the files."

"And?"

"They were all 68 accounts."

"The 68's are IRA's if I remember correctly."

"Exactly. I was able to memorize a number on one of the files. When he left the area, I immediately jotted down the number. He had just inadvertently narrowed my search efforts dramatically."

"Hmmm."

"I went to work on that account, along with several other similar IRAs. I combed over them, looking for anything out of the ordinary. But after several hours of trying to find something, I was at a dead end—nothing suspicious was showing up. Then, late in the day, I remembered something that the system analysts had told me last year when we first set up your new software. It was about a special code."

"A special code?"

"Yes, there is a special code that the tellers can use to file maintain an IRA account when a simple mistake has been made when entering account information. This is unique to this software. I hadn't seen it before, so subsequently, I had forgotten all about it."

"Why the code?"

"The reason for the code is that IRAs are a lot more complicated and difficult to work with than normal savings accounts. So sometimes, underpaid and overworked tellers will make a minor mistake when entering the data—it happens on a fairly regular basis. The tellers just aren't as comfortable with IRAs as they are with normal savings accounts. You can hear them grousing under their breath every time a customer mentions an IRA."

"Yes, everyone hates IRAs. Go on."

"So to avoid a bunch of red flags clogging up the system as the result of some harmless mistakes, banks are provided with this code. Using it, a teller can pull the account information out, play around with it and then put it back in. Actually, they could transfer money from the account. The changes would go totally undetected— even during routine Federal audits. Such maintenance is not part of your normal data analysis so it wouldn't show up."

"What about teller fraud? Couldn't the teller use the special code for his or her advantage?"

Josh chuckled, "You're always one step ahead of me, Alex. But the answer is no. There is definitely oversight. Such entries must be provided to the controller of the institution on a daily basis on a special read-out that is separate from your system analysis. If there is anything that looks suspicious, he would catch it in a minute. Any teller that didn't report such maintenance would be fired immediately."

Alex's smacked his lips, the ice rattled as he set the empty glass on the table. "So, the only one who sees these entries is Jack Montrose?"

"That's right, but he's supposed to share that information with us."

"Let me guess—he hasn't been doing that."

"That's correct. But that's not the worst of it."

"Oh?"

"Are you sitting down?"

Alex sighed, a long groaning sigh.

"For the remaining few hours of the day, I was able to examine literally dozens of IRA's using the code."

"Montrose was working on the same group of accounts, wasn't he?"

"Yes, so I used account numbers that were at the other end of the spectrum from the account number I discovered at the cooler. He was definitely watching me, but he didn't really know what I was doing."

"How did you get the code without him knowing?"

"From a slender, giggly, nineteen year old teller named Arial. She knows I'm the bank's auditor, so she thought it was her job to help."

"We're you able to gather any more information?"

"Did I ever!"

"Really?"

"Yes, almost half of the accounts I checked had been tampered with. Using the code, they took money from the accounts late summer of last year and then put it back in at various times starting early this year. Judging by Montrose's frequent visits to the office, I'm sure the process is still going on."

Alex stood and walked to the kitchen to mix another drink. "Pardon the ice machine Josh; I think I'm going to get drunk."

Josh laughed nervously, "No problem, I might do the same."

Alex filled his glass and set the empty bottle of tonic water on the countertop. "How much money are we talking about?"

"Most of the accounts I've seen were carrying substantial balances, usually well over one hundred thousand dollars and typically five or ten thousand dollars had been removed. In a few cases, it was twenty thousand. There was no rhyme or reason to the amount of the withdrawals. But based on the information I have gleaned so far and projecting this information out across the broad base of accounts in this category, I would say that we are looking at possibly tens of millions of dollars being extracted from these accounts. This game they're playing looks big, Alex—very big!"

The shocked bank president leaned against the counter. "Oh, wow! How much has been paid back?"

"I'm not sure. The accounts I examined had all been paid back, but I've only scratched the surface. I found a motel and will be staying up here tonight. It will be another day or two before I get through all of the accounts. Louie said I could work through the weekend. He's been a great help."

"I'll bet. Just put anything you need on our tab."

"Thanks, but I expected the worst with these surprise audits, so I have extra clothes and toiletries with me."

Suddenly, Alex felt warm; he began to perspire. "I

just can't understand why they would go to all the trouble to take the money out and then pay it back."

"Whenever people extort money, they usually plan to pay it back, but it rarely ever happens. In this case, it's happening—too early to tell why."

Alex scratched his head, "Hmmm....it doesn't make sense."

"These kinds of things never do at first."

"I guess so. Please keep in touch. I will have my cell with me at all times."

"Okay, Alex."

There was a long pause. "We must keep all of this confidential. This information will explode if the media gets wind of it. We need to stay as discreet as possible until we can gather enough evidence to make our case."

"No question about it," Josh replied. "Stay in touch."

"Okay, good-bye."

Alex ambled across the room and fell back in his chair. His head was buzzing. He felt certain that the situation in Chicago was the product of another scheme by his chairman, Barnes O'Brien. After all, the point-man, Jack Montrose, was hand-picked by Barnes. But why take the money and pay it back?

Alex felt helpless and frustrated. He had watched the opportunistic Barnes use his position as chairman to become a player of great power and influence at Midwest Consolidated, far beyond that of a typical chairman. Barnes had managed, in a little over two years, to swing control of the vote on the board to his side. He had also managed to bring a controller on board who seemed to work more for him than for Alex. And, in a clandestine move while Alex was out of the country on vacation, he succeeded in changing the basic mortgage underwriting guidelines at Midwest allowing for subprime mortgages.

These moves angered Alex, but what angered him most was that Barnes had been able to do all this right under his nose and without breaching any federal or state banking regulations. That is, until now. Barnes may have finally reached too far. The embezzlement of funds from private savings accounts was indeed a serious violation of Federal regulations. The corner of his mouth curled up in a smile, as he sipped on his vodka and contemplated possible negative ramifications this would have for his long-time nemesis. "A little jail time might do the old lout some good," he whispered. His thoughts were interrupted by his phone.

"Hello Barnes, I was just thinking about you."

The reply was swift and sharp, "What the hell is Dulin doing snooping around in Chicago and why wasn't that audit cleared by the board?"

The aggressive comment angered Alex. "That's none of your business, Barnes. I'm running this bank—not you!"

"That's BS, Alex! A surprise audit at our largest office is definitely the business of the board. You should have at least called to inform me." Alex could hear a muffled 'son-of-a-bitch' on the other end.

"That's a ridiculous assertion on its face, Barnes. There is no bank policy that requires me to inform the board about every audit that takes place. The board discusses the annual federal, state, and internal audits each year in January and sets a tentative schedule. What happens after that is entirely up to me. Besides, Montrose has been running up there all year without your blessed 'board approval' and I haven't heard you complaining about that." Alex's frustration was growing.

"You're out of line here, Crane, and you know it."

"I know no such thing! And by the way, Barnes—how did you happen to know about this audit in the first place? I didn't tell anyone and I'm certain Josh didn't."

There was a pause, followed by a throat clearing, "Why...I...uh ran into Jack at...uh CVS a little while ago. He was getting some beer for the weekend. We're neighbors you know."

"Oh, is that right?" Alex was incredulous. "Let me get this straight. Jack stopped at the drug store to get a six-pack of beer after a long, hard week of work. He runs into the Chairman of the Board on his way to the check-out counter and before you know it, he's telling you about an audit that Josh Dulin was doing in Chicago today. Wouldn't a quick "hi" and "how are you" seem more logical?"

"Well...uh I don't know. He was just talking I guess."

"I don't believe you ran into him at the drug store Barnes. I think he called you on his way home, which is totally out of line for a man in his position. The controller answers directly to me. To divulge such confidential information to a board member behind my back is reason for possible dismissal."

"Now listen here, Alex. You can't fire a man just for talking to me. He knows I'm interested in what is going on at the bank. He was just making small talk there at the convenience store."

"I thought it was a drug store."

"Well, drug store, convenience store, what the hell's the difference?"

Alex loved having the aggressive Barnes on the defensive, but he was bluffing with the dismissal threat.

He needed Jack Montrose right where he was until he could get to the bottom of this deception.

"I'm very concerned about the level of involvement of my chairman in the day to day operations of this bank, it doesn't seem healthy to me. You've got your nose in everything."

Alex could hear Barnes puffing nervously on his cigar. "Well, with all the losses we're having and so forth, I just…uh was afraid something was going a little wrong in Chicago, that's all."

"Your concern for our bank's well-being is very touching, Barnes. But I would suggest, in the future, you leave the management of this bank up to me."

"Leave it up to you, yes. Well, I have to go now. Ellen and I are going out to dinner." Barnes turned his phone off. The abrupt ending was Barnes's way of saving face. Alex had put him back on his heels and he didn't like it. But Alex knew that Barnes would stay very much involved in the bank's business—now more than ever.

The next several days would be difficult for everyone. The recently discovered scheme was like a ticking time bomb ready to explode. Alex felt sick inside as he turned on the TV and contemplated the future. As the picture beamed in, he was momentarily distracted from his troubling situation by loud applause as the crowd, surrounding the beautiful tenth green, cheered for a smiling Phil Mickelson. The popular pro golfer lifted a putt from the hole, nodded at the appreciative crowd and walked quickly to the next tee. "He plays a simple game and then goes home," Alex groused. "I envy him."

Chapter 10

"Ever see so much corn?" Nicky laughed as she sat in the front seat working on her latest knitting project.

Alex adjusted the collar on his golf shirt and turned down the radio. "It's good to get away for a few days."

Nicky's hands dropped to her lap, she smiled at her husband. "It certainly is. I just love going up to the lake; it's so relaxing. And with all that is going on at the office, you needed to get the hell out of Dodge for awhile."

A broad grin spread across Alex's face, surprised by the locker-room epithet from his prim and proper wife.

"Look honey, there's someone at the wishing well!" Nicky exclaimed.

Alex glanced over at the ancient well that sat just off the road about fifty feet from an old bait shop. A man in a crumpled ball cap and black waders was holding a milk cartoon in his left hand while cranking vigorously on the well-rusted handle with his right hand.

Available to the public, many of the fishermen, who rented the one room cabins that dotted the shorelines of nearby lakes, used the well as a source of drinking water. The old cabins, many of which were constructed in the early part of the twentieth century, were often without running water, leaving the occupants to their own devices. But for Nicky and Alex, the well was not a source of water, but the exciting symbol of their entry into the beloved lake region of northern Indiana, and more importantly, it reminded them that they were only ten minutes from their final destination, Lake Wawasee.

"Not much longer," Alex mused. Still shaken by the revelations from Josh Dulin the night before, he was really looking forward to some time away.

"I know, I'm getting excited." Nicky quickly went back to her knitting, wanting the last few minutes to pass as quickly as possible.

As was the custom in the hospitable Indiana, Alex nodded and smiled at many of the vacationers as he drove through North Webster, a popular resort community, just south of Lake Wawasee. A few minutes later, their turn was in sight.

"South Shore looks busy."

Nicky smiled and looked over at the legendary golf course that pushed in against Highway 13. "Sure is. Maybe you can get a game with Al Fox and the boys. The grandkids won't be here until Saturday evening."

"We'll see."

"Don't worry about me, honey. Millie called me yesterday and invited me to go to Shipshewana for some shopping with her and the girls tomorrow. So, you're on your own."

Alex squirmed as he turned right onto Vawter Park Road. "Well…uh actually, Al called me yesterday also. We have a tee time at South Shore at noon tomorrow."

"You rascal," Nicky poked him playfully.

A short time later, the turn signal chimed as Alex turned left and guided the SUV up the narrow drive to their large lake home. He stopped just outside the open garage door as was his custom. Nicky was the first one out of the car with Alex close behind. They both stood, as was their custom also, and admired their lovely home for a few seconds before unpacking. Nicky breathed deeply, wanting to inhale as much of the fresh lake air as humanly possible. Then, not unexpectedly, they heard the somewhat over-exaggerated squeals of neighbor Millie as she came rushing past the stone landscaping wall next to the garage, her thin arms open wide for the coming hug.

"How are you? Oh my goodness! So good to see you both! You look wonderful!" Then, much to Nicky's annoyance—as usual—she hugged Alex first, a long, hard hug. 'I'm on the driver's side he would always say. I'm the first one she comes to.'

After a much shorter hug, Millie and Nicky began talking about their shopping trip to the Amish settlement at Shipshewana the next day.

"It will be wonderful tomorrow, Nicky. They've opened two new shops recently. One is a kitchen shop—your favorite!"

"Oh great!" Nicky exclaimed. "I can't wait."

"What's Larry up too?" Alex asked.

"He's out fishing, what else? I swear, I feel like the man has a mistress out there on that lake somewhere, with all that fishing he does. Oh well, I guess there are worse things he could be doing."

"That's for sure." Alex stood politely quiet next to the open rear hatch on the SUV. Anxious to unpack, Nicky stood quietly also.

Getting the hint, Millie spoke, "Well…uh, I best be going. I've got lots to do." After a quick departing hug for both, the slender neighbor started home. She stopped suddenly near the edge of the drive and turned around. "Oh, by the way, are you guys expecting company?"

Alex paused while reaching for the suitcases. "The kids are coming up Saturday evening. Why do you ask?" Nicky peered over the hood of the SUV.

"Well, two men in a black sedan pulled in to your drive earlier this morning. They got out of their car looked around briefly. They were dressed in suits. They looked like businessmen. One of them was writing notes on a pad. I thought maybe it was company that got here a little early or something."

"Hmmm....that's funny. We're not expecting anyone but the kids. I can't imagine who that might have been," Alex mused.

"Did the car have those dark windows?" Nicky asked.

"I'm not sure, but I think so. I hear my phone, I'd better get going. See ya tomorrow!"

Nicky looked quickly at Alex, eyebrows raised.

"What?" he replied.

"Black sedan, dark windows."

"I heard the county is doing assessments for property taxes here. It was probably the folks from the assessor's office."

"The last assessor I ran into was wearing a ball cap and a golf shirt. Millie said these guys were wearing suits. "

"Quit worrying, honey; we're up here to have a good time, alright?"

"Okay, okay." She slid the suitcase off the tailgate and grunted slightly as she lifted the heavy case with both hands and struggled to the front door. A suitcase in each hand Alex hurried ahead and firmly planted his knee against the front door, holding it open.

"Dinner at The Frog tonight? We can take the woody."

Nicky paused, giving her smiling husband a quick peck on the cheek. "I love The Frog. You know that."

"Good, after we unpack, I'll go down and get the old boat uncovered and start it up. We can be at The Frog by 7:30."

"Wonderful, my dear!"

. . . .

The sleek Chris-Craft woody banged against the waves as a smiling Alex, his hair blowing wildly in the stiff breeze, guided the ancient boat across beautiful Lake Wawasee. Wawasee was Indiana's largest natural lake at more than three thousand acres. It had a fully developed shoreline that included the homes of some of the wealthiest people in the country. Property on the exclusive lake, known for its crystal clear water, sold for over fifteen thousand dollars a front foot. So a home with a hundred feet touching the lake would be valued at approximately one and one half million dollars. It was an intoxicatingly wealthy area that had attracted Indiana's best and brightest for well over a hundred years.

"Slow down, honey," Nicky shouted. "Let's enjoy the ride."

Alex shoved the throttle arm down; the bow of the boat suddenly dipped and then surged forward, eventually settling in the lake. A few seconds later, the backwash gently nudged the boat forward. The powerful engine made a thick chugging sound as it settled in at idle speed and moved slowly through the choppy lake. The old wooden boats or "woodies", as the locals called them, were the only boats on the lake that could make such a sound and Alex loved it. They were the original speed boats on the lake and held a special place in the hearts of the lake's residents.

A short time later, the lights of the legendary Frog Tavern glowed ahead as Alex approached the mouth of the narrow channel that led to the popular eatery.

"There's a place over there." Nicky pointed to an empty spot at the north end of the long pier that bordered the restaurant. An expert boatman, Alex glided forward and carefully maneuvered the beloved woody into the narrow spot. He tossed a looped rope over the large wooden post, jumped out of the tipsy boat and reached back for Nicky, who was busy yanking the rope tight on the rear post.

Inside, the popular haunt was buzzing with activity. Carol, their favorite waitress, approached.

"Table for four okay with you guys? Don't have any twos," the waitress shouted over the noisy crowd.

"That's fine, Carol," Nicky replied.

Alex nodded at a few familiar faces as the waitress led them to their table, laying the one page menu on the table in front of them. "How you two doing?" the harried waitress asked.

"Fine Carol, busy place tonight," Alex observed.

"Yeah, it's a nice weekend for a change, everybody's up here. A drink to start with?" she asked.

"Sounds like a winner," Alex quipped.

"I'll have a glass of Riesling," Nicky ordered.

"Bud Light for me," Alex smiled. "Got any of those frosty mugs tonight?"

"Sure do. Comin' right up."

. . . .

"Got another iced tea back there, bartender?"

"Yeah, be right with you."

Herbert "Hawk" Barger had been an agent with the FBI for more than thirty years and during that time had distinguished himself as a gritty, take no prisoners type of agent. He gained fame as the lead agent in the break-up of a huge numbers racket in his hometown of Chicago some twenty years earlier. He felt he held some status in the bureau and didn't like being on assignment at some lake in Indiana on a Friday night. And to make matters worse, the assignment interrupted his usual Friday night ritual—an evening on Rush Street in Chicago, ducking in and out of his favorite bars and restaurants well into the wee hours of the morning.

Hawk's day job was to sit at a desk in the field office on West Roosevelt Road and give orders to the many agents on assignment in the greater Chicago area. Special assignments, such as these, were usually left to the new guys or rookies. But his boss had told him he needed his 'best' for this stake-out, and, as was the case so many times before in his illustrious career, Hawk was put temporarily on special assignment. And this meant that his time was their time until he could get back to his desk job and a more predictable schedule. He turned to his young partner, Jake Collier, seated on the bar stool next to him and groused, "Where's that motel again?"

"Goshen."

"How far is Goshen from here?"

"Fifteen minutes—it's the closest motel I could find that had a room available. They're having a bass tournament on the lake this weekend and all the local motels were booked."

The bartender banged Hawk's iced tea on the bar, seemingly a little annoyed that the two men weren't buying the more expensive alcoholic drinks. Hawk shot him a hard stare.

"Look here," Jake ordered as he slipped a photo from the inside pocket of his suit coat and pointed it toward Hawk.

"It's a picture of that Crane fellow."

"So what?"

"Look over there, near the corner of the room. See the guy with the good lookin' chick—the guy in the ball cap?"

Hawk looked over his thick shoulder. "It's some guy with a good lookin' broad, so what?"

"It's him, Hawk, it's Crane."

As if to accommodate the curious agents, the unknowing Alex lifted his hat higher on his forehead as Hawk turned to look.

"You're good, Collier, you're good. It's him alright."

"The work-up said they liked to go to The Frog. We hit it right."

"He's kind of nice looking for an old guy," Barger mused.

"Yeah…and he's a rich bastard too; they say homes cost over a million bucks on this puddle." Collier shook his head.

"Hmmm… a million, that's steep." Hawk turned

slowly back toward the bar. "Think I'll stay on Rush Street and leave these rich folks alone."

"Me too."

. . . .

Away from his work and trying desperately to forget the stunning events of the day before, Alex looked admiringly at his lovely wife's pretty blue eyes, pouty lips, and tanned skin. "You look lovely tonight, my dear," he said softly.

Nicky smiled at someone behind him. Suddenly he felt two hands crash on his shoulders.

"Crane, you old rascal, didn't expect to see you up here."

With Nicky laughing out loud, Alex spun around to greet his good friend and attorney, Ted Blue, "Why, hello Blue, how are you?"

"P...pretty darn good if I don't s...say so myself."

"And how are you, Carrie?"

"Great thanks, and let me apologize for my drunken husband. We got up here about noon and he's been at it ever since. I'm afraid my little teddy bear is feeling no pain." She grabbed his cheek with her forefinger and thumb and shook it—a little *too* aggressively, Alex thought.

"Well...uh won't you have a seat," Nicky offered.

"Don't m...mind if I do. T...thought you'd never ask," Ted replied.

Carrie frowned, "Are you sure you want us to sit down?"

"I hate to tell you this Carrie, but he's not much better when he is sober." Alex mused.

"Have you eaten?" Nicky asked.

"Yes, we ate a little while ago," Carrie replied. She leaned closer and whispered to the surprised couple. "I'm so sorry. Ted hardly ever drinks, but when he does he really makes up for lost time. We won't stay long."

"Oh....heck, stay as long as you want. We just ordered a large pizza. You can help us eat it. It's too big for us." The gracious Nicky smiled warmly.

Alex smiled at his drunken friend, "I'm glad you came up to the lake; I've been wanting to talk to you."

"What a...about?'

"That ten grand you owe me from our poker game last week."

"I'm not that frickin' drunk, Crane!" He poked Alex in the shoulder nearly knocking him off his chair. A smiling Alex righted himself and scooted back to the table. "I'll settle for five."

"Okay five, you're gonna need it when Barnes and Vito get d...done with you."

Alex's smile quickly faded; the shocking news from Chicago on Friday rushed through his mind. "What do you mean, Ted? What about Barnes and Vito?"

"T...they're not cooperating with my inquiry. They say they need to talk with the SEC, b..before they can give us any branch filings. S...something smells, if y...you ask me. I think they're stalling for time."

With Dulin's discoveries in the Elmwood Park office, those branch applications didn't seem as important at this point. But something kept telling Alex that they could be part of a bigger picture.

"Alex! You promised me you wouldn't talk business. So please, can't this wait until later? I think Ted would be better able to answer your questions at another time dear." Nicky sounded serious.

"Okay, okay." With everything that was at stake, it was excruciating for Alex to end the conversation with his attorney, but he had made Nicky a promise long ago not to talk business when they were at the lake.

"H…Heck, you can always come to w…work for us, Alex," Ted started to fall off his chair.

Alex and Carrie leapt from their chairs at exactly the same time. "We'd better get going," she said red faced. "I think Ted needs to go home."

Alex hooked his arm around Ted's waist, Carrie grabbed under his arm. They struggled as they lifted the tall man to his feet.

"Did you come by boat?" Alex asked.

"No, we drove the Expedition," Carrie replied.

"Q…quit your fussing Crane, I'm okay." Ted pushed Alex's arm away, as he stood, still leaning on Carrie. "Carrie can g…get me to the truck."

"Sure?"

"H…Hell yes, Alex!"

"I'll call you Monday," Alex said.

He watched as his friends struggled to the main entrance, pausing briefly as two men in suits and ties approached the door. The larger of the two men motioned for Ted and Carrie to go ahead of them. Both men then turned and nodded at Alex. Nicky, her back to the door, didn't notice. A chill went up Alex's spine at the gesture from the over-dressed men. This was lake country; even the wealthiest of the wealthy dressed very casually at The Frog. Shorts and tank tops were the normal attire. Who were these men in suits and why were they at The Frog? Could they be the same men their neighbor Millie noticed earlier in the day? And what about the black sedan that Nicky had mentioned earlier in the week? Things were starting to add up and Alex didn't like it one bit.

Nicky smiled, "He'll be okay honey; don't worry."

"Oh yes…yes. Carrie will take good care of him," Alex chuckled nervously. "He'll be so embarrassed tomorrow."

"I know. Excuse me, honey, I have to run to the ladies room. If Carol comes, order me another glass of Reisling."

"Okay."

Alex took a long sip of his beer and watched as Nicky made her way to the ladies room. The men at the door were being too obvious; something wasn't right here. It was a blatant attempt to intimidate Alex and his family. The stakes in this game of big money were ratcheting up. He slid his iPhone from his pocket and checked to see where Nicky was—she was waiting near the occupied ladies room. This gave him the time he needed; he quickly pushed the speed dial.

"Hello, Barnes?"

"Yeah."

"Sorry to bother you. Hope you aren't in the middle of dinner."

"No, I just finished having dinner at St. Elmo's and now I'm having a drink with my lovely Ellen."

Alex glanced over at Nicky; she was still waiting and peering out the large window at the channel. "I'm up at the lake, Barnes."

"Well, isn't that nice, good for you. Hope you're having a great time."

"Not really, Barnes. Seems these two gentlemen in dark suits have been following us around for a couple days. You know anything about that?"

There was a pause on the other end. "Well…uh, hell no, why would I know anything about something like that?" Barnes was speaking quietly, apparently so Ellen couldn't hear him.

"They're dressed to the nines; they look like Federal agents to me. You're the guy with ties to the Government Barnes, tell me about it." Alex could hear Barnes excusing himself from the table. A few moments later he could hear the sound of the traffic outside the restaurant.

"Now you listen to me, Alex, I don't know anything about this."

"Things are getting real messy, Barnes. Attorney Blue told me that Vito isn't cooperating with a routine audit and now a couple of goons in black suits are following my wife and I around at the lake. I don't like it and I'm getting a little nervous."

"Like I said Alex, I don't know anything about this. So if you'll excuse…"

Alex interrupted, "I want you to call some of your big shot friends and get these guys outa here. My grandkids are coming up tomorrow for the weekend. I don't want my grandkids to see those guys, Barnes—got it?" Alex was incensed. He never dreamed his denial of the TARP money would lead to something as dark and menacing as this.

Barnes replied nervously, "I really must be going."

Nicky was working her way back to the table. "Just fix it, Barnes. Nicky's coming, I gotta go."

"How can I fix it?"

Fuming, Alex covered his mouth, "Fix it, you hear me? Fix it!" Alex quickly slid his phone back into his pocket. Nicky spoke briefly to some folks at a nearby table and then settled into her chair. Carol was close behind with the pizza.

"I'm starving," Nicky said.

"Another Riesling for my lovely wife and a Bud Light for me, Carol."

"Right away!" The busy waitress squeezed the pizza into the middle of the cluttered table and hurried off.

"Who was that?" Nicky queried.

A startled Alex replied nervously, "Oh, sorry about the phone, I...uh I called Carrie to see how Ted was doing."

Nicky's eyebrows rose. "And how is he?"

"Not so good, he got sick just before they got to the car." Alex raised his mug immediately wanting to change the subject. "Here's to another great weekend at the lake, my dear."

Nicky smiled, their glasses clicked. She reached forward and gently rubbed his arm. "No more business calls, okay?"

"Okay."

"And we'd better eat quickly and get back to the cottage. You have to get up early and go to the shooting range."

"You're right, six A.M. rolls around pretty fast."

Chapter 11

Friday night was Louie's night on the town, and that meant a night on Rush Street. The predictable evening always started with a late dinner at Butch McGuire's. The legendary restaurant, with its Hugh Hefner nudes decorating the walls, fit Louie's nostalgic look at life to a tee. Not a big player in Chicago politics, the frumpy bank president was still a well known figure in the many bars, restaurants, and coffee shops on the famous stretch that was located just a few blocks north of the loop in downtown Chicago.

....

With the bright red lights blinking on the towers atop the famous Hancock Center behind him, Louie speared his last chunk of filet, chewing it slowly until it was gone. A dainty eater for a large man, Louie dabbed his puffy lips gently with the cloth napkin and then laid it neatly on the table. He glanced at the melting ice in his whiskey and water. There was enough brownish residue left for one final swig. He lifted the rounded glass and sipped it empty.

"Rachel!"

"Yes, Mr. Campano?"

"Check please." Louie glanced at his watch. It was 10:36.

"Coming right up."

Louie left his table and shared niceties with a few familiar patrons at the bar before paying his tab and exiting the comfortable environs of the well-known eatery. Once outside, he waved his huge arm in the air and quickly hailed a cab. He always left his car parked in a nearby parking garage for safe keeping, choosing to use the more efficient cab system to navigate the busy streets of the bustling playground. Over the years, Louie had gotten to know most of the drivers. The drivers jealously protected their territories. And like most other folks who frequented Rush Street, Louie had his favorite cabbies.

A few seconds later, a shiny yellow cab veered to a sudden stop at the curb in front of Louie. He hurried over and climbed into the backseat.

"How ya's doin' Louie?"

"Fine Maurice, and how are you?"

"Pretty good, I guess." The cabbie laughed nervously. "Where ya headin' man?"

"Condos."

"Okay."

Maurice was not one of Louie favorites. Although he was a friendly sort, he was one of the younger drivers on the circuit and Louie knew it would be an exciting ride. It didn't take long for the action to start. Horns blared as the young daredevil gunned the cab and pulled out in front of several passing cars on Rush Street. Maurice shouted profanities and waved his fist at the other drivers as he forced his way into the busy traffic.

Louie grabbed tightly onto the armrest as the young cabbie wove his way in and out of traffic, spewing his colorful epithets along the way. This ride to the condos would be a long one for Louie.

"This traffic is getting worse all the time. These A-holes don't know how to drive," Maurice bellowed. The young driver was always just one aggravating event away from totally losing it.

Louie had hooked up with Maurice a few weeks earlier. That night Maurice had informed him that he had found religion and would not be using foul language any more. Louie found this promise amusing as another profanity laced diatribe came blaring from the front seat, followed by a muffled, "Forgive me Lord." Suddenly, Louie jerked violently forward as Maurice slammed on the brakes. Falling forward, Louie glanced through the front windshield at the light above as it blinked from yellow to red.

"Scuse me." Maurice said apologetically.

His heart pounding rapidly, Louie collected himself. "I'm in no hurry Maurice."

"I know ya ain't, Louie, but I am. I got me a lot a bills to pay and I owe support on three keeds on top a that. Gotta get me as many rides a night as I can."

The light turned green, the engine revved, Louie's head bumped against the headrest.

"You gotta a woman or something in those condos, Mr. Campano?"

Louie's brow lifted, surprised and annoyed by the personal question from the aggressive cabbie. "Maybe," he replied.

"You sure go there a lot."

This time Louie refused to answer the inquisitive

driver, temporarily ending the line of questioning. Several minutes later the cab came to an abrupt stop.

"Here ya are, brother. Be careful in there, man, those keeds get expensive," the young driver grinned slyly at Louie.

Louie handed him a twenty. He always gave the cabbies more than enough to cover the ride. Then he gently patted Maurice's bony shoulder and said, "Take care."

Louie quickly exited the cab and hurried into the vestibule of the thirty story condominium complex located just off Rush Street. He stepped inside the sealed cubicle and pushed the buzzer for Room 3025.

"Yeah?" came the terse reply.

"It's me, Louie."

There was a click on the speaker and then a loud buzzer sounded; Louie reached quickly for the door handle before the buzzer stopped and pushed through to the inside. A few feet down the hall, he stopped near the elevators and pushed the top button.

The Tower Condos were located on the west edge of the Rush Street area and housed some of the most expensive units on the upscale North side. A base unit, featuring just one bedroom and roughly a thousand square feet, would set the buyer back over a million dollars. With a monthly maintenance fee of six hundred dollars, it was indeed pricey.

There were only four units on the top floor; each of them was well over four thousand square feet. Louie couldn't imagine in his wildest dreams what they would cost. But he loved being invited to the upscale condo for the weekly parties. It gave him a chance to hang out with the upper crust of Chicago's busy night scene.

Louie exited on the thirtieth floor. Then, as usual, he paused to admire the surroundings in the wide hallway. No matter how many times he made this visit to "The Tower" on the top floor, he was always overwhelmed by the lush carpeting, expensive oils, and fresh flower arrangements that decorated the beautiful corridor.

As he approached Room 3025, music and animated conversation could be heard. Louie recognized the mellow saxophone sounds of his favorite jazz musician, Boney Jones. The folks in Chicago loved jazz, it served as a kind of national anthem for the city of broad shoulders. If you frequented the night scene in Chicago, you had to love jazz—it was a given.

Louie nervously adjusted the neck on the black turtleneck. He glanced down at his protruding belly. He was hoping the generous sweater he was wearing would cover as much of the huge outcropping as possible. Finally, he pushed his glasses up on his nose and tapped lightly on the door. Using the doorbell was out of the question for the reserved Louie. A few seconds later the door cracked open.

"Louie! Come on in my boy! Come in!" The stylishly dressed greeter swung the door open wide waving toward the bar. "Have yourself a drink!"

"Thanks, Tommy—good to see you," Louie replied.

Tommy "The Greek" Chaconas, owner of the condo, also owned the entire Tower Complex, as well as thirty other condo developments, in the greater Chicago area. He was an extremely wealthy man by anyone's standards.

"Make yourself at home, Louie!" Tommy smiled warmly and went back to his lady friend, whose long shapely legs extended from beneath the deep V in her evening gown as she sat precariously on the arm of a nearby leather chair.

Louie scanned the stunning room. It was decorated in mainly black and white décor, with lots of glass shelving, expensive lighting effects and delicate knick knacks on the shiny shelves.

Several people nodded or mouthed a quick "hi" to the likeable Louie. From the corner of the room, Louie received a long range grin and nod from Frank Miller, owner of Miller Brothers Inc., the largest brewery in Chicago and a long time customer of his bank. The room was full of Chicago's finest.

Attractive ladies in long evening gowns—their ample bosoms exposed for the consumption of the male guests—worked the room, smiling and making small talk. A man in a plaid vest stood behind the long bar at the back of the room, busily creating the requested elixirs for the guests.

As Louie made his way to the bar, he noticed two ladies in long gowns leaning over a glass table in the corner of the room. They giggled as they pushed a white powder into lines on the table top. Occasionally, they leaned over for a quick snort. This didn't surprise Louie; many of the party goers used cocaine as their escape mechanism for the night. Others chose not too. The casual demeanor of the young ladies was an indicator of the total acceptance of this behavior by the others. Cocaine, or blow, as most users liked to call it, was part of the night scene on Rush Street and Louie knew it.

"Whiskey and water?"

"Yeah, thanks Nick."

The cherubic banker looked at his watch; it was now

11:17. He would stay until 1:00 A.M. and then make his way back to the parking garage near Butch McGuire's, hoping to be home in Elmwood Park around 2 o'clock. Contrary to most of the others in the room, Saturday was a work day for Louie. If Louie got lucky and paired off with one of the lovely "escort" ladies, he would, of course, have to adjust this schedule. So far, after several years of attending these gatherings, Louie had only got lucky once, but it was a doozy. The unexpected event gave the lonely man a fuzzy feeling for several days afterward. Unfortunately, the intriguing lady had never shown up again. Self-deprecating by nature, Louie assumed it was because she didn't want to have to spend another night with him.

"Here you are, sir."

"Thanks." Louie dropped a five in the tip glass, wrapped his thick fingers around the drink and walked over to one of the many large windows in the expansive living room and looked out at the dazzling lights of the big city below.

Chapter 12

"What the hell's the name of that lake?"

"It's like I told ya Jake, Wawasee, with the accent on the ee. 'Wa-wa-see'. Got it?"

Slightly aggravated, Jake leaned on the stirring wheel and looked away from his partner. "Alright, alright, calm down a little."

Hawk knew that Jake didn't like following some family around a lake in Indiana anymore than he did. They were trained to go after bad guys, like the legendary Al Capone or someone who was trying to do harm to our country, like the infamous Aldrich Ames. This assignment was chump change, even for a young agent.

"It's only 8:30. Maybe we can catch a little of the Cub's game. How far is the motel?" Hawk asked.

"Just up the road."

"There's a Walmart over to the right; stop for a minute. I need some toothpaste."

The turn signal flashed on the side of the road as they turned into the huge parking lot just as the song, Chicago, blared out from his cell phone.

"Hmmm…kind of late for a call." Hawk lifted the phone from the small tray in the middle of the armrest.

He shot a glance at Jake. "It's Wade. Wonder what he wants?"

Jake shook his head and pulled to a stop at the back of the lot. "We'll soon find out. I'll activate the hands-free so we both can hear."

Hawk nodded and then spoke, "What's up boss?"

"I'm calling you and Jake off this assignment for now."

"Oh yeah, what happened?"

"Dunno, got a call from D. C."

"D. C. you say!" He threw a surprised glance at Jake.

"Finish your report and head back home. Try to get a refund for the room. If you can't, just forget it."

"Okay, you're the boss."

"See ya Monday, unless something comes up."

"Okay."

Hawk turned off his phone and loosened his tie. "I guess this is a little bigger operation than we thought. First time in all my years that I've been called off a job from D.C."

Jake smiled. "Can you do the report on your laptop on the way home?"

"I don't know why not."

"Still want that toothpaste?"

"No, let's stop at the motel and see what we can do about the room and then get out of here."

"10-4."

Chapter 13

"Come on, baby! Come on down!" Vito screamed. His face was flushed and sweaty and covered with a big, swarthy smile. The dancer moved sensually down to her knees in front of him. He pulled back on the G-string and carefully stuffed in the five spot. The loud, pounding music seemed to ratchet up a few decibels as the all but naked dancer stood and wiggled her way down the runway to the next customer.

"I think she likes me!" Vito bragged.

"She likes your cash, that's all," the man seated next to him shouted over the music.

Vito felt a vibration on his leg. "I'm getting a call," he laughed. "Hope it's not the old lady!"

"Better not answer it."

"I won't if it's her."

Vito chuckled nervously as he checked the screen. He put his hand over his ear and moved away from the bright, flashing lights of the long runway. "Barnes, is that you?"

"What the hell's all that music? Where are you?"

"Uh...I just stopped for a few drinks after work. What's up?"

"Are you in some topless bar, Vito?"

Vito featured himself a tough guy from the mean streets of West Chicago. He had been an associate for the mob since his youth and he didn't like the way the older Barnes talked to him. Sometimes it bothered him more than others—this was one of those times.

"Yeah, so what? You're no angel yourself, Barnes! Besides, it's none of your business what I do in my spare time!"

Barnes, apparently agitated by the strong response from a person he had so little respect for, paused. He finally spoke, "Listen up Vito, this thing is escalating."

By now Vito had made his way out of the noisy bar and was walking toward the back parking lot, "Escalating, what do you mean?"

"Alex sent Josh Dulin up to Elmwood Park for a surprise audit and a couple of guys, probably Feds, are following Crane around at the lake."

"What? An audit at the Chicago office! I knew it, damn it I knew it!" Vito couldn't believe his ears. He slammed his fist against the fender of a nearby pick-up. "Now you listen to me, Barnes! I didn't bargain for any of this. I got involved in this mess just to make some quick cash, that's all. I'm just a securities dealer; this isn't my problem!"

"The hell it isn't, Vito! You're involved in this up to your eyeballs!"

"That's bull and you know it! Don't call me again unless it involves me."

Barnes was becoming angry. "This was your baby from the get-go, Vito. I wouldn't even know Ed Moretti if it wasn't for you!"

"I asked you to help Moretti with his campaign, that's all."

"Why'd you ask me, Vito? Why did you ask the Chairman of the Board of the biggest bank in the Midwest? You know why—because you wanted me to skim money from my bank for your buddy's campaign. So cut the crap!"

"I know nothing about that!"

"What about that night at the club, Vito?"

"What night?"

"That night you and I were having dinner at the club with Montrose and you laughed and said that we could take funds from the Elmwood Park office and big Louie would never know the difference."

"I must have been drunk."

"You weren't that drunk. You're the one who strong-armed Louie's controller, Paul Rizzo, into quitting so Montrose would have free reign at Louie's office."

Frustrated by Barnes right on assessment of the situation and no match for him intellectually, Vito abruptly ended the call and angrily clicked off his phone. He began pacing back and forth in the parking lot. The ramifications of their little game could be far reaching, and like Barnes, he was very worried. He punched in another number and pushed the phone to his ear.

"Yes Vito, what is it?"

"Barnes just called and told me that a couple of Federal guys, probably FBI, have been following Crane and his family around at their lake home.

"Hmmm…the FBI—doesn't surprise me."

"Why do you think the feds are following Crane and his family around anyway?" Vito asked.

"Intimidation."

"For what reason?"

"Midwest Consolidated is key to the President's reelection plans and the bank has a huge presence in Missouri, Illinois, Michigan, Indiana and Ohio. Moretti carried Illinois and Michigan pretty comfortably in the last election, so they should stay in his camp. But it was close in Missouri, Indiana and Ohio and if he doesn't carry those states in the next general he won't get reelected. And, all three states have a history of voting Republican in the Presidential elections." There was a pause.

"Go on."

"In addition to their corporate center in Indianapolis, Midwest has major offices in St. Louis, Cleveland, Cincinnati, and Columbus, along with scores of smaller branches spread throughout all those states, as well as hundreds of mortgage originating offices. Plus, in addition to the offices, there are all those ATM machines and electronic banking centers tucked all over the place. If Midwest fails, the party in power is going to look real bad in those states. Thousands of people could be laid off and tens of thousands of account holders could be affected. The media would have a field day; they love to demonize the banks. It would bode poorly for the Presidential election. Barnes feels that the only way Midwest is staying afloat is to keep the bailout money and Crane wants to pay it back."

"But why the goons on Alex?" Vito said quizzically.

There was a long, exasperating sigh. "Well, my cerebral friend, because the current administration, including the President, is watching Midwest Consolidated very closely. If Crane insists on repaying the bailout money, the party feels the bank could fail— Crane feels otherwise. The fall mid-term elections don't look good for the Democratic Party and Moretti is desperately afraid that he will lose the general. Alex Crane has a great big bulls-eye on his back right now and they want him to know it. They are attempting to intimidate him so that he will keep the TARP money—at least until after the Presidential elections."

"Makes sense and thanks for the info."

"Anything else?

"Naw and I better run, got some people waiting inside." Vito was mum on the audit. As far as he knew, only he and Barnes and Montrose knew about it and he wanted to keep it that way.

"Okay, Vito, and tuck one for me, will ya?"

"Smart aleck," Vito snorted.

The bright lights flashed along the runway, the loud music pounded as the anxious broker wiped his forehead dry with his handkerchief and re-entered the seedy nightspot just in time for his favorite dancer's next set.

Chapter 14

Red lights reflected across the crowded room, but the party-goers paid little attention as the corporate helicopter drifted slowly past the large thirtieth floor window. The two men inside the glass bubble leaned forward to try and get a better view of the festivities in the lavish top floor condo. Still standing by the window, Louie smiled at the curious gawkers.   After a few seconds, the chopper rose and darted away. Louie felt a tap on his shoulder.

"Louie, my friend! How are you?"

Louie wheeled around at the sound of the familiar voice.

"Fine, Ben," a surprised Louie replied. "What are you doing in town?"

"Ed sent me home to take care of a few loose ends from the campaign. The women are looking pretty hot here tonight. Tommy must be doing his homework."

Louie nodded at the powerful Ben Ramsey. Ramsey occasionally made an appearance at Tommy's get-togethers, much to the dismay of the others. Cocky and abrasive, he rubbed a lot of people the wrong way.

"You makin' any money over there in Little Italy, fat boy?"

"I'm trying, Ben, I'm trying."

"Good. I better move on, Louie, I got some catching up to do."

Alone again, Louie headed for the nearby guest bath for some necessary relief. The sound of the soft music faded as he closed the door to the small room. A short time later, with drink in hand, he opened the door and reentered the party. As he made his way to the big room, he hesitated in the darkened hallway just outside the half-bath. Certain no one was watching, he did what he so often did. He slid his cell phone from his pocket and snapped several one-handed pictures of the party. It was a nervous habit of his—a way for an introverted guy to pass some time at a party. He didn't do anything with the pictures. When the memory card filled up, he would print the pictures and throw them in a catch-all drawer in his den.

Suddenly, the mouth-watering scent of teriyaki marinade drifted into the narrow hall. Louie dropped the phone back in his jacket pocket, stepped back into the light of the room and made his way to the hors d'oeuvre table.

Chapter 15

Early morning dew glistened on the rod iron fence as the silver Mercedes pulled onto 116th Street. It was 7:30 A.M. on Monday morning and Barnes was beginning his daily commute to his law firm that was located just west of the circle in downtown Indianapolis. An early riser, he took pride in the fact that he was always the first partner to arrive at the office each morning. That meant being there no later than 7:50. The drive from Carmel to downtown Indy was no more than fifteen to twenty minutes, unless there was a delay, so he was leaving in plenty of time. The powerful engine of his Mercedes revved as he shifted from first to second and raced down the road, slowing occasionally for the annoying round-abouts as he made his way to North Meridian Street and the final leg of his journey.

Barnes felt conflicted as he drove past the lavish estates on North Meridian. The events of the past weekend were not to his liking. Barnes looked at the world as a game or a contest—like prize fighting—or an even more accurate description, ultimate fighting. He would do almost anything to gain the advantage in the rough and tumble world of politics or business. He'd take someone's best shot, bounce up and kick them in the groin while smiling from ear to ear. But he drew the line when it came to family—or the family of anyone involved in his iniquitous games.

As it was with the mobsters he had grown up with in Boston, families were off limits. That's why, as requested by Crane, he had called Party Chief, Bill Worthem, to try and get the goons off Crane's family. Worthem had contacted him later that evening, leaving a terse message on Barnes's phone, "Request granted on temporary basis." A small player in a big game, Barnes realized that he was pushing his luck with the request, but true to his own sense of values, he knew he had to try. And as the message implied, he had won—at least for now. But inside, he knew that much bigger challenges lie ahead. The audit in Chicago could cause him terrible harm; the whole house of cards could tumble down if the scheme to divert funds to the Moretti campaign was uncovered. He would face personal humiliation along with possible jail time. Everything he had worked for all his life would go up in smoke. It was a terrifying thought.

. . . .

The room felt a little muggy. It was 7:53 and the air conditioning didn't kick on completely until 7:50 each day. The room was just beginning to cool down as Barnes made his way to his desk. His office was surprisingly small and cluttered. As the main partner in the firm, Barnes could certainly have a large, expensively furnished office—the other partners did. They had turned their expansive offices into small living rooms with separate conference areas, but Barnes felt more comfortable in his little office. "Everything is just an arms-length away," he would explain when asked about his modest surroundings. Then he would add, "And that's the way I like it".

Smoke soon filled the air as Barnes lit up his one and only cigar for the day. Although he promoted a smoke-free office and was banned from smoking at home by a health conscious wife, he managed to get a few drags from his cigar every morning before the rest of the staff arrived. Everyone, including his many clients, knew the harmless dance and thought nothing of it. The smell of stale cigar smoke would hang in his office for half the day, but Barnes could honestly say that he never smoked during normal business hours. After one last hard drag, he punched out the cigar in a small metal ashtray and then put it in his bottom desk drawer.

Hearing voices by the front entrance, Barnes grabbed a thick file off his desk top and headed to the front of the building. When he arrived, he was surprised to see Party Chief, Bill Worthem, standing near the door.

"Good morning Bill, what a nice surprise. You haven't been to my office for awhile."

The thin man with a shiny, bald head, wearing a gray pin-striped suit, smiled at his occasional golfing companion. He stepped forward, hand outstretched, and the two men shook hands. "Got a minute?" he asked.

"Why certainly, Bill. Why don't we step into the conference room?"

The stocky partner led Bill through the door into the conference room that was located near the front door.

Inside, an attractive lady in a blue business suit, smiled broadly at the men as she finished making the coffee.

Barnes introduced the young lady, "Bill, I'd like for you to meet our next partner here at O'Brien and Son, Amy Connelly. She's kind enough to make our coffee every morning."

The blushing lady smiled and nodded. "Thank you, Barnes," she said, pausing next to her beaming manager on the way out of the room. "Can I help you with anything, Mr. O'Brien?"

"Yes, would you please have someone type this for me?"

"Certainly." The helpful attorney took the file from Barnes's outstretched hand and left the room leaving the two men alone.

"Coffee, Bill?"

"No thanks, I've only got a few minutes. I'm on my way to a party event in Crawfordsville. The local sheriff is having trouble with his reelection bid."

Barnes nodded.

Worthem walked around and took a seat at the other end of the table as if to say "This may be your office, but you're not in charge." Bill Worthem was a tough political operative who had headed up the Democratic machine in Indianapolis for more than twenty years. An attorney by trade, he didn't shy away from confrontations and was considered "One of our top party leaders" by President Moretti after helping him carry Indiana in the last election. Many in the media were speculating that after the recent resignation of a key White House counsel, the President would tap Worthem for the job.

The powerful party man cleared his throat. "That

was quite a brash move Friday evening. You rattled some chains—that's for sure."

Barnes seemed irritated by Worthem's abruptness. "What's going on here Bill? When did this cops and robbers stuff start?"

The corner of the party boss's mouth turned up in a dismissing grin. Ignoring Barnes question, he continued, "I'll try and make this clear; the party doesn't like our local fund raising chairman sticking his nose into Government business. There are reasons for everything we do. We need you to keep your thoughts to yourself and go about your business."

Barnes slammed his fist on the table, "Local fund raiser is it? I raised millions of dollars for that campaign and I don't like being threatened by some over-ambitious party hack!"

Worthem took a deep breath, trying to ignore the insult. "You heard me, Barnes, keep your mouth shut. No more calls to me or other party officials about FBI activities."

"Now, you listen to me Bill; I'm no fan of Crane. In fact, I'd like to break him in half but I don't like his family being followed by guys in dark suits."

"We need Midwest to keep that TARP money. It's imperative that Midwest Consolidated be in good shape for the next Presidential election and Crane is standing in our way. We have our way of dealing with such things—Crane's family will not get hurt."

"I hope not."

He gave Barnes a sharp stare and went on, "The Ambassador to Ireland will announce his retirement at the first of next month. Right now, close aides of the President have told me that you are the leading candidate for that job. One more episode like Friday night, Barnes, and I guarantee you that the closest you'll ever get to Ireland will be at O'Haver's" Pub on Saint Patrick's Day."

"Don't threaten me, Bill!" Barnes stared angrily at the party chief. "A lot of cash came out of Elmwood Park during the campaign and I've got a whistle too."

"It's obvious that you're not thinking clearly. We must keep that particular situation out of all dialogue. You're being irrational with such threats. As it stands now, you're highly regarded in the party, but that could change in a hurry. The bottom line is, what happened Friday night is none of your business."

"Every time you put those goons on Crane's family, he's going to call me. He's not going to call you or President Moretti."

"Just tell him you are a local fund raiser and you know nothing about it."

Barnes laughed sarcastically, "You've got it all figured out, don't you Bill? Well, you don't know everything."

Worthem's brow lifted.

"There's an audit in process at Midwest's Elmwood Park office as we speak Bill. It seems Crane's auditor, Josh Dulin, is on to something. He's starting to uncover our little scheme to raise campaign funds."

"Like I said, Barnes, I don't like talking about that situation."

"Oh…I'm sure you don't. But you'd better start looking for a good attorney, you might need one."

"Moretti will deal with any audits in due time. He's the most powerful man in the world and he can get plenty serious when he has too. In the meantime, I would suggest that you continue to tow the party line."

"Like I say Worthem, you better watch your backside."

The exasperated party boss shook his head in frustration. He stood and walked slowly toward the door. Pausing next to the feisty attorney, he spoke quietly, "Think about it, Barnes, you've become a very, very wealthy man and you're past sixty years old. You have a wonderful family and you are about to fulfill your life's dream. You have a nice retirement ahead of you." He leaned closer, his face only inches from the aging attorney. He was almost whispering now, "Our President is trying to hold on to his power and he will stop at nothing to do so. Keep your future bright, Barnes. Keep your nose out of our business."

The office door closed behind him; Barnes stood motionless. He felt very warm and perspiration began to dampen his shirt. The tough Irishman had been shaken by the ominous threat from Worthem. Sudden laughter out in the lobby shook him out of his thoughts. It was time to greet the other partners and staff for the day. He stood and paused before leaving the room. For the first time he understood the totality of the situation in which he was involved. Moretti's charming, smiling face flashed through his mind. To think such an apparently nice man could be the source of such intimidation was indeed shocking. He wanted to savage Worthem. He wanted to tear him apart, but he knew that he had no choice but to "tow the party line" and it infuriated him. "That pompous ass!" he moaned just before he opened the door to the lobby.

Chapter 16

"I gotcha Grandpa! I gotcha!" The diminutive seven year old shouted in glee, clutching tightly to Alex's lower leg. The two friendly warriors struggled across the thick lawn on the warm summer evening. Suddenly, Alex rolled to the ground, covering his head with both hands. The excited seven year old crashed on top of him, punching Alex, for all he was worth. Nearby, Nicky was busy tightening the straps on granddaughter Katie's lifejacket, preparing her for a much anticipated boat ride. Alex's son and daughter-in-law, Jarod and Missy, played volleyball in the side yard with a young neighbor couple.

"You haven't got anybody, you little troublemaker!" Alex lifted the hysterically laughing boy above him, shaking him gently and then dropping him to his chest for a tight hug. Nearby, Jarod gathered up the loose volleyball, glanced over and smiled at the doting grandfather. With her lifejacket secure, granddaughter Katie ran toward her grandpa.

"Time for a boat ride, Grandpa!" she shouted.

Many years ago, Alex had appointed himself commodore of the small stable of boats they kept at their lake home. It was a job he coveted and one he would not relinquish to anyone.

"Yeah Grandpa, boat ride!" the exuberant Eli shouted. Alex set the giggling boy carefully on the ground.

Nicky hurried over and slipped a lifejacket around Eli's shoulders and strapped it tight. She smiled at her husband. "Better get going, dear. It's getting late and we still have to put some food in these kids' bellies and get them ready for bed. And, you have an early trip to Chicago in the morning."

Alex jumped to his feet and brushed the grass clippings from his bathing suit. "Okay kids, let's get going." Alex raced toward the boat.

The two happy children ran toward the long pier, shoving each other along the way. "Which boat, Grandpa?" eleven year old Katie asked.

"Let's take the pontoon; it's easier to get off and on for swimming. Don't get in the boat until I get there!" he commanded.

"You can grill some brats and dogs for the kids when you get in," Nicky suggested.

"Okay, honey. I'll take them to the sandbar for a little swimming and then we'll head back. Give us about an hour."

"No longer than that, please. The day's kind of gotten away from us."

"Okay." Alex hurried over and helped the children into the large pontoon. He then lifted the thick ropes from the pier posts, tossed them in the boat, and joined the children inside the wobbly craft. Soon they were cruising through the rough waters of Lake Wawasee. Alex glanced back at the shore as Nicky hurried into the house to get things around for dinner.

Alex felt at peace as he bounced across the choppy lake toward the popular sandbar, a shallow spot in the lake that the locals had adopted as their favorite swimming hole.

Fortunately, the two menacing men who had been shadowing them earlier in the weekend had not reappeared since his call to Barnes. But Alex understood that all was not over; he knew things would get worse before they got better. This situation was escalating and he feared that things could get rough. He also understood that his family was a point of vulnerability for him. If attempts to intimidate or frighten his family continued, he would protect them at all costs. For the time being, it appeared that Barnes had rectified the situation and he prayed it would stay that way.

Earlier that day Alex had received an e-mail from Louie Campano requesting a meeting in the Chicago office on Tuesday morning. The office was only a two hour drive from their cottage, so he and Nicky and the kids had decided to stay at the cottage for a couple more days. Alex would drive up to the meeting on Tuesday and then return to the lake in the afternoon. They would then drive back to Indianapolis Tuesday evening.

Louie had assured Alex that the meeting was routine. He said all he needed was a little time with him to go over some pressing issues at his office. But with the recent discovery at that office, Crane wasn't sure what to expect. He trusted Louie, but he also wondered if the congenial manager had become an unknowing pawn in this treacherous game.

A huge wave suddenly appeared in front of the boat. The pointy pontoons knifed into the dark wave sending a cold spray of water splashing through the boat, completely soaking Alex and the children. The children screamed in delight, shouting in unison, "Do that again, Grandpa! Do it again!" Alex, not nearly as excited about the frigid experience as the children, hoped that he had just experienced his last tsunami wave for the day.

Moments later, a large cluster of anchored boats came into view. Alex pulled back on the throttle and began looking for an opening among the bobbing watercraft. Finally, he located an acceptable spot. He tossed the anchor overboard and killed the engine. Soon, the kids were in the lake, screaming and splashing in the clear water. Alex was beaming. He loved these times at the lake with the grandkids—he wouldn't trade them for anything.

. . . .

Their lips blue and shivering beneath the large beach towels, the exhausted children huddled in the captain's chair next to their grandpa for the trip back to the cottage. Alex accelerated slowly, hugging the shoreline and avoiding the large orange buoys that marked the restricted swimming areas. In their exuberance, he and the children had stayed too long and it was starting to get dark—Grandma was not going to be very happy.

Alex surveyed the approaching wetland with its tall reeds and frog infested lily pads. He gazed in delight as graceful sea gulls dive-bombed at the hull of the cruising boat. A flock of Canada geese honked as they flew overhead in perfect formation in the darkening sky.

"What a paradise!" Alex sighed. Unfortunately, his melodious trance didn't last very long. A powerful engine roared behind him. Alex glanced to the rear. A boat was fast approaching, too quickly for this time of day when low throttle was required. It was a large speed boat with a high, menacing hull. The two dark figures in the front were indiscernible against the setting sun. Alex's pulse quickened. He scanned the isolated bay that bordered their lake home for any signs of other watercraft, but there were none around. The trailing boat moved closer. With only four Department of Natural Resources officers assigned to cover more than one hundred lakes in the vast resort area, enforcement on the lakes, for the most part, was left up to the residents. This type of behavior at dusk was unusual. *Who could they be? Who would so blatantly break the rules?* Alex glanced over at the frightened children and then back at the menacing craft.

The mysterious boat seemed to be picking up speed as it came closer. The sky was continuing to darken, reducing visibility. Alex felt trapped. He couldn't turn right inside the swimming buoys and a left turn would throw them right in front of the fast approaching boat. The dark craft was now only a hundred feet away and coming hard. Heart pounding, Alex saw the final swimming buoy just before the wetlands. He gunned the boat toward the last buoy. His arm went over his face for protection against a flock of low flying mallards. He spun in his seat; one of the darkened figures in the boat raised his arm and jabbed it toward them. Alex leaned in front of the children to protect them. The outboard engine whined, pushing the cumbersome craft forward.

"What's the matter, Grandpa?" Katie shouted. "Why are you pushing against us, Grandpa?" Eli bawled. The children hugged tightly to his legs.

The boat was now right on top of them; panic

flooded through the normally cool Alex. The unexpected intruders had caught him totally off guard—his heart was in his throat. The hull of the speeding boat was just a few feet from the struggling pontoon and the driver's arm was pointed directly at them. Alex kept himself between the boat and the children, bracing for the assault.

"Who are those men, Grandpa?" Katie screamed.

"We're gonna die!" Eli cried.

Suddenly the huge hull peeled left and a voice shot out, "Stay out of the way, old man!"

Alex spun around to see a muscular teenager showing him his middle finger. He and a companion whizzed past, howling in laughter. The big waves from the passing boat pushed the pontoon toward the shore. Alex spun back around; the pontoon was racing toward the large boulders that lined the shoreline in the wetland.

"Grandpa! Grandpa! Look out for the rocks!" Katie screamed.

Alex grabbed the throttle and yanked hard, slamming the motor into reverse. The hundred fifty horse engine sputtered and groaned as it strained mightily to stop the momentum of the heavy boat.

The shaken children clung mightily to their grandpa, waiting for the crash landing on the rocks. The big engine revved violently and then finally caught hold.

Wide-eyed, his face wet with perspiration, Alex watched in disbelief as the long vessel came to a stop just inches from an enormous boulder. He crammed the boat into neutral and fell to his knee, hugging the children.

"Who were those men, Grandpa?" the older Katie

asked. "Why did they try to run over us?"

Alex pulled them closer. "Everything is okay; it was just some crazy kids." With one arm around the children, Alex reached for the controls, backed the boat around and out of the reedy area. He looked across the lake at the large speed boat as it disappeared into a distant bay. "Smart alecks," he mumbled.

The frightening episode was a stark reminder to Alex of the threatening situation he had been cast into at the bank. Although these were just a couple of drunken kids, something deep inside told him that it could have just as easily been a real provocation. Alex prided himself in keeping his emotions under control. That event, along with the two goons earlier in the weekend, had thrown him off his game. He vowed to never let that happen again. Mentally tough and fit, he would be ready for the next threat. Real or not, he would be ready.

With the children back in their seats and starting to calm down, Alex guided the boat back to deep water and continued their trip across the bay to the cottage.

Chapter 17

"Thank you, Esther."

The steaming black liquid splashed in the thick mug. He took a deep breath, the scent of fresh brewed coffee smelled wonderful. Butch lifted the cup, filled to the three-quarters level as he demanded, and gently blew across the rim of the cup dispersing the ropes of steam. Esther took her leave and retired to the maid's quarters.

Alone, the aging mobster took a sip. He savored the warm beverage for a moment before looking out his dining room window and giving his daily nod to the statue of the Patron Saint Maurice that was located at the end of a long courtyard. A devout Catholic, he felt a connection to the powerful warrior Saint, standing in full battle armor and leaning against his shield. The inscription below the statue explained how the courageous Saint had died in an epic battle in 286 A.D. fighting for his beliefs. Alonzo "Butch" Ferinni understood that kind of sacrifice—often fantasizing his own death in a blazing gunfight with a rival gang while defending his turf.

On this typical hot summer day, the large house was quiet as usual. There was no one in the living area but Butch. His seventeen year old son was away at military school in Indiana. His wife, nearly twenty years his junior, was still slumbering in their expansive master bedroom on the second floor. As was their routine, he would be long departed before she made her way downstairs later in the morning.

Butch listened as a large lawn tractor groaned to life in the front yard. His groundskeeper had started his work for the day. He would work the front yard area until Butch left the premises, knowing better than to disturb his boss's morning ritual.

Butch Ferinni was a powerful man in the declining, yet still active, Chicago crime syndicate. Revenues from his construction business and waste management company, along with some diminishing revenues from bookmaking and gambling machines, allowed him to maintain a nice life style.

Growing up on the rough West Side of Chicago in the heavily Italian neighborhood of Elmwood Park, Butch had known from the time he was a small boy watching the long black limos drive slowly down the red brick streets of his neighborhood that he wanted to be a made man. His quest began at age nineteen when he became an associate, running errands for the soldiers and capos in the Elmwood Park area. After a few years, he was elated when he was made a soldier himself. Possessing a charming personality and not afraid to use violence when called upon, he soon caught the eye of the Elmwood Park boss, Joseph "Jo Jo" Piazza. After taking out a couple of "bums" from an opposing outfit, he was elevated to capo by Piazza. Shortly thereafter, he was made an Under Boss when George "The Boogey Man" Egidi was arrested by the Feds and given ten to twenty for racketeering.

A mercurial personality, whose emotions could turn on a dime, the young Under Boss soon became both respected and feared by the other mob bosses in the Chicago area. Although prone to periodic gestures of great generosity, he would cut the legs off anybody who stood in his way. A loyalist to a fault, he resisted the temptation to move to the exclusive River Forest community with many of his mob friends when he started to move up in the organization. Instead, he chose to remain in his hometown of Elmwood Park.

Always in awe of his long-time mentor, Piazza, a devastated Butch was made boss in 1970 when Piazza came up missing while vacationing in the nearby Wisconsin Dells. Incensed by the death of his beloved boss, Butch vowed revenge against the rival gangs, but fortunately for his unsuspecting adversaries, a park ranger found the body of Piazza on a hiking trail deep in the Dells. The resulting autopsy revealed that Piazza had died of a massive heart attack while taking a hike in the scenic woods and a blood bath between rival gangs was avoided.

"Hey, boss," the gravelly voice shot out of the nearby speaker.

"Yeah?"

"Mr. Compano has arrived; he's here at the gate."

The silverware jumped as Butch violently slammed his huge fist against the oak table. "He's what?"

The voice quieted, it was almost inaudible. "He's at the gate, sir."

Embarrassed and red-faced, Butch tried desperately to compose himself. His old school chum had arrived and Butch was incensed by his guard's action. He spoke with calm rage, "How long have you known Mr.

Compano, Johnny?"

"For many years, sir."

"And you have humiliated him by holding him at the gate?"

"I'm sorry sir, but you said we had to be extra careful with all…."

Butch interrupted, "You idiot! Apologize to Mr. Compano and then have Esther greet him at the door and bring him to me."

"Yes sir."

Butch abruptly clicked off the speaker, leapt from his chair and hurried around the room partially closing the blinds on the many windows in the large dining area. The rising sun was pouring into the room and he wanted the lighting just right. His anger over the incident at the gate was starting to subside and he was now excited by the arrival of his old friend, Louie Campano. Johnny's behavior would soon be forgotten and there would be no retribution against the scolded guard—Butch loved him like a son. He could now hear Campano's voice out in the main vestibule. He watched as the large doors pushed open and Esther escorted him into the room. Arms wide apart, Butch rushed forward.

"Louie! Louie! How are you?" The two large men embraced, followed by several aggressive slaps to the back.

"Come-in! Come-in!" Butch waved his arm toward the large oak table.

"Coffee, Mr. Compano?" Esther asked at just the right moment.

"Yes Esther, and sweetener please."

Esther smiled warmly and hurried off to fetch the coffee while the two men made their way to the table to talk and enjoy the beautiful view of the courtyard.

The reserved Louie waited by his chair before sitting. Butch, already seated, pointed to the chair inviting him to sit down.

"Sit down, Louie."

"Thank you, Curly." Louie grinned sheepishly. He was the only human being on the planet that could get away with calling the hardened mobster Curly. A childhood nickname given to Butch because he had a mop of black curly hair as a boy, Ferinni had stopped the use of the old name long ago. He felt it was inappropriate for a tough guy gangster. Louie knew this and would only say it once as a gesture of affection for the old days; the rest of the time he would call him Butch.

A seldom seen broad smile spread across Butch's pocked face. He rubbed his balding head. "I wish I still had those curls. It is so good to see you my friend!"

"Likewise, amico mio."

Still smiling, Louie scanned the lavish room, looking out toward the beautifully landscaped courtyard and the ever vigilant Saint Maurice. "You've done very well for yourself Butch. I'm always very impressed when I come to your wonderful home."

Almost without notice, Esther set a cup of coffee in front of Louie and refilled Butch's cup, and left a warming carafe on the table before exiting the room.

Butch smiled, "And who would have thought, when you were making those big holes in the defensive line for me so many years ago in high school, that you would end up the president of a large bank?"

The humble Louie's face flushed. "We have been blessed—that's for certain."

"I agree and I thank you for coming, Louie. I hope I haven't interrupted your busy day."

"Oh no! Since Midwest took over, I have plenty of time. They're running everything out of Indianapolis now."

"Hmmm....I see, like I prefer to run things from my home," the mobster laughed heartily.

Louie wagged his head. "I guess so." He stared at Butch, waiting for more information to explain why Butch had requested this visit.

"I will get to the point, Louie. It's like I told you on the phone. I am thinking about putting in a pool for my Maria. She has seemed down lately and I think it would perk her up a little to have a nice pool; it would give her something to look forward to each day. Come outside and I will show you what I mean."

Louie nodded. The two men picked up their cups as Butch led the way through a thick glass door and out to a large stone patio.

"You see that landscaped area between my patio and the long courtyard?"

"Yes."

"I was thinking that it might be a good spot for a pool. Do you think it is a big enough area?"

A puzzled look crossed Louie's face. "Well, actually, to tell you the truth, it looks a little small." Not wanting to bring a negative tone to the upbeat conversation, Louie was a little tentative. "I'm....uh not sure a pool would fit there. But I'm a banker, not a contractor. I think you need to talk with a contractor."

The smile suddenly drained from Butch's face. His dark eyes squinted into the morning sun. "I know you must think it is odd that I bring you out to my home and ask you such questions."

Louie stared quizzically at his somber friend.

Butch exhaled and sat down on the stone wall that bordered the patio. "My life is not what it appears. I don't want to build a pool, Louie, I need the cash for another reason."

A concerned Louie stepped closer to his friend. "What's the problem, Butch?"

"It's Maria."

"Maria? What's the matter with Maria? Is she okay?"

"Well…uh physically, she's fine. But she's got this problem and I'm not sure what to do about it."

"Please, go on."

The mob boss took a deep breath, "You understand the nature of my business."

"Why yes, of course."

"Well you see the Feds have been on a rampage lately and our bookmaking business has almost dried up. And, with the weak economy, the revenues from our other businesses have also been down. " Tears glistened in the sagging eyes of the hard man, embarrassed by his diminished status. He continued, "And…uh Maria, well she has this problem." He clasped his hands around the warm coffee mug and continued. "It's not easy being married to someone like me. Maria has very little life of her own. Respectable ladies here in town don't have much to do with her. And unfortunately, her family lives in Florida and Colorado, so she is alone a lot. This is not a very exciting life for her."

"I understand. It's not what you see in the movies."

"No, it's not."

"It must be difficult for her."

"It is. And my Maria, she gets depressed, and when

she does, she shops and then she shops some more. Most of it is done on online. She has run up over two hundred thousand dollars in credit card bills in the past few years."

"Hmmm...."

"I had no idea; the UPS man comes late in the afternoon when I am gone. She has been hiding most of the goods in our attic."

Louie sat down on the edge of the wall and took a sip of coffee. "I see, and you need two hundred thousand to pay off Maria's shopping debts."

Butch nodded.

"Maybe we could do an equity line." He glanced toward Butch.

"I refinanced the house two years ago. Remember?"

"Oh yes, I forgot. We went to full equity on that one."

"Yes, I used that money to buy the waste management company."

"That's right, I remember now."

Butch scooted over next to Louie and laid his arm across his shoulders. "Our friendship goes back a long way and I think I'm putting you in an awkward position. Please forget what I said just now. I will get the money elsewhere."

Louie spoke softly to his life long friend, "You forget something, Butch Ferinni. Many years ago your father, God rest his soul, loaned my father twenty thousand dollars on a handshake so he could start Compano Federal. There would be no Compano Federal or Midwest Consolidated, or whatever we call it, without the generosity of your father."

"But that was my father. It was not me."

"You're right Butch, it was your father. But I know as well as I know my own heart, that you would have done exactly the same. I have no doubt of that. I will gladly do this loan for you."

"Thank you, you humble me."

Butch initiated another quick hug and the two men strolled through the house and out to the front drive. They paused by Louie's truck.

"I will have a six-month non-secured note for two hundred thousand dollars with an indefinite number of renewals prepared for you. I have several appointments Saturday but I could do your loan before office hours. Could you stop in early Saturday morning—say 7 A.M.?"

"I'll be there Saturday morning at 7:00 A.M. And, thank you so much Louie."

"My pleasure." The two men shook warmly. Then Louie walked to his old truck, opened the squeaky door and climbed in.

"Oh, Louie."

Louie paused, his generous posterior hanging awkwardly over the side of the badly worn driver's seat, "Yes, Butch?"

"If you ever need anything and I mean anything, you let me know, okay?"

"Okay," Louie said as he slid over, stuck the key in the ignition and started the truck. He slid the gear shift into drive, lifted his thumb in the air and pointed it toward Butch. As he pulled out of the compound, he repeated the same thumbs up gesture to a smiling Johnny and disappeared around the corner.

Chapter 18

Traffic was heavy on the Eisenhower and the exit ramp for Harlem Avenue was fast approaching. Uncomfortable driving on the crowded expressway in the best of circumstances, Alex truly despised the morning rush hour around Chicago. To add to the confusion, he heard a beep on his handheld. He quickly snatched his phone from the center console and attempted to read the text message while speeding toward his exit. The terse message, from Josh Dulin, read: *Just finished review. Took longer than expected. Can we meet at your office at 8 A.M tomorrow?*

A horn blared as Alex swerved onto the exit ramp. He slammed on his brakes to keep from running into a beat-up Domino's Pizza car in front of him. "Chicago traffic," he mumbled.

Once safely off the ramp and on North Harlem Avenue, Alex fumbled with his cell, attempting to send a quick text back to Josh. Not very adept at this new way of communicating, he found it maddening. He clumsily poked the letters o and k and then hit reply as he slammed on the brakes once again as the approaching stoplight turned from caution to red much faster than he expected. His anxiety level rising, Alex took the momentary pause to check out the GPS on his dash for the best route to Café Winberie's on Oak Park Avenue.

Louie had e-mailed him earlier that morning informing him that some surprise visitors would be at the meeting today. In order to accommodate the growing guest list, Louie had to relocate the late morning meeting to a larger room at Winberie's, instead of their original meeting place, Big Al's Bar and Grill in Elmwood Park. Alex was disappointed, he liked big Al's.

Arriving at Winberie's, Alex turned off Oak Park Avenue and navigated his way through the crowded parking lot at the popular eatery. Finally locating a parking spot, he carefully pulled into the narrow space, glanced at his watch and hurried inside. A smiling hostess directed him to the meeting place at the rear of the warmly decorated restaurant. When Alex arrived at the room, Louie Campano was pacing outside waiting on the tardy Alex.

"Alex, so good to see you!" The big Italian gave Alex a giant bear hug. "Betcha hit some bad traffic."

"There were two accidents—one near Gary and another just after I got on the Eisenhower." Alex smiled and straightened his tie, still reeling slightly from the powerful hug administered by his old friend.

Louie grunted, "Should have left a little earlier. Barnes and the others didn't have any trouble."

Barnes! The name exploded inside his head. What in the world was Barnes doing here and who were "the others" Louie just mentioned. Alex now realized that his meeting was going to be much different than the one to which he had originally been invited.

The observant Louie, sensing Alex's concern, spoke up. "I'm sorry for the confusion. This all just fell together this morning; I wasn't really certain who all was coming. Oh well, the more the merrier!" Louie smiled and pushed the door to the room open. "Follow me," he said.

Once inside, Alex quickly surveyed the room. Seated at the end of a long table in the center of the rectangular room was a man he had never met but recognized immediately from seeing him on television so many times. It was Ben Ramsey, the former college roommate of President Moretti at nearby DePaul University and now, his Chief of Staff. Alex was shocked to see Ramsey in attendance. His presence gave weight to the importance of this impromptu get-together. Insiders say the President takes his cue from the former Illinois Senator on topics, such as, the controversial health care legislation and cap and trade. His presence troubled Alex.

Seated just to Ramsey's left, a stoic Barnes sat staring straight ahead, still smarting from Alex's dressing down a few days earlier. Begrudgingly, he turned slightly and acknowledged Alex with a rather weak attempt at a smile.

To Ramsey's right, two aides, who had several memos scattered on the table in front of them, busied themselves with various recording devices.

Seated next to Barnes was Louie's secretary, Ava. She smiled at Alex and mouthed the word hello. Louie quickly took a seat next to her. Behind Ramsey, two blocky security guys stood with hands clasped and legs apart. Slightly intimidated by a hard stare from one of the guards, the former Navy Seal remembered his pledge to stay on game no matter what the situation. He gathered himself and smiled confidently at the guard as the aggressive Chief of Staff hurried around the table toward him with his hand outstretched.

"Ben Ramsey, Alex, it's a pleasure to meet you." He smiled broadly. "I hope we haven't overwhelmed you with this sudden get-together."

The two men shook firmly, Alex made direct eye contact. "Certainly not, I've learned recently to expect almost anything."

"Please, have a seat." Ramsey pointed to the end seat.

Alex dropped his briefcase on the table and found his seat. A single legal pad and ballpoint pen lay on the table in front of him. It contrasted greatly with all the recording devices, attaché cases full of files, and laptop computers being employed by Ramsey's aides at the other end of the table. It was soon obvious who was in charge of this meeting.

"Coffee, Crane?" the preppy Chief of Staff asked. The last name salutation was a mild power play by Ramsey. Slightly inappropriate, it indicated Ramsey's need to show dominance.

"Yes, thank you. Black, with a shot of Jack Daniels, please—I could use a drink right now." Alex said dryly, exhibiting an irreverent sense of humor in response to Ramsey's gentle put-down.

Ramsey chuckled nervously; his brow lifted as he looked over at a dubious Alex. He turned to his right and mumbled, "Cybil."

A shapely blond in a gray business suit jumped to her feet and hurried to the coffee pot. She quickly poured a cup and delivered it to Alex. "Sorry couldn't find any Jack." She grinned flirtatiously at the handsome CEO and hurried back to her seat.

Ramsey returned to the head of the table. Alex slumped back in his chair and assumed a relaxed position. Cool on the outside, he was buzzing with anxiety on the inside.

"I would like to thank all of you for coming today. I realize Chicago traffic can be overwhelming, especially when you're not used to it," Ramsey said.

The gall of this man; this was a bank meeting called by Louie and this guy invites himself at the last minute and then takes charge of the meeting. Alex was fuming.

Ramsey went on, "I particularly appreciate Alex and my good friend, Barnes, driving all the way from Indianapolis to be here with us."

Barnes threw an over-exuberant smile at the powerful man. Alex nodded lazily.

"I know there are some banking issues that you gentlemen need to discuss, but you will have to do it later. We plan to fly back to Washington at 11:30 and therefore, time is of the essence. So, I will get right to the point. First of all, the President wanted me to tell you personally just how appreciative he is of the support given him by all of you here at Midwest Bank during the last election. He looks forward to continuing this close relationship in the years leading up to his reelection campaign. He sends his warmest regards."

All of you? Alex thought.

"Your chairman, Barnes O'Brien, and the President have developed a particularly close personal relationship over the past several months. He looks forward to the possibility of more involvement by Barnes in his administration."

Barnes smiled smugly.

Ramsey turned to his right, "Okay, Cybil."

His assistant and the other aide immediately began packing up all the recording equipment and stuffing legal pens and pads into a large briefcase that suddenly appeared from under the table. Cybil then went around the table, smiling warmly and collecting all the pads and pencils and stuffing them in the briefcase. She smiled at Ava and pointed at the door. With Louie's nod of approval, Ava rose and started for the back of the room. Then, along with the security guards, Cybil and her colleagues also headed for the door. When she passed by Alex, she leaned over and whispered, "Please put your briefcase on the floor, Mr. Crane." At the same moment, he received a reinforcing stare from Ramsey. Alex reluctantly set the case on the floor next to his chair. The door shut behind him.

"What's this all about?" a befuddled Louie Campano asked.

"Oh…uh sorry Mr. Campano. I didn't mean to alarm you. It's just that I have some very personal concerns from the President to discuss with all of you. It would not be appropriate for the staff to hear," Ramsey replied.

Louie looked quizzically at the powerful man.

Alex unexpectedly jumped into the conversation, "Let me explain, Louie. With the staff being part of the meeting, if only briefly, Mr. Ramsey can now charge this expensive trip from Washington to Chicago to the taxpayers. If it were totally off the record, someone else would have to pony-up for the trip."

Ramsey chuckled nervously, "You're a smart man, Alex. You may want to come to work for us someday."

Not amused, Alex stared at Ramsey as the smile drained from his face. The tension was mounting in the room.

Ramsey continued, "It appears Mr. Crane is in no mood for small talk so let's get right to the point, shall we? My economic advisors and I have just spent a great deal of time reviewing the financial statements for Midwest for the past two quarters. And to make a long story short, even after receiving twenty-five billion dollars of bailout money, Midwest is still experiencing substantial losses. Income is down and the bank's net worth is shrinking as we speak. I think we all know that in the past election, the middle of the country was the tipping point for our victory. Without Ohio, Indiana, and Missouri coming into the fold, we would not have carried the election. Midwest Consolidated is the largest bank in the central states, with offices in Michigan, Missouri, Illinois, Indiana, and Ohio. The failure of a bank with this asset size would send shock waves throughout this part of the country and would certainly not bode well for the party in power." Ramsey paused and glanced at the others. "Would my more knowledgeable banker friends like to comment on that assessment?"

Obviously uncomfortable talking about numbers, Louie turned toward Alex.

Alex spoke up quickly, blocking any attempt by Barnes to jump in and control the discussion. "If you mean, do I think that you, the President and the Federal Government could do a better job of turning that situation around than we could? The answer is a resounding no."

Ramsey's eyes went wide with shock and anger at Alex's terse remark. Alex, for all practical purposes, had cut off all debate.

Barnes spun toward Alex; his face contorted in rage. "Why, you pompous ass! This bank is in a hell of a mess and you know it! If we try to pay back that money, we'll go under!"

Alex's eyes narrowed. A competitive man by nature, his frustrations were growing. "We can work out of this situation without the bailout money. Our commercial paper is doing fine. Our bond managers tell me the worst is over in the foreclosure area and the secondary market should be stabilizing in the near future. Our deposits are good, and even though our net worth is down, it is still above industry averages. It has been a difficult and challenging task to work out of the subprime crisis, but we are now on our way to doing just that." Alex paused and glanced at Barnes. "Maybe our chairman would like to explain to Mr. Ramsey just how we got into this mess in the first place."

His head tilted back, the arrogant Barnes stared menacingly at Alex.

Alex leaned forward in his seat. "Okay, Barnes, then I'll tell him why. We got in this mess because *you* got us involved in subprime mortgages, without my knowledge, so you and your friend, Vito Taglioni, could get rich."

His displeasure and outrage growing, Alex turned toward Ramsey. "And that could have never happened without help from Ben here and his cronies at the Fed. This whole thing stinks to high heaven and you all know it."

Louie Campano sat wide-eyed, shocked by the damning allegations from his usually polite colleague.

A stunned Ramsey attempted to regain control of the meeting. "Now Crane, let's stop with the mudslinging, shall we? We have some issues that are very important to President Moretti to discuss here today."

Emboldened by Ramsey's comment, the street fighter in Barnes took over. He calmly removed his glasses, pulled out his handkerchief and began cleaning the lenses as he spoke. "Ben, it's obvious that Mr. Crane does not share our concern for the future of Midwest. It is also obvious from his comments that he still intends to pay back the bailout money and put our bank in further jeopardy. But I can assure you sir, that the Board of Directors at Midwest does not share this view. I will call for a vote at the next meeting, at which time I am confident the board will reject the payback. So, Mr. Crane can make all of the scurrilous allegations he likes, but you can rest assured, Ben, that at the end of the day, Midwest will keep that money."

Alex was incensed by the arrogance of his chairman. His legs were shaking from anger, but he kept his cool. He wanted to mention the audit at the nearby Chicago office in the worst way, but he dare not. Even though he was sure that Ramsey had gotten wind of the audit, it was too early for Alex to play his hand on the audit.

Alex spoke calmly, "I know that you have been working overtime to sway the board to your side Barnes, but I'm not so sure you have the votes. I can assure all of you here today that I will do everything in my power to insure that we pay back that money. I'm more determined than ever, and nothing said here today, will alter my resolve."

Ramsey's face bled white; he had been sent to Chicago to insure that Midwest would keep the bailout money and it was now apparent that he had failed. He and the President had underestimated just how tough and determined Alex Crane could be. The President would be furious with him.

He took a sip of water and spoke almost inaudibly, "Gentlemen, it appears we have a stand-off. I was very much hoping that we could work together here today to solve this very difficult problem, but it appears that this is not going to happen. It's obvious to me that Mr. Crane is steadfast in his determination to gamble with the future of Midwest consolidated." He then paused for a second, cleared his throat and issued this warning. "I hope for everybody's sake that Barnes prevails. There is no room for negotiation here. The President is determined to carry the Midwestern states in the general election and he will be gravely disappointed by Mr. Crane's refusal to cooperate. The President doesn't take rejection well and he will not let anything or anyone stand in his way." The powerful man's words sent a chill up Alex's spine. Louie sat in stunned silence.

Ramsey turned toward Barnes and said softly, "Keep in touch." Then he quickly exited the room, avoiding any eye contact with Alex.

There was muffled conversation for a moment outside the door and then the hall fell silent. Ben Ramsey and his contingent had left the building.

His anger subsiding, Alex felt sick inside as he watched Barnes slip on his thick glasses and stand to leave. A man of honor and integrity, Alex knew he had thrown down the gauntlet today and that the President and his Chicago thugs would now be after him with renewed vigor. Right now, he wished he were like his friend Louie—single with no wife and family. A warrior by nature, Alex had no concern for himself, only his wife and family. He knew these men would stop at nothing to get what they wanted. War had been declared today and he must prepare for it.

There was an eerie silence in the room. All the emotions that had been lying under the surface had broken loose during this impromptu meeting with the President's Chief of Staff.

Louie finally broke the ice, "Well gentlemen, I think it would be best if we just share e-mails in regard to the few items I needed to discuss. I don't believe any of us are in the mood to continue this meeting." He face broke into a half smile. "Meeting adjourned."

Barnes shook Louie's hand and thanked him for hosting the meeting and then paused next to Alex on his way out of the room. Alex sat staring straight ahead. "Alex, I want you to know that I admire your determination on this matter, but I…"

Alex wheeled around in his chair and interrupted the chairman. "Cut the crap, Barnes. Politeness does not become you." Alex had reached ground zero with Barnes, and the gloves were off. "In the past couple of years, with your secret meetings and back room deals, you've managed to turn my life into a virtual time bomb, ready to explode at any moment. I rue the day I ever brought you on the board—it was a huge mistake. And, I'm not going to compound that mistake by turning my back as you and your political hacks try and destroy everything I've accomplished over the past thirty years!"

Barnes grimaced and then spoke slowly. "I've been hoping you would come around, Alex, but it's obvious you have no such intentions. And, these "hacks" that you just referred to, happen to be the President of the United States and his close aides. You have taken it upon yourself to lock horns with the most powerful man in the universe. And, to make matters worse, today you managed to embarrass and humiliate his Chief of Staff. Better watch your backside, Alex. Things could get ugly." Barnes hurried out; the room was now empty except for Alex and Louie.

Alex smelled garlic as Louie fell into the chair next to him and laid his hand on Alex's arm. "Ya got your hands full, my friend. These boys play rough."

Alex smiled warmly, "I know. I know they do, Louie. Thanks for your concern."

"I love my bank and I don't like what I am seeing." He squeezed tighter on Alex's forearm. "I'm with you on this—I promise you that."

"Thank you, Louie, thanks a lot." Alex appreciated the support, but there was little his office manager in Chicago could do. But the kind gesture made him feel better, if only for an instant.

"It's going on twelve. How about some lunch?"

"Well...uh I really should be..."

The local manager interrupted, "This place has got a mean Stromboli sandwich."

"Okay Louie, on one condition."

"Yes?"

"You let me buy."

"It's a deal, boss."

Alex lifted his briefcase from the floor and the two men exited the room. He felt Louie's arm slide gently over his shoulder as they made there way to the restaurant area. "You've been good to me, Alex. You've always been good to me."

"Thanks, Louie."

. . . .

Alex set his fork on the table. "You're right, Louie. That was a great sandwich and the soup was wonderful."

"Glad ya liked it, Alex." Louie smiled and lifted his hand slightly to acknowledge two men who were in the process of being seated at a table across the room. A chill shot up Alex's spine; they were the same two men he had seen at The Frog Restaurant the previous weekend at the lake.

"Friends of yours, Louie?"

"Yeah, that's Hawk Barger and his pal Jake; they're FBI guys. Want to meet 'em?"

"Oh no, no. I have to get going. I need to pick Nicky up at the lake and then head back to Indy."

The waitress laid the check on the table next to Alex. He quickly scanned the check, as was his habit. Satisfied that it was accurate, he stood to leave.

"Thanks for lunch, boss. I wish you didn't have to rush off."

"I do too, but Nicky is waiting for me at the lake."

Louie stood and the two men shook hands.

"Parked out back?" Alex asked.

"No, I'm in the front lot."

"Okay, then I will be in touch."

"Let me know if you need anything."

"Will do." Alex hurried to the check-out counter near the back entrance of the room. He glanced discreetly at the two FBI agents. The older one with the square jaw was smiling at him—just like he did at the lake. Alex set his briefcase on the counter, reached for his money clip and paid the check. Taking a quick glimpse over his shoulder at the agents, he hurried through the back door to the parking lot.

Chapter 19

The afternoon sun filtered through the faded blinds as the orange rubber ball bounced off the small rim and then fell harmlessly to the floor. A nearby agent jumped from his chair and clumsily chased the elusive little ball around the office, finally corralling the exasperating orb next to the copy machine.

"Watch this," Jake Collier bragged. Faking a few dribbles, he juked left and right, and then with an awkward attempt at a hook shot, he let the little ball fly. It seemed to hang in the air forever as it floated toward the basket. The other office workers in the large room paused briefly and then roared their approval as the ball swished the net, took one bounce and fell into the hand of Hawk Barger.

The famed agent grinned and shook his head. "You looked like Jordan on that one!" he exclaimed.

All heads turned as the door to the windowed office at the far end of the room swung open.

Head agent, Wade Ellis, stepped out into the office and scowled. He seemed annoyed by the festive atmosphere in the usually business-like office. "In my office, Barger," he groused.

A collective groan moved through the office and a

red-faced Hawk quickly maneuvered his way across the room to the boss's office and pushed the door shut. The others watched as a frowning Ellis leaned on the corner of his desk. His head moved back and forth as he barked at Hawk and then handed him a file. Barger quickly thumbed through the bulging file. Animated conversation followed with Ellis finally throwing his hands in the air and shaking his head. Then Hawk, always a bit antagonistic toward those in authority, glared at his boss and then nodded in the affirmative. A few seconds later, he exited the room.

A wide-eyed office staff watched as the enigmatic agent hurried over to his partner's desk. Jake, still gloating from the lucky shot of a few minutes earlier, spoke up, "Well, did you finally get fired?"

"I wish. We're on assignment. You better go home and get enough stuff for a couple of days. I'll pick you up at sixteen hundred."

"Where we going?"

Always deathly curious about the secret destinations of the higher-paid, big shot agents in the office, the word processors and laptops fell silent as the nosy workers strained mightily to hear what the agents were saying.

Aware of the attention, and speaking loud enough so all could hear, a grinning Hawk replied. "We gotta tail Cindy Crawford for a couple of days at a nude beach in California. The boss thinks she's working for Al Qaida."

There was a chorus of boos, followed by a showering of paper-wads and other harmless missiles, as the ducking agents grabbed their briefcases and scurried from the office.

Chapter 20

Alex glanced over at the large sign to his right that read, South Shore Golf Club. The parking lot was almost full on this warm Tuesday afternoon in late August. Alex waited for a couple of oncoming cars to pass and then turned left onto Vawter Park Road.

A short time later, he turned and carefully drove up the narrow drive to his lake home. Alex could see Nicky talking to their neighbor, Millie, near the garage. She had all the bags packed and arranged them neatly on the ground next to her. Alex pulled close, hopped out of the car and approached the gabbing women.

"Hello ladies." He gave Nicky a peck on the cheek and the friendly neighbor a quick hug. "Sorry I'm a little late. Louie and I got to talking."

"No problem. We're all packed and ready to go and it's only four. We should be home by six-thirty. Jarod said he would pick up the kids around seven, so we should have plenty of time."

Alex glanced at the side yard, "By the way, where are the kids?"

"They're out front wading in the lake. Why don't you load up and I'll go get them."

"I'll let you guys get packed. See you next time!"

Millie smiled warmly and disappeared through the large bushes that separated the two houses.

Alex stuffed two small travel bags under each arm and lifted the two larger suitcases. He hurried around the SUV, stacked them in the rear compartment and slammed the gate closed.

"Hi Grandpa!" Little Eli, arms outstretched, rushed to greet Alex. Katie, almost twelve, arrived a short time later and gave her grandpa a big hug, pinning her giggling brother against his belly. The hug broke up and the kids quickly piled into the backseat. Then Alex and Nicky got in the front and buckled up. Nicky reminded the kids to do the same. The SUV turned around and drove slowly down the drive for the trip back to Indy.

. . . .

"Look at those rich guys! They probably play golf every day. Are we ever going be rich like that, Hawk?"

"Working for the FBI—are you kidding?"

Hawk peered through the car windshield. Their vehicle was positioned at the back of the parking lot of South Shore Golf Club, tucked neatly between a large delivery truck and an SUV. They were out of sight of the passing autos, but they had a clear view of the intersection of Vawter Park Road and State Road 13. They were patiently waiting for Crane's SUV to appear.

Jake snickered, "Look at that fat boy; he just missed the ball a mile!"

Hawk shook his head, "You're just jealous."

"Who me? I love being poor." The aggressive agent smiled sarcastically.

Hawk interrupted, "Look! There he is—back

already."

The men watched Crane's Escalade pull onto State Road 13 and head south.

"Buckle up, buddy. We're going to Indy."

. . . .

"Your text message beeper just went off." Nicky looked up from her knitting.

"It did?"

"Yes darling, and are you ever going to get your hearing checked?"

"My hearing is fine."

"You didn't hear the beeper and I did."

"I was thinking about something."

"You're hopeless."

Normally, Nicky would read him the message, but today he didn't want her to see it with all that was coming down with Barnes and company. He hoped she didn't notice the change in their routine. He took his IPhone from its holster and opened the message and saw it was from Josh Dulin. Alex read, *I would like to move morning meeting to my office at same time. No answer necessary unless this is a problem.*

Chapter 21

"Benching 250, hmmm….pretty good for a guy your age."

Flushed and perspiring heavily, Alex dropped the heavy weights on the rack and sat up. "Got to try and keep up with you young fellas, Tony."

"You must've done ten miles on the tread earlier. Got a triathlon coming up or something?" The gym owner grinned.

"Not really, just got back from a weekend at the lake, drinking beer and eating everything in sight—you know how that goes."

"I've seen you come here after a weekend at the lake before, but I've never seen you work this hard."

Alex grinned at his old friend. He loved his evenings at Tony's work-out complex on the Northwest side of Indianapolis. Lifting and sweating with the young guys brought back memories of his high school days as a star half-back and made him feel macho and young again. Because he was in exceptionally good condition for a man of fifty-five, he was able to do aerobic exercises much longer that most of the young guns at the popular fitness joint. Alex prided himself on his muscular frame and fine condition, attributes he felt necessary to meet the many stressful challenges of the fast changing banking industry. Lately, he felt a more pressing need to keep himself in the best physical shape possible. He snatched his towel off the top of the bench and aggressively rubbed his peppered black hair dry.

"See ya, Tony."

"Take care Mr. C. See you next time."

Alex draped the towel over his damp neck and headed for the exit. After a few quick jabs at the punching bag dangling by the front door, he stepped out of the air-conditioned center into the warm Indiana night. As he walked toward his car, he paused to admire the nearby Pyramids, which are three, thirty-story, office buildings that resemble the Egyptian Pyramids. The stunning buildings on Indy's Northwest side were known to all the folks in Indiana. Anyone giving directions to a nearby business would simply say it was near the "Pyramids" and most people would know where to go. Alex was proud of the support his bank had given the developers over the years to maintain and improve the dynamic structures. Alex stepped off the shallow curb, walked to his car, slid in and started the engine. He was soon climbing the nearby entrance ramp onto the always busy I-465 for his trip home.

Several miles down the road, Alex glanced in his rear view mirror. An SUV he had noticed after leaving the work-out center was still behind him. His cell rang; he tapped the control of the steering wheel and answered the hands-free.

"Yes, dear?"

"Where are you?"

"Just left Tony's."

"Would you pick up some milk on your way home

please?"

"Certainly, dear."

"And don't forget to get skim for my diet."

"I know dear, good-bye."

"Bye."

Alex glanced in the side mirror. The dark vehicle was still behind him but staying at a safe distance. There were hundreds of folks who frequented the restaurants and shopping on the Northwest side each evening—it could be anybody. But Alex had made a vow to himself to be more vigilant after the embarrassing incident at the lake last weekend.

His exit was fast approaching. Alex peeled off 465 onto the long ramp to I-65 North. The trailing vehicle took the same exit, staying at the same safe distance. The shadowy SUV's precise distance from him bothered Alex. A typical commuter would drift a little—forward and back, side to side, but there was absolutely no wavering with the SUV. It was obvious that this vehicle was on a mission.

On full alert now, a few miles up I-65, Alex swerved to the right onto 334, the exit to his home in Zionsville. The other auto made the same exit and was now close behind. Its bright headlights pushed up close to the back of his BMW—almost touching it.

Alex's pulse quickened, he leaned over and popped the glove box open, removing his loaded forty-five revolver and laid it on the passenger seat next to him. He had been granted a permit to carry the gun as part of increased security efforts after the failed extortion attempt of a few years earlier. The former military man had won several awards for his shooting prowess during his days as a Seal and he wasn't afraid to use a firearm.

He had put the gun in his glove box that evening after the disguised threat from Ramsey at the Chicago meeting.

Suddenly, Alex felt a hard jolt to the rear of his car. He flew forward, and his elbows crashed against the steering wheel. Fighting to maintain control of his car, the light flashed green at the end of the ramp. He gunned it onto 334 toward Zionsville. The menacing SUV stayed glued to his backside. Alex glanced right at the well-lighted convenience center at the end of a long road. He felt it would be a safe place to confront his pursuers. He suddenly took a sharp, aggressive turn to the right. Midway through the turn, his car's engine began to stall and sputter. He glanced down at the fuel gage—it was below E. In all the recent confusion, he had neglected to fill the tank. His car drifted to the side of the road. He was now alone on a dark road with someone aggressively pursuing him. His training as a Seal had taught him how to kill. He could snap a man's neck or puncture his trachea within seconds, but it had been years since he had been in the military. And, although he was in excellent physical condition, the good life of fancy restaurants, expensive country clubs, and genteel surroundings had undoubtedly softened him. He wondered if he still had the mustard to confront his tormentors.

The trailing SUV abruptly backed off as if confused by the slowing vehicle. The sputtering suddenly ceased, the engine groaned and then went dead. The vehicle rolled to a stop. With no trace of a moon, it was ugly black outside. Without hesitating, Alex put it in park, snatched the forty-five off the seat and dove toward the passenger side, slamming down on the handle and opening the door as he flew across the seat. A few seconds later, he crashed headfirst onto the roadside. Pain shot through his shoulder as the small stones along side the road dug into his work-out suit. He quickly rolled to his feet and ran toward the back of his auto. He fell across the trunk, pointing his loaded forty-five directly at the mysterious SUV. The shiny barrel glistened in the bright lights of the approaching vehicle, which was now just a few feet away. All the instincts of a young Navy Seal suddenly came rushing back to him. He popped the safety on the deadly revolver and prepared to fire. He was in his element—he was ready to rumble.

Suddenly, the SUV slammed on its brakes and skidded on the loose gravel that covered the crusty side road. Alex lifted his forearm to protect against the flying stones. Screeching to a stop, the big vehicle's rear tires were soon spinning in reverse with its headlights off. A huge cloud of dust exploded around the SUV as it did an abrupt 180 and accelerated back onto 334 heading toward I-65. A short time later, its lights came on illuminating the smooth surface on 334.

Perspiring heavily and shaken, Alex lowered the gun, breathed a quiet sigh of relief and dusted himself off. His shoulder was aching from the fall on the rocks a few moments earlier. Not wanting Nicky to know of this harrowing encounter, he checked his rear bumper for damage. Fortunately, the rubber bumper guards had protected his car well. His sweatsuit had also survived the fall in fairly good condition. There was a slight tear behind the left arm, but otherwise it looked presentable. He looked across a field as the large vehicle raced down I-65 toward Indianapolis. Still angry, he kicked the ground. "You guys haven't seen the last of me," he murmured.

He leaned inside and placed the revolver in the car's glove compartment. He picked up the work-out towel that had fallen from his neck and dried his face and neck. He bumped the passenger door closed and hustled across an open field to the nearby service-center for a can of gas and a gallon of milk.

. . . .

"What the hell was that all about? Sissified bank president, my ass!" Jake hollered. "And why'd we run anyway? We shoulda taken him out!"

Hawk Barger spoke quietly, "We had to leave the scene. We had no choice."

Hawk was upset. He didn't like running; it went against every bone in his body. But in this case, he had to. It was obvious to him that Crane was ready to fight. He and his partner had been dangerously close to having a bloody incident with a high profile bank president. Hawk had done the right thing. He did what any experienced agent would do—he backed away from the confrontation before it escalated into something tragic. But he felt cowardly—he felt like less of a man and he resented Jake's comments.

"We caved! We wimped out and you know it!" Jake barked.

Agitated and conflicted, Barger quickly wheeled to the side of the road and crammed the car into park. He unbuckled his seatbelt and leaned toward the passenger side. He violently grabbed Jake's shirt collar and yanked him closer. Their faces were only inches apart. Barger's face was red with rage, "You listen to me, you sorry son-of-a-bitch! If you're ever going to amount to anything in this organization you're going to have to get a hell of a lot smarter than you are right now!"

Jake sat wide-eyed; Hawk yanked harder on his collar. "Alex Crane is a civilian Jake. He's not a terrorist or some other form of enemy combatant. He is the president of one of the largest banks in the country! Think about it! If we would have harmed that man in any way, we would have been disgraced! We would have lost our jobs and more than likely, we would have gone to jail!" Hawk released his grip, pushed Jake hard against the seat, composed himself as best he could and buckled up.

A proud man, Jake stared straight ahead, not saying anything. An angry Hawk checked the rearview mirror, gunned the powerful engine and merged back onto I-65.

. . . .

Alex wound his way through the up-scale neighborhood of the large two and three story homes with well-manicured lawns and a large man-made lake that meandered its way through the center of the subdivision. The whole scene was highlighted by a four-level fountain that seemed to reach for the sky from the middle of the lake.

Alex was still reeling from his encounter with the SUV and was trying desperately to make sense of it all. The two FBI agents who had been observing him earlier in the week drove a dark sedan, not an SUV. Would Ramsey have involved the CIA or possibly the Chicago mob? He lifted his cell and punched the speed dial.

"Hello?" It was a cool response from Barnes, who had caller ID. Not to call Alex by name was purposeful and underlined the growing tension between the two men.

"Got a minute, Barnes?"

"I'm in the middle of something here, I only have a minute. What is it?"

"Someone was tailing me again tonight; they rammed the rear of my car on the exit ramp off of 65. I brandished my handgun and they backed off and drove away."

Barnes cleared his throat, "Handgun? Sounds like the Wild West to me! Please quit bothering me with these things. Like I told you before, I have no idea who might be harassing you. You're calling the wrong person."

"I don't think so," Alex said calmly.

With the dispute between himself and the administration ratcheting up, anger seemed inappropriate. In the military he learned that when the enemy becomes more defined, the dialogue becomes more formal.

"Was Nicky with you?" Barnes asked.

"No."

There was a long pause. "Like I said Alex, I know nothing about your problem tonight."

"I don't believe you."

"Listen Crane, you should take your money and retire to that beautiful lake up north. It would save you a lot of grief. And besides, I know that's what Nicky wants. Good-bye."

Barnes' insightfulness about Nicky annoyed Alex; she must have mentioned something to him at a recent office gathering or something. Alex dropped his phone back into its holster and turned toward home. He could see the light in the second story window. Apparently, Nicky had decided to retire early to do some reading. He saw her slender silhouette move gracefully past the sheer window covering. A few seconds later, she pulled the curtain shut and the window went dark.

Alex turned into the open garage door and pulled to a stop. The spacious garage began to darken as the heavy garage door clattered shut behind him. Alex hurried inside. Three empty suitcases from the weekend were neatly placed next to the top of the basement stairs across the hall from the garage door. Alex gathered up the cases and took them to the basement, tossed them on the luggage shelf and hurried back upstairs. He paused at the end of the kitchen counter and flipped on the intercom.

"Nicky?"

"Yes, dear, what do you want? I'm starting to take off my make-up."

"I'm going to be on the computer for a little bit; I should be up shortly"

"I may be sleeping, so please be quiet."

"Okay."

"How was your work-out?"

"Fine, thanks."

"Good-night, dear."

"Good-night."

Alex opened the refrigerator door and grabbed a recently opened bottle of Chardonnay. He filled the wine glass Nicky had left him on the counter. Then he hustled across the dining room to his small den. He dropped in the chair in front of his computer, turned it on and fumbled for the elusive mouse.

Louie Campano never had his cell phone turned on. He only used it for out-going calls, so Alex knew if he wanted to get a message to his Chicago manager, he would need to send him an e-mail. And, Louie probably wouldn't see the message until he opened his computer at work the next morning.

Alex clicked on Outlook Express and pulled out the keyboard. He located Louie's address and began typing: *Good Morning Louie, Would you please call me on my cell phone at your earliest convenience. Important! Regards, Alex.*

Hot and tired, Alex took a sip of his wine and turned on ESPN to see if his beloved Cubbies had beaten the Dodgers that day. He groaned as the score scrolled across the bottom of the screen—Los Angeles Dodgers 6, Chicago Cubs 2. He shook his head, turned off the television and made his way to the bedroom, hoping for a good night's sleep.

Chapter 22

Louie took a bite of his Payday, savored the sweet flavor for a moment and swallowed. A contented smile crossed his face as he licked his lips and took another bite. He loved Paydays; he kept a stock of the legendary candy bars buried deep in the bottom drawer of his office desk. Every morning without fail, he ripped one open and enjoyed the salty peanuts wrapped around the tasty nougat center. As the day progressed, he would sneak another one whenever possible, sometimes devouring as many as ten in one day. He was certain that no one knew about his secret addiction—not even Ava. Somewhat self-conscious about his weight problem, he would be embarrassed if anyone found out. He quickly tossed the last chunk in his mouth and gave it a few extra chews just as his phone line lit up.

"Uh…yes Ava?"

"Alex Crane on one."

"Okay." Louie finger-nailed a peanut fragment loose from between his front teeth and pushed the button to line one. "Hello Alex!"

"Good morning, Louie. Did you get my e-mail?"

Louie shuffled in his seat, "No, I haven't checked the internet yet today."

"That's okay. I've only got a minute; I'm on my way to a meeting with Josh Dulin."

"Tell Josh hello for me."

"Will do. Hey, uh…listen, Louie, I've got a question for you."

"Okay."

"Remember those FBI guys we saw at lunch the other day?"

"Yes, Hawk Barger and Jake Collier."

"How well do you know those guys?"

"I know Hawk a little bit; I bump into him down on Rush Street occasionally. I don't know Jake as well."

There was a pause. "Keep this under your hat, okay?"

"Oh sure, you can trust me, Alex."

"With all my disagreements with the administration on the bailout money, I think Ben Ramsey has put a couple of Federal agents on me. A car with dark windows has driven slowly past our house several times recently and then someone was watching us up at the lake last weekend. When Nicky and I went to dinner Saturday night, these two guys made a point to smile and make eye contact with me as they left the restaurant. I'm almost certain that it was that fellow, Hawk, and his friend. And, I don't think their appearance at lunch Monday was an accident. They wanted me to see them again; I think they're trying to intimidate me."

Alex was a good friend, but Hawk was somewhat a friend of Louie's also. He wanted to stay out of this if at all possible so, he stayed non-committal. "Is that right?"

"Yes, and last evening I was followed closely by a black SUV when I left the gym. The driver ended up ramming me in the rear when I exited to go home. It wasn't the same vehicle that has been shadowing me; I think they may have brought in the CIA or something this time."

Louie had seen Hawk several times around Rush Street in a large black SUV. And one evening over a drink, he had told Louie that the office in Chicago housed several such vehicles. Louie felt this was pretty much public knowledge and he felt he could tell Alex without betraying a trust. "I've seen Hawk around in a black SUV."

"Hmmm….is that right?"

"Yeah, a couple of times. The FBI provides them to their agents."

"That helps. It probably was this Hawk fellow and his friend again."

"Be careful, Alex."

"Oh yeah?"

"Yeah, Hawk is the best. He's nobody to mess with."

Neither am I. Alex thought. "Thanks for the tip, buddy. I'll talk to you soon."

"Stay safe."

Chapter 23

Louie poked nervously at the colorful screen once again. He squinted menacingly at the machine as an automated voice scolded him, "Please make another selection, the icon you selected is incorrect." His frustration growing, Louie poked the screen again—this time with his knuckle. The annoying voice once again scolded him, "Please make another selection, the icon you selected is incorrect." Beads of perspiration appeared on Louie's forehead. Fist doubled, he fainted a punch at the obnoxious machine. Becoming more and more aggravated, he felt a sudden tap on his shoulder.

"Can I help you, Mr. Campano?"

"Oh…uh hi, Julie," a red-faced Louie replied. "I'm trying to print some pictures from my cell phone."

The slender girl stepped in front of Louie. "I know, Mr. Campano."

Louie grinned sheepishly. It was the same every time he came in—one of the girls at the CVS ended up helping him download and print his pictures.

"You should ask one of us to help you. This thing can be tricky."

Louie smiled as the young lady rapidly navigated through several screens.

"Six by four again?"

"Yeah."

"Doubles again?"

"Yes," he said quietly.

"There you go, Mr. Campano. Just call for me if you need anything else."

Louie watched as the colorful pictures started sliding into the opening at the bottom of the tall machine.

"She makes it look so easy," he mumbled.

A few minutes later, he gathered up the stack of pictures and stuffed them in the gold envelope with red lettering that Julie had left for him and started for the check-out line.

"That will be $12.95."

Louie slid out a ten and three singles from his money clip and handed them to the checkout girl.

She waited for the receipt to print, took a nickel from the drawer and handed them both to Louie. "Thank you, Mr. Campano and have a nice day."

"You too, Julie," Louie said softly as he turned and pushed through the nearby doors and ambled toward his dirty pick-up.

Once inside the truck's smallish cabin, he opened the envelope and balanced the pictures between his belly and the center bar on the stirring wheel. He flipped through the pictures quickly, laughing and shaking his head at some of the scenes. Suddenly, his eyes went wide. He grabbed one of the pictures tight and pulled it closer for a better look. He quickly tossed the others on the passenger seat and sat up, staring at the shocking image. He suddenly looked away and glanced out the driver's side window as if taking a much needed break.

"On my mother's grave!" he muttered as he went

back to the vivid picture. It was one he had taken at the recent party at Tommy the Greek's condo on Rush Street. It was a perfect picture of Ben Ramsey, President Moretti's Chief of Staff, leaning over a well-lighted glass table with a small straw stuck in his nose and reaching toward a narrow line of a white substance. A sexy lady in an evening gown, with her ample breasts protruding, was laughing and leaning over the other side of the table with a straw in hand awaiting her turn. There was no doubt about it—Louie had captured one of the most powerful men in the world in the act of snorting coke.

Feeling warm and starting to perspire, Louie thought back to that evening. After relieving himself, he had stood in the shadows of the darkened entryway to the bathroom. With a drink in one hand and his cell phone in the other, he had taken several rapid fire pictures of the chaotic room—a nervous habit of his when he felt bored or alone. He didn't remember taking any of Ramsey. He was stunned as he scanned the damning image. There was an unwritten code among all the big-shot party goers on the windy city's North Side—just like in Vegas, *"What happens at Tommy's, stays at Tommy's!"*

Aside from Tommy's hired "hostesses", many of the party goers were married men or women looking for a quick lay. But regardless of their motivation, they all assumed the others would obey Tommy's motto. The sight of the President of the United States' right hand man snorting coke with a sexy lady in a posh condo on Chicago's North Side would be a story of enormous proportion. All hell would break loose and a media firestorm would ensue. Every tabloid journalist in the country would be licking his chops at his or her opportunity to gain new insights into the juicy story.

Frightened by the possible enormity of the situation, Louie felt it was imperative for him to get rid of the photos. Although he was no lover of Ben Ramsey, he grew up with the President and was a trusted member of the Rush Street night scene. He knew what he had to do—he would hurry home and cut the radioactive photos into a thousand pieces and flush them down the toilet, never to be seen again by human eyes.

Placing the photos on the dash, he quickly scanned the remaining photos looking for other possible explosive scenes involving the charismatic Chief of Staff. Finding several, and with his hands shaking, he stuffed the pictures back into the envelope and turned the ignition key starting the truck. The engine revved loudly as he pulled out of the busy parking lot and gunned it down Harlem Avenue toward home.

Chapter 24

"How's the weather in Scottsdale, honey?"

"It's hotter than Hades out here!"

"Sorry to hear that. How are your meetings going?"

"Boring as usual, but at least I've played some good golf courses while I've been out here. We're going to play a course at Desert Mountain early tomorrow morning before the heat suffocates us. Then our last meeting is in the afternoon. I will be flying out at 11:30 A.M. the next day."

"Miss you."

"Same here, pumpkin. I'll call you if anything comes up."

"Okay." Lisa cringed, she hated the name "pumpkin".

"Bye, Edward."

"Bye."

The light ahead turned green. The expensive gold bracelet slid down her slender arm as she reached for the turn signal and turned right off Meridian Street onto Market. Lisa Carl was on her way to her part-time job as a secretary-receptionist at a health spa. She had left for work early so she could make a stop downtown and talk with her investment broker. Guiding her Mercedes

Roadster off North Meridian onto Market Street, she pulled into an open parking place.

"Lucky me," she murmured. She filled the parking meter with dimes and hurried around the front of the building to the entrance.

Lisa was a wealthy woman and enjoyed a great deal of status in her hometown of Indianapolis. Well educated, and with a Bachelor of Arts degree from the University of Virginia, Lisa had never had a real job. Fortunately for her, she had married Edward Carl, owner of a local software company, right out of college. Edward Carl was twenty years her senior and one of the wealthiest men in Indianapolis. His hefty income was more than enough to support Lisa in a fashion she never dreamed possible while growing up in a working class neighborhood on the city's Southside.

Attractive and likeable, she had used her husband's great wealth and notoriety, along with her involvement in many charitable and civic events, to become somewhat of a celebrity in the Midwest metropolis. A physical fitness addict, she had a firm and shapely figure along with striking good looks. Able to afford expensive clothes and fine jewelry, she was always dressed in the latest fashions. Lisa was the secret crush of many a man in the fast-paced business world of the dynamic state capital, but the achievement of which she was most proud was her invitation to join the Board of Directors for Midwest Consolidated Bank a few years earlier. To be on the board of the giant conglomerate was a wonderful achievement for a non-career woman who worked part-time at a health spa. Many, in the local business establishment, were shocked when the appointment was announced in the Indianapolis Star two years ago, wondering how a person of such limited achievement could be given such responsibility. As for her part, she jumped at the opportunity, and by most accounts, had become a competent and thoughtful member of the board.

She waited for an opening and then ducked inside the fast-moving revolving door and hurried inside the busy office. Claudia, the receptionist, smiled at her, and then stared openly at Lisa's short tight skirt and see-through silk blouse, which was all the more revealing because with Edward out of town, Lisa had chosen to go braless. Finally, looking away from Lisa's barely covered chest area, the stunned receptionists muttered, "Oh hi Lisa, how are you today?"

Unabashed and smiling broadly, Lisa replied. "Fine, thank you."

"Are you here to see Mr. Taglioni?"

"Yes, and he is expecting me."

The red-faced receptionist pushed the direct line to her boss. "Mr. Taglioni, Lisa Carl is here to see you."

"Send her right in."

Lisa quickly lifted a small mirror from her purse, fluffed her blond hair and checked out her make-up. Apparently satisfied, she stuck the mirror back in her purse and smiled at Claudia.

"It's okay, Lisa." The secretary pointed toward Vito's office.

"Thank you."

Vito was fumbling nervously through one of the many stacks of papers on his desk when Lisa walked in. His eyes grew wide; he gawked at her unfettered breasts as they bounced under her transparent blouse.

"Why…uh hello Lisa. How are you?"

She reached her hand forward, "Just fine thank you. So good to see you again, Vito."

Vito straightened his tie and laid his reading glasses on the desk top. He took her outstretched hand and cupped it firmly between both of his, extending the greeting for as long as possible. He attempted to look at her face, but his eyes kept wandering down to the extraordinary scene below. He looked at the back of the room to be sure the door to his office was closed. "Th…thank you for stopping by," he said awkwardly.

"Oh, no problem. I don't have to be at work for an hour, so we have plenty of time to talk or whatever."

She arched her back and lowered her firm backside slowly to the edge of the leather chair. Lisa felt naughty and a little guilty. She wasn't sure why she became such a vamp whenever Edward was out of town, but it always seemed to happen. Oh well, theirs was a marriage of convenience anyway. They weren't very close; she gave the old man a trophy wife to show off to his friends and he gave her all the security and material things she would ever want. On top of that, she had learned, just a few days earlier, that Vito was the one who had convinced Barnes O'Brien to add her to the Midwest board. She was hoping that her meeting with the handsome Vito would allow her the opportunity to show her appreciation. There had always been an animalistic energy between her and the charismatic securities dealer.

Vito turned his back slightly and took a quick shot of breath spray. He hurriedly jammed the small canister back in his pant pocket and smiled. "You look lovely today, Lisa."

"Thank you."

"And how is Edward?"

"Oh he's fine. He's out in Arizona right now." She crossed her legs very slowly giving the very attentive Vito a great view of her upper thigh area in the process. *You naughty girl!* she thought.

"Oh...uh well...uh, that's good." Vito was trying desperately to compose himself. To have a beautiful, successful woman like Lisa walk into his office in an outfit like that, was a dream come true for a man like Vito. His fantasies were running wild.

"What can I do for you, Vito?" she smiled flirtatiously.

"Well, Barnes...uh wanted me to talk to you about the bailout situation at Midwest Consolidated. Being Chairman of the Board, he didn't feel it was appropriate for him to talk to you."

Lisa glanced down; the cool air-conditioning in Vito's office had caused two protrusions to pop out on the front of her blouse. She looked over at Vito and smiled. He was literally shaking in his boots. He couldn't keep his eyes off the ever improving vision in front of him.

Lisa arched her back a little more. "I haven't quite decided yet—I may need a little more convincing." In reality, Lisa had studied Alex's proposition carefully to repay the TARP money and had decided to support him. But her sexual energy was on high alert and she didn't want this moment to end. A little white lie wouldn't hurt at a time like this.

Responding to the tease from the seductive beauty, a thrilled Vito ambled over and locked the door to the office. Returning to his desk, he flipped on the inter-com. "Claudia, we are discussing an important project. I don't want to be disturbed."

"I understand, Mr. Taglioni."

Inside the office, Lisa spoke softly, "Do you have a copy of the proposal I can review?" The rich board member batted her eyes.

This was a play to get next to Vito and he loved it. "I believe so," he replied. Growing more and more excited, his eyes darted back and forth from her thigh-high skirt to her see-through blouse. He fumbled clumsily for a file—any file. He slid one off a nearby pile and scanned the label. It read: "Miller Trucking Company." "Yes, yes. Here it is. The bailout file."

"Can I come around and take a look at it?" Not waiting for an answer, the shapely vixen once again unwound her legs, sinuously giving Vito an even better view this time. Then she slowly stood and gyrated around Vito's desk, forcing her excited breasts firmly against his shaking shoulder.

"This must be hard for you," she murmured.

"Yes I am hard…uh,,,uh I mean, yes it's really hard filling in for a man like……" Breathing heavily, he failed to finish the sentence.

She smiled and rubbed the back of his head, running her fingers back and forth through his curly hair. Without missing a beat, she carefully slid her hand across his shoulder toward his chest.

Vito was completely helpless—he didn't move.

Then, she loosened his tie and unbuttoned the top buttons on his shirt, gently sliding her hand under his shirt and caressing his chest. "You have such beautiful pecks!"

"Momma Mia!" Vito moaned as he suddenly jumped to his feet and swiped his desk clean with a wild swing of his arm. File folders, supplies and an empty coffee mug went crashing to the floor. He turned and grabbed Lisa by the waist, gently lifting her and laying her on the desk. His hand shaking, he slowly unbuttoned her delicate blouse exposing the partially hidden treasures he had been ogling for the past several minutes. He quickly kicked his shoes off, slid off his trousers and jumped aboard. Bare legs and groping hands were soon flying in every direction as the two lovers wrestled frantically on the oversized desktop.

. . . .

Outside, the straight-laced Claudia suddenly stopped what she was doing and listened intently at the moaning and groaning now coming from Vito's office.

"You animal!" Lisa shouted.

Realizing that Vito and Lisa's business meeting had evolved into something much different, she quickly leaned down and turned up the music on the inter-office sound system. The increase in volume caught the attention of some of the clerk typists. They paused and looked over at the slightly embarrassed receptionist as Olivia Newton John belted out her famous line, "Let me hear your body talk, body talk!" on the blaring speakers. Muffled laughter filled the room as Claudia tried desperately to ignore the growing chorus of groans and exclamations coming from inside Vito's office. Finally, in desperation, she put her hands over her ears and sat motionless, staring down at her desk.

. . . .

Straightening his tie, Vito could hear Lisa grumbling in his poorly lighted bathroom. A short time later, she emerged. Several strands of her rather long, blond hair were shooting straight out from the back of her head. Her mascara was slightly eschew and her lipstick was pushed high on the right side giving her mouth a quivering look.

"Vito dear, you may want to invest in some better lighting for that bathroom!"

"Sorry, I guess I never really noticed."

She frowned. "I must be going. I have a couple of more errands to run."

"Oh...uh Lisa, I hate to bring this up at a time like this—it seems kind of inappropriate." Vito struggled to say the words, "But it's about the TARP money."

"What about it?"

"Well...uh have you made up your mind now?"

She shrugged, "My, how delicate of you," *Does he really think I would make my decision based on what had just taken place?"* Lisa was feeling guilty and embarrassed. Flirtatious and sexy by nature, this was the first time she had ever done such an outrageous thing in her life. Oh, she'd had her share of trysts along the way, but never on a man's desk in a crowded office in the middle of the day. And to top it all off, the ever sophomoric Vito was now asking her if their shallow, juvenile act of a few moments earlier had somehow influenced her vote on one of the most important issues to ever confront Midwest Consolidated Bank.

Vito grinned sheepishly, "Well, you did say you needed some convincing."

Lisa breathed deeply and tried to remain calm, "Yes, I certainly did." She shook her head in disgust. "Oh,

Vito."

"Yes?"

Would you please send Claudia away from her desk? I need to get going and I really don't want to see her right now."

Vito punched the intercom, "Claudia, would you please go to the third floor and get the Hollingsworth file?"

"Gladly, Mr. Taglioni."

Lisa stood in the center of the room gently tapping her foot, allowing time for Claudia to leave the receptionist area before exiting Vito's office. She stared blankly at the floor, not speaking to Vito.

Vito was undaunted. "Was that a yes a moment ago?" he asked boldly. "I need some brownie points with Barnes real bad right now."

Lisa looked at Vito with empty eyes. She wanted to treat the unbearable lout to a slow, painful death by torture, but the recent explosion on his desktop was just as much her fault as it was his. She decided to play along with him. "What do you think? You stud muffin you!" she said flirtatiously. Feeling somewhat nauseated, she gave him a wink and exited the office.

"Jackass," she whispered as she closed the office door behind her and hurried past Claudia's empty desk. Her pointy hair drew a nervous chuckle from nearby workers.

Inside his office, a wide grin spread across a confident Vito's face. His cell phone rang almost immediately.

"Yes, Barnes."

"Did she show up?"

"Yeah, she just left."

"And?"

"It looks good! Read good!"

"Good work, my boy. I owe you one."

"You know me, Barnes. I got a way with the women."

"Yes, yes, you certainly do. I'd better run. We'll talk later."

"Good-bye, Barnes."

"Good-bye."

. . . .

Barnes was ecstatic. He had gotten what he wanted from Vito—a positive response from Lisa. It wasn't a firm yes, but he didn't need a firm yes right now. He and Edward Carl were very old and dear friends; they played golf together regularly at the club and went on an annual fishing trip together to Northern Minnesota. He knew that if there were any lingering doubts at all in Lisa's mind, he was certain that his relationship with Edward would trump them.

He quickly opened his bottom desk drawer, pulled out a cigar and lit up. Soon, the strong aroma permeated his messy office. He leaned back, threw his feet on top of this desk and stared aimlessly across the room. His thoughts took him far away to the American Embassy in Dublin, at 42 Elgin Road, Ballsridge, Dublin. He will never forget that address. During one of his several trips back to his homeland, he had visited the embassy. He was mesmerized by the building with its bold, round architecture. He vowed, that day, to do everything in his power to someday be the Ambassador to Ireland and occupy an office in the stunning edifice located in the heart of his beloved homeland. Now, with Lisa's vote apparently secured, he had taken one more step toward making that dream come true.

Chapter 25

It was afternoon and the long shadow from the giant Soldiers' and Sailors' Monument had darkened the board room at Midwest Consolidated. Arms full, Erica bumped the light switch with her elbow and paused for a second as the lights fluttered on. She walked around the long table and laid one of the seven folders she was carrying in front of each of the large, leather chairs. After distributing the folders, she lifted the ice water pitcher and filled each of the glasses. On her way out, she made a stop at the end of the table to test her recorder she had put there earlier.

A short time later, Alex Crane entered the room and took his seat at the head of the table. He flipped open the file Erica had placed on the table and began a quick review of the information. Alex preferred to have his board meetings in the morning when his mind was fresh, but with Lisa Carl, Barnes O'Brien, and Strom Winslow all still gainfully employed, Alex scheduled the monthly board meetings at 4:00 P.M. so as not to interrupt their busy work schedules. Cliff Williams, Seth Boardman, and Jack Mathews were all retired and they also liked the late afternoon meetings because it gave them a chance to get in a round of golf before the gatherings. The typical board meeting didn't last too long. Alex would brief the board on the topics that were on the agenda. Then, after some discussion, a vote would be taken—almost always in favor of Alex's recommendations. But Alex knew that this meeting would be much different. There was only one topic today and it was his controversial recommendation to pay back the TARP money to the Federal Government.

Tensions had been mounting for weeks over the contentious issue and the battle lines had been clearly drawn with Barnes O'Brien leading the opposition to the proposal and Strom Winslow heading up those in favor. Strom had called Alex at home that morning and told him that he had spoken to the other board members several times over the past few weeks and felt confident that they had three of the four votes necessary to carry the issue. Lisa Carl was the wildcard and he just couldn't get a handle on which way she was leaning. The aggressive lady usually voted with Alex on less important matters, but her husband, Edward, was a good friend and golfing buddy of Barnes. So, in the past she had split her vote between Alex and Barnes on more significant issues. Alex was certain that Barnes had been lobbying Lisa in everyway possible. He felt that her vote was very much up in the air at this point.

As expected, Strom was the first board member to arrive at 3:45; this gave him and Alex a few minutes to talk again before the others arrived.

"Afternoon, Strom."

"Good afternoon, Alex." The big man had a blank expression on his face. Alex had been looking for a warm smile or an encouraging "thumbs up" from his old friend, but he got neither.

"Well, the big day's finally here."

Strom closed the door behind him, strolled over and fell in the chair closest to Alex—his usual spot. "Yeah, it sure is." The big man opened the file that was lying on the table and scanned the cover page.

"Any new insights on Lisa's vote?" Alex got right to the subject, as he was anxious to find out if Strom had gathered any new information on Lisa since their last discussion earlier that day.

"Well, yes I have. I had lunch with my daughter, Amanda, today. Claudia Harper, Vito's secretary, is a good friend of hers. Claudia told Amanda that Lisa paid Vito a visit the other day."

"Vito's right in the middle of this. Barnes may have asked him to intercede."

Strom's right brow lifted, "Yes, I believe he did. Claudia told Amanda that things got very heated in Vito's office.

"Hmmm...that's not like her, she's usually very easy to get along with."

"Not that kind of heat."

"Really?"

Strom coughed a nervous laugh. "Claudia's desk is right next to the door of Vito's office—she could hear everything. I guess they were really going at it and on his desk, none the less."

A wide-eyed Alex stared at Strom in disbelief. "You're kidding?"

"Claudia said that several other staffers in the office could hear them. She told Amanda that she was embarrassed to death."

Alex fell back in his chair. "If this gets out, it will be the talk of the town."

Strom looked over at his shocked friend. "It's already out—Amanda said it's all over town."

"Well, you know us, Strom, we're always the last to know."

Strom's smile quickly faded. "I'm sure our buddy, Vito, thinks he won her vote. I'm sure he feels she'll do anything for him now."

"Yeah, and Barnes and Lisa's husband, Edward, go way back. She's undoubtedly been getting a lot of pressure. It doesn't look good."

"I agree."

Still stunned at the revelations concerning his only female board member, Alex fumbled nervously through the stack of papers left by Erica. "I still can't believe Lisa would do something like that."

"I guess we know how to get her vote next time."

"Strom!"

"Just kidding."

Both men laughed heartily. Suddenly, the door to the office swung open and Lisa Carl walked in.

"Am I interrupting something?" she asked. She studied both men's faces a little longer than usual, attempting to detect if their laughter had something to do with her weak moment with Vito. Both men broke eye contact with her, which in effect, gave her the answer.

Glancing up from the table, Alex cleared his throat, "Oh no, you're not interrupting anything. Please come in. Strom and I were just reminiscing about old times."

Lisa shot the men a hard stare and then took a seat at the far end of the table. She looked different today. She was dressed much more conservatively than normal—donning a gray business suit with a ruffled silk blouse protruding just above the buttoned jacket. Her lovely face was high-lighted by a minimal amount of make-up, and her usually flowing blond hair was pulled back in a tight bun. It appeared that she was trying very hard to present a new image to the board in the aftermath of her scandalous event with Vito. Alex was certain that that the juvenile display by her two fellow board members had taken her aback.

"What's the matter, my girl? Are you mad at us?" Strom said jokingly, attempting to relax the tense atmosphere. "We've been saving your usual seat." He pointed across the table at the seat next to Alex.

"Thank you, but this is fine," she said quietly.

"Are you sure? You look a little lonely down there," Strom replied.

Alex watched the unfolding scene with rapt attention concerned that he and Strom had inadvertently offended the single most important vote on this issue.

"Yes, I'm sure; this is fine."

"But where is Jack going to sit? You took his seat," Alex interjected.

The sound of Alex's voice seemed to soften the dour expression on Lisa's face. She batted her eyes a few times and replied, "Oh well, I guess I don't want to take Jack's seat." She lifted her purse off the floor, slowly rose and took her usual seat at the front of the table next to Alex.

Alex breathed a sigh of relief.

It was now almost four o'clock. The door opened once again and in walked board members Cliff Williams, Seth Boardman, and Jack Mathews. After a few friendly greetings and niceties, the three board members took their seats and quiet conversation ensued. A few minutes later, Barnes O'Brien appeared at the door. As usual, he was the last to arrive.

Erica followed Barnes into the room and took her customary seat at the other end of the table. She immediately turned on the tape recorder and laptop and prepared to record the proceedings.

"Good afternoon, Barnes," Alex said politely.

"Good afternoon," Barnes replied. He greeted the other members by name, giving a particularly warm smile and hello to Lisa Carl. Alex wondered if Barnes knew about the incident at Vito's office.

Wasting no time, Alex lifted the small gavel at the head of the table and tapped if firmly on the small oval base.

"Ladies and gentlemen, we have but one item on the agenda today But it is indeed, an important one. I realize there has already been a lot of discussion on repaying the TARP money, so I would like to open up the meeting for any final remarks and then we will take the vote."

Barnes quickly rose from his seat. He lifted the sweaty glass from the table and took a sip. His chin pushed firmly against his neck, he grabbed the inside of his vest with both hands and launched into a lengthy diatribe about the "sorry state" of Midwest Consolidated's financial health. Well prepared and convincing in his arguments to keep the TARP money, the battle-tested attorney strolled around the room, often waving his arms in the air and patting the other members on the shoulder. At one point, he bent down and whispered something in Lisa's ear. Smiling broadly, he continued his rant. Lisa seemed embarrassed by the gesture. Barnes ended by returning to his chair and slamming his fist on the table, and demanding that his board take control of this bank from a misguided and over-zealous manager who was jeopardizing the future of Midwest Consolidated Bank to advance his own narrow ideology.

Exactly what you're doing, Alex thought. After a few more questions and comments from the other members, a determined Alex took the floor to defend his position to give back the money. He cited the ever growing control of the bank by the Federal Government and the need for Midwest to stay independent and viable and not become a failed victim of another Government take-over.

Lisa Carl sat quietly throughout the discussions, never asking a question or offering her opinion. After some closing arguments by Strom Winslow on the importance of staying free of Government control, Alex called for the vote.

"As I call your name, please respond by saying aye if you are in favor of paying back the TARP money and nay if you are opposed. I will start to my left with Strom and move around the table. And, I remind you, that a simple majority of four will support the motion and by the same token, a simple vote of four will defeat it. Speak clearly so Erica can hear you and record the correct answer."

"Strom Winslow."

"Aye."

"Barnes O'Brien."

"A huge nay, the correct vote." He smiled smugly and winked at Lisa. She smiled back at him. Alex's heart sank. He collected himself and continued.

"Seth Boardman."

"Nay."

"Jack Mathews"

"Nay."

"Cliff Williams."

"Aye."

The vote was now three to two against repaying the TARP. Alex would be the final vote. Lisa, as expected, would determine the outcome.

"Lisa Carl," Alex announced.

Lisa paused before answering. Her eyes were filled with tears. She looked briefly at Barnes and then at Alex. "Aye," she said softly, but loud enough for all to hear. Her shoulders collapsed, her eyes went down.

Alex was elated, "My vote is aye," he said quickly.

"The motion to repay the TARP money has passed the board by a vote of four to three," Erica announced.

Barnes jumped to his feet and this time he slammed both fists on the table; the entire room shook from the power of the blows. "What the hell, Lisa? What are you doing? You damned floo…" Barnes stopped short of finishing his rant, realizing that he was about to call one of his best friend's wife a floozy. His eyes darted around the room at the others. His face was pale and ashen; his thick hands were shaking. His whole world had just fallen apart in front of him. He was beside himself.

Lisa blushed at the dressing down from Barnes. Then her eyes grew dark and she glared back at the pompous attorney.

Alex proceeded to wrap up the meeting. "The motion has been carried to pay back the TARP funds. As with all Government programs, I'm sure this one will take some time to implement. Hopefully, it will be completed by the end of this fiscal year in December."

Barnes slammed his briefcase shut and stormed

from the room.

"We're adjourned," a beaming Alex announced.

Chapter 26

Butch purposely arrived a little late hoping that most of the people would be inside already. Embarrassed that he could no longer afford a limo and chauffeur, he didn't want the townsfolk to see him driving his own vehicle. He turned off the engine on the black Hummer with darkened windows and started to open the door.

"Just a minute." His diminutive wife rustled around in her large leather purse and pulled out a small plastic bottle. She flipped the lid off and carefully jiggled two oblong tablets into her shaking hand. Then, she opened wide and tossed them in her mouth. She lifted a bottle of water from the center console and washed them down. She dropped the bottle back in the holder.

"I wish you wouldn't take so many pills, Maria. It makes me feel bad—like you're not happy or something."

Her sad, empty eyes stared at Butch. "I told you, Butch, I have a chemical imbalance. I was born with it. It's nothing you did. We'd better get going or we'll be late." She pushed her door open and slid out of the SUV.

A disconsolate Butch exited the vehicle and hurried to catch up with his fast-walking wife. They were soon inside an old elementary school that was located in a working class neighborhood in Elmwood Park. Maria stopped in the large vestibule area and looked both ways. "It's this way Butch. The gym is this way."

"I know," the aging mobster whispered as he and his eloquently dressed wife hustled down the shiny hall past the many pictures of young athletes holding up trophies and smiling at the camera. Up ahead, a voice on the loud speaker asked the crowd to take their seats. Suddenly, Butch grabbed his wife's arm from behind. "Look here, Maria."

Maria sighed, "What is it? We have to get going; everybody is getting ready to sit down."

"I know, I know, but look here." He pointed to a picture behind a small trophy inside the aging trophy case. "See the little fat boy on the back row grinning from ear to ear?"

"Yes, I see him."

"That's me! It's little Alonzo. We had just won the sixth grade football tournament. Wasn't I a cute little guy?"

Maria frowned and shook her head. "You were fat and frumpy looking if you ask me. Let's go."

She wrestled free from his hand and hurried toward the gym. A dejected Butch trailed along behind, straightening his tie as he struggled to keep up.

Maria paused unexpectedly just outside the gym door and turned toward her surprised husband, her eyes clouded over. "I'm sorry, Butch, you were a darling little boy. You really were." She gave him a peck on the cheek, grabbed his hand and pulled the beaming wise-guy through the wide door to the gym.

Once inside, the crowd reacted immediately. There

was applause and cheers throughout the packed room. Several folks rushed forward to greet the smiling Ferinnis. A beaming master of ceremonies shouted into the microphone, "They're here, our honored guests are here! Let's make them feel welcome. What do you say, folks?"

Chapter 27

Vito, a little hung over and sporting a nasty headache pushed the button on his speaker phone. "Yes?"

"You have a call from Jay Underwood up on the third."

Jay was Vito's in-house investment guy. Very smart, and he had the unenviable task of overseeing all Vito's many investments. It was a job no one wanted. Jay had lasted an entire year—which was a record for First Financial. His office was in the posh VIP room on the third floor where First's best and brightest operated. The company's big hitters loved the VIP room and having their own investment area made them feel important.

"I wonder what the hell he wants," Vito mumbled.

"What's that, Mr. Taglioni?"

"Oh nothing. Put him through."

"Right away."

"Hello, Jay. How are you today?"

"Fine, sir. Sorry to interrupt your busy day."

"Oh, no problem. Just feeling a little under the weather today—if you know what I mean."

There was a short chuckle on the other end. Everybody in the office knew of Vito's extracurricular activities. The seasoned broker made light of it. "It happens to the best of us."

"What can I do for you?"

"I just called to congratulate you."

"Oh yeah, what for?"

"With your recent purchase of ten thousand shares of Verizon common stock, you are now the largest account holder for First Financial Securities. I want to thank you personally for having trust in me."

"Oh really?" The arrogant owner knew almost to the penny what his investments were—he checked them almost daily. But he wanted to hear Jay say it. "Just what is my portfolio right now?"

"Two hundred and seventy-three million!"

"Hmmm…it's getting up there alright and during a down market. Good job, Jay."

Jay had managed to protect his boss's money in the recent downturn by investing mainly in small and mid-cap companies. Since the subprime crisis reared its ugly head, Vito's portfolio had actually grown over ten percent, at a time when most investors were experiencing thirty to forty percent drops in value—Vito was very happy with Jay Underwood.

"Glad to see you're earning your money, Jay. Keep it up."

"Sure will, boss. Thanks."

Vito smiled and fell back in his chair watching the large fan circulate above. The awesome value of his holdings had never seemed to completely register with him before, but after hearing the words "top investor in the company", he had a sense of the vast amount of money he had accumulated—most of it earned in the past few years as a result of his corrupt subprime deal with Barnes.

The deal, he and his unlikely bed partner, Barnes O'Brien, had forged some two years earlier, was paying off. Barnes had used his substantial political equity with the Democratic Party machine to help get Vito necessary branch approvals to expand his business to several other cities. The plan, so far, had gone just as they hoped it would. The deal gave Barnes forty per cent of all the profits for providing legal counsel and assisting in the formation and marketing of the huge mortgage-backed bonds. Vito received sixty per cent for providing the vehicle to sell the bonds and finding investors willing to spend tens of millions of dollars.

Barnes was a wealthy man before the scheme had been hatched; it was all about power and political ambition with him. But for Vito, who was struggling financially at the time, it was strictly about the money. Ever since he was a small boy he had longed to be a rich man. His father, a simple baker's assistant, would occasionally take Vito with him to the upscale River Forest community near their home in Elmwood Park to deliver a cake. Vito would sit and gawk at the huge estates owned by the local mobsters, doctors and attorneys. And today, for the first time, he fully realized that he had done just that. It sent a chill up his spine just thinking about it. He could blow five hundred dollars a night in a local Indy strip club and never miss it. The purchase of his lavish new home in the exclusive suburb of Carmel, valued at over three million dollars, had hardly made a dent in his enormous holdings. He had a new Mercedes, a membership at one of the finest country clubs in Indianapolis and still had a whopping two hundred seventy million dollars to spare. But even better for Vito, his enormous wealth seemed to gain him cover for his bad boy behavior. And fortunately for him, his beautiful wife, a former model, seemed to tolerate his indiscretions as long as Vito kept her checkbook fat.

"Mr. Taglioni?"

"Yes, yes what is it, Claudia?" Vito glared menacingly at the speaker phone he had forgotten to turn off.

"Cliff would like to see you."

"Okay, send him in." Vito sat up, poked the phone off and glanced toward the large oak door.

The office manager cracked the door slightly.

"Come in!" Vito said impatiently.

Cliff walked hesitantly across the threshold to the office, turned quietly around and pushed the door gently closed and released the doorknob without making a sound. The hard-driving Vito found his young office manager's entry ritual amusing and his charming personality disarming. It was difficult for him to get as angry with Cliff as he did with the others. Cliff was smart and diplomatic, the perfect fit for his mercurial boss.

"Good afternoon, sir."

"Good afternoon, Cliff. I hope you have some good news for me about the branch filings with the SEC—particularly the Chicago office."

"Well, I have some news that's for sure. I will let you decide whether it is good or not." He cut a nervous grin.

"Go ahead."

"As I suggested, I contacted our man at the SEC. I told him about the request from Ted Blue for copies of all of our branch approval files and our unfortunate discovery that there was basically nothing in the Chicago file except the original application."

"And?" the impatient Vito snorted.

"He told me that it would be difficult to create a duplicate file because the empirical data and demographics have obviously changed since the time of application. He said he would look into it and get back to me right away."

"This doesn't sound good." The surly boss, still basking in the splendor of his staggering wealth, sat up in his chair. "Did he get back with you?"

"Yes, a few hours later."

Vito slid to the edge of his chair. "Okay, continue!"

"It seems as though another large securities firm had applied for a branch approval in Chicago around the same time as First Financial. He said we could use the data from that request to create a file for our Chicago office. All the information in our file will now be dated around the time of the original application."

"So, by copying the information from the other file and putting it with the original application, we pretty much have what we need." Vito exclaimed.

"Bingo!"

Beaming from ear to ear at his own brilliant deduction, Vito went on. "I'm sure there was some data from that file that couldn't be used,"

"That's correct, but he felt we could extract enough information to create an "adequate" file for Mr. Blue. He said the SEC would take responsibility for the less than complete file, while at the same time insisting that in the midst of the largest housing boom in our country's history, less than totally complete files were quite normal and our file met all of their important specifications."

"Wonderful! Wonderful! Good job Cliff. There'll be a bonus in this for you."

"Thank you, sir."

"One more thing, Cliff."

"Yes?"

"I don't remember any other firms opening up in Chicago around that time or anytime since for that matter.

"You're absolutely right and there's a reason for that."

Vito's brow lifted.

"That application hasn't been approved yet. It's still pending."

Vito grunted a coarse chuckle. "I guess Moretti and his boys have been taking good care of us."

"Guess so." Cliff looked anxiously at the clock on Vito's desk. "Sir, if you'll excuse me, I have a two o'clock."

"Oh, please go ahead."

The office manager hurried from the office. As the door swung shut, his cell phone blared. He quickly answered, "Yes, Barnes?"

"Are you sitting down?"

Chapter 28

"Wasn't that a wonderful lunch? Let's hear it for Louise and her staff back there in the kitchen. Come on, loud enough so she can hear, come on!" Those in attendance applauded politely for the popular cook and her staff at St. Celestine Elementary School. A few seconds later, a smiling, gray-haired lady, reluctantly stuck her head out from a door at the back of the multi-purpose room and waved at the appreciative crowd. She pushed the door open further and pointed at her staff that was still busy working inside the steamy kitchen. They smiled and waved their utensils and damp towels at the crowd.

"Thanks again to you and your staff, Louise. You're a jewel." The emcee smiled warmly.

Nearby, Butch Ferinni fidgeted in his seat, as he nervously waited for the coming introduction. Maria squeezed his hand gently to reassure him.

"Thank you all for coming today. It looks like we've had a pretty good turnout for our friend, Butch Ferinni!" A burst of applause erupted throughout the room.

The emcee paused and cleared his voice. "Ladies and gentlemen, it has been my pleasure to serve as President of the Elmwood Park Chamber of Commerce this past year. And nothing gives me more pleasure than what I am about to do. Butch Ferinni and I go back a long, long way. Believe it or not, we were classmates together here at St. Celestine elementary school. I was just a little kid, skinny and sickly from a severe bout with pneumonia as an infant. It was not unusual, I'm sorry to say, for some of the boys here at the school to pick on me from time to time."

A groan spread across the room.

The emcee smiled and turned toward Butch. "That was until one day when Butch Ferinni saw a much larger boy punch me and knock me to the ground right out there." He nodded toward the playground outside the back windows. The emcee smiled and looked over at a blushing Butch. "Butch was playing catch football nearby, and when he saw the bully knock me down, he ran over as fast as he could and kicked the larger boy right here!" He lifted his ample backside toward the crowd and pointed at it. The crowd burst out in laughter. "Then he told the boy if he ever saw him near me again, he would beat the crap out of him. Butch wasn't the biggest boy in school, but he sure was the toughest." He looked at Butch again. "I'll never forget that day." A slightly embarrassed Butch smiled broadly.

The animated emcee quieted the crowd, and then went on for several minutes describing the many charitable contributions made to their community by Butch Ferinni.

"I don't know who came up with the idea of giving out a Citizen of the Year Award first, but I do know this—in all my years serving this community, I have never seen a more deserving candidate for this award than the man I am about to announce. Ladies and Gentlemen, the winner of the Elmwood Park Chamber of Commerce's Citizen of the Year Award, Alonzo "Butch" Ferinni. Let's hear it for Butch!"

Those in attendance jumped to their feet as the aging mobster stood and approached the podium. He grabbed the large plaque from his friend and lifted it toward the crowd, beaming from ear to ear as the applause continued.

Chapter 29

"Damn it, Barnes! I thought you said Montrose reassured you our little plan for skimming money from the bank was foolproof."

"He did. It's just that Crane got suspicious and sent Dulin up there to snoop around and he may have figured out what Jack was doing."

Vito shook his head as he stared out at the noisy traffic on Meridian Street. "May have?"

"Well, yes. We're not certain that he knows, but Montrose thought he was acting very secretive that day. He wasn't sharing and discussing things with him like he usually does. For that reason, he thinks Dulin may be onto something. Anyway, we can't take any chances—we have to assume he knows."

"Oh damn! If Crane knows about this we could all be going to prison," Vito snorted. "I don't know why you had to get me involved in this thing. Now you've gotten both our asses in trouble."

Barnes frowned, "Don't go there again, Vito. Just shut up and listen."

Vito glared at Barnes.

"There's more."

"More?"

"Yes. We just had our monthly board meeting at Midwest and the board voted in favor of paying back the TARP money."

"What?"

"Yes, and your friend Lisa was the deciding vote. She voted with Alex in favor of the payback."

Vito's face turned beat red. "Why, that snooty bitch."

Barnes shot back, "I guess you weren't as convincing as you thought."

"Listen Barnes, I did my best. I tried to help. Edward's your best friend. What about that?"

"It really doesn't matter who's at fault. The fact is, it happened. And now, we've got a giant mess on our hands."

"The question is how do we get out of this situation?"

"It's going to take a while to implement the payback. In the meantime, Ramsey will have to do something about Crane. If he's no longer president, I can replace him with Montrose. When that happens, I will ask the board to revisit the TARP issue. Montrose will be the deciding vote and we will be able to rescind today's decision."

"Good luck on that one. Crane doesn't look like he's going anywhere to me."

"I told Ben Ramsey about the board's vote. He called me back a short time later and said he had just gotten off the phone with the President and said he had never seen him so upset." There was a deafening pause.

Vito dropped down in his chair. "And?"

"He says the gloves are off. Nothing is off the table at this point. He told Ramsey to 'Capone him' if necessary."

"Capone him? Do you know what that means?"

Barnes continued, "Yes, and I wouldn't want to be Alex Crane right now. The President can't wait any longer; there is too much at stake. He feels he must act now."

"Do you think they're serious?"

The usually bellicose Barnes spoke almost inaudibly. Vito had to strain to hear him. "I've seen enough of these guys to know that they will stop at nothing to get what they want."

Vito shouted, "They want to kill Crane?"

Barnes interrupted, "Quiet down, Claudia may overhear you."

"I'm not stupid, Barnes. Claudia is out to lunch."

"Listen to me closely, Vito. Ramsey may need your help."

"My help? Oh Mother of Jesus!" Vito groaned.

"Here's what we need you to do."

Chapter 30

"How did you manage to get us out of there early, my dear?"

"Yesterday, I told Sammy that I had a meeting and we couldn't stay for the whole thing."

Butch pushed the passenger side door shut and hurried around to the other side and quickly climbed inside the Hummer, hoping to get behind the dark windows before anyone saw him.

"You shouldn't have told them your limo was picking us up. You shouldn't be embarrassed because you have to drive yourself. Most of the made guys drive themselves now."

"Okay Maria, okay. Just knock it off please." Butch exited the school parking area, and gunned it down 77th Avenue, anxious to get away from the school parking area as fast as possible.

"You shouldn't have lied to them. It will be a lot more embarrassing if people find out we don't have a limo," Maria groused.

"Like I said Maria, knock it OFF!"

Maria knew her limits; she knew she had pushed far enough. She didn't want to see the ugly side of her volatile husband, so she stopped talking.

Butch's cell rang. He quickly flipped it open. "Vito, you dog! How the hell are you?"

"Okay Butch, how about yourself?"

"Couldn't be better. And what is my big shot, rich guy friend doing calling me on this fine day?"

"I may need a favor from you, Butch."

"Oh yeah?" Butch never liked Vito much, but tolerated him because of his powerful connections.

"Yeah, well…uh Moretti's having some problems."

"Oh yeah?"

"Yeah."

"And how is Eddie? Got the big head yet?"

Vito forced a chuckle, "You know Ed. He was never short on self-confidence."

"I know, but I'm proud of him.—very proud!"

"Yeah, so am I."

"So what kind of problems is Eddie having? I can't imagine the President of the United States having any problems."

"He's in a jam, Butch. It seems as though some people are working against him; they're trying to bring down his presidency."

"That's a shame, but what's that got to do with little ole Alonzo?"

Maria was getting curious. She turned toward her husband and listened carefully. He shrugged his shoulders at her. "Oh I see….I see, well…uh Maria and I got some shopping to do, so why don't I call you later."

"Sorry, I didn't know Maria was with you. Do you think she heard…."

The wise-guy interrupted, "No, no problem."

"One last thing Butch, do you have a number where I could call you that can't be traced back to you? These cell phones are easy to track. I have an apartment that I use occasionally for some of my extra-curricular activities. The phone's in my buddy's name. I'll bet you have a place like that?"

Butch's brow narrowed. Prone to violence, the hard-bitten gangster had always been faithful to his Maria. "Hell no, I don't!"

The playboy, Vito, thought everyone was like him, always looking for a good lay. Ferinni's response stunned him; he realized he had made a horrible misjudgment.

"Hey Butch, I was just joking. I know how much you love Maria."

Butch knew Vito was blowing smoke, but not wanting a confrontation with his important friend, he accepted the apology and went on. "I can always get an untraceable phone if I need to.

"Okay, you still on line with the same address?"

"Yeah, sure."

"I'll e-mail you the number I was talking about. Call me at that number after seven."

"Okay, Vito. Good talking to you."

Maria squirmed in her seat. "What the hell was that all about?"

Butch didn't answer.

"What does Vito want with you? He never calls you."

"Ah, Moretti needs a little work done on his house. He wants me to do it."

She popped a blue pill in her mouth and washed it down. She looked directly at her husband, her tired eyes pleading, "Vito's a weasel; I don't like him."

"Oh hell! Vito's not that bad. Besides, I ain't making him any promises—even if it is for Ed Moretti." He waved at the sentry at the front gate to his mansion and then put the gas to the big SUV. It soon disappeared behind the stone walls that surrounded the large enclave.

Chapter 31

"Yes Vito, what is it? I'm at work. I told you to never call me at work."

"I'm calling about the board meeting today."

The line got quiet. "Oh, yeah."

"Yeah."

"What about it?"

"You know what about it."

"Listen, that's none of your business. I have customers waiting; I have to get going."

"You stabbed me in the back, you two-faced whore."

"Listen Vito, you've called me three times in the past week. Every time you get worried, you call me. I don't want you to call again."

"You promised me."

"I did no such thing. I never told you how I would vote."

"You led me to believe you would vote against Crane and you know it."

"I did no such thing! That was an embarrassing, humiliating day for me, Vito. People are starting to talk. I just want to forget what happened that day and I just want to forget you!"

Vito grunted, "You have no idea what you did today.

You have no idea of the consequences."

"I did the right thing. That's what I did—the right thing."

"The hell you did!"

"I've got to go."

The phone went dead on the other end. Dismayed, Vito slumped in his chair and stared blankly across his cluttered desk top.

Chapter 32

"Hey Gus! Ya up there, Gus?"

The broken screen door squeaked as it opened at the top of the rickety stairs. A thin man, wearing a sleeveless t-shirt with an unshaven face, stuck his head out the door. He blinked and then quickly shaded his eyes against the afternoon sun. "Yeah, Ginny?"

"Made beans and cornbread for supper. Five o'clock, if you're interested. Better join us—you could use a little meat on those bones."

Gus winced; he didn't like the reference to his thin frame. He was plenty healthy and ate like a horse. He was very seldom sick and was very strong for his size. "Is Pudge gonna be there?"

"Yes, I wouldn't invite you if Pudge wasn't going to be here."

"Okay Ginny, see you then. Thank you." He stood and watched as his benevolent landlady disappeared under the stairs.

Gus liked living in Michigan City, Indiana on the shores of beautiful Lake Michigan. He found the people in the old factory town to be generous and friendly. Now nearing retirement, he had arrived in the city eleven years ago, broke and with all of his life's posses-

sions crammed into the trunk of his small car. He had
migrated here from Illinois after he found out his ex
was having an affair with the local Chief of Police.
Angry and shaken, and anxious to put some distance
between himself and his adulterous former wife, he
filed for divorce and moved to Indiana. Lonely and
alone, and looking for a new beginning, he found his
way to the lakeside community, just a thirty minute drive
from Chicago.

Shortly after arriving in town, he took a job as
dishwasher at the trendy Matey's Restaurant that was a
few blocks from the lake and very near the new Blue
Chip Casino. The Blue Chip was the most exciting thing
to happen in Michigan City in over a hundred years. On
his days off from Matey's, he would deal a little
blackjack at the five dollar table on the glitzy gambling
boat. Well liked by the gamblers for his dry wit and
friendly demeanor, Gus soon decided to quit his job at
Matey's and became a full-time dealer at the casino.

"Gussy," as the customers like to call him, soon
found himself dealing to the high rollers at the hundred
dollar table, the highest max allowed on the boat. While
not getting rich by any means, Gus did well enough,
with his tips and a small hourly wage, to pay his three
hundred fifty a month rent to Pudge and Ginny, buy a
2004 Honda Civic and make an occasional trip to Des
Moines, Iowa to visit his sick daughter, Darcy.

A few hours later, clean shaven and sporting dark
slacks and a nicely pressed white dress shirt, Gus went
whistling down the stairs to Pudge and Ginny's
backdoor. He always stood at the door until one of
them saw him and invited him in. He felt it too
aggressive to knock on the door, even though this event

happened at least once a week.

"Come on in, we won't bite ya," an apron-clad Ginny shouted from the steamy kitchen.

Having received the necessary invitation, Gus carefully pushed the crooked screen door open and stepped inside, just as Ginny's husband, Pudge, an obese man with a huge protruding belly, came rumbling into the kitchen from the nearby living room. Pudge worked nights at one of the nearby steel mills in Portage and had an appetite nearly as big as his bulbous body.

"Sit down," he ordered. "Can't eat dinner standing up."

Ginny slipped off her apron, hurried over and set the beans and cornbread on the table. Soon, they were all seated and after a poor attempt at grace by Pudge, the steamy hot beans and luscious cornbread started moving around the beige, Formica-top table. Pudge's job at the mills paid very well, but due to three previous marriages and lingering child support payments, the Hoffman's lived a rather meager lifestyle.

Pudge's small, beady eyes shot a hard stare at Gus from beneath his thick brow. "How's business at the boat?"

"The action's been pretty good lately. I think with the slow economy, folks are stickin' closer to home. The house had a record month last month."

Pudge grunted.

"Thanks for eating early, I appreciate it." Gus said sincerely. The Hoffman's normally ate at six o'clock, except when they invited Gus. Gus had to be at the casino at six-thirty, so they ate at five to give him time to eat and then get around for work.

"You don't have to say that every time," Ginny

scolded. "We know you appreciate it."

Gus smiled warmly.

Pudge glanced at Gus. "Ya know somethin' Shorty? We've known you eleven years and I still don't know a darn thing about you. I mean you seem like a nice guy and all, but we know nothing about your past."

"My past wasn't very exciting; it would bore you." Once again, Gus was irked by the reference to his small stature. There was a time when a man would have felt his rage for such a comment—but not today and not Pudge Hoffman. He had done too many nice things for Gus.

"You weren't one of those Italian gangsters or something, were you?" The big man exploded in laughter at his own absurd observation. His big belly hit the table, spilling his coffee all over the white tablecloth.

Ginny jumped to her feet and glared at her husband, "Apologize to Gus, smart aleck! He can't help it he's small." Ginny grabbed a dish towel from the nearby counter and quickly soaked up the mess.

With a mixture of soup beans and cornbread dripping from his mouth, Pudge muttered an almost inaudible, "Sorry."

Ginny smiled at Gus. "I looked up Clemente on the computer the other day and it means gentle and merciful."

"Thanks Ginny and it's okay. I know Pudge likes me," Gus winked at the big man.

Pudge's eyes softened and a smile slowly appeared at the corner of his mouth and then spread clear across his chubby face. Soon the two men were sharing an impromptu high five across the table, with Pudge's belly once again bumping the edge, spilling Gus's coffee this time.

"I love ya Shorty, I sure do." Pudge said.

A beaming Ginny joyously announced, "I baked a cherry pie today. Can you stay for dessert, Gus?"

"I could never turn down your cherry pie, Ginny."

"I really am sorry, Shorty." a sincere Pudge implored again.

Gus took a deep breath, "I know you are Pudge, but do me a favor, will ya?"

"Sure, anything."

"Don't call me Shorty."

"Oh…okay. Sorry again."

"No problem."

"How's your daughter feeling these days, Gus?" the repentant steelworker asked.

"She's tired a lot—not much energy."

"Why doesn't she get that heart taken care of?" Ginny offered.

"She has a rare heart disease. It requires a very delicate operation and will cost about two hundred thousand dollars. She works at a convenience store and they don't provide insurance.

"Oh my, that's a fortune."

Tears welled in Gus's eyes. "Yeah, I know. I wish I could pay for it. I've been saving, but I've only got about twelve thousand in the bank so far—not near enough."

"You poor thing!" Ginny rose from her chair and threw her arms around Gus, hugging him tightly. "I've been praying for Darcy every day."

"Thank you, Ginny," Gus said softly.

"I wish I had two hundred thousand laying around here somewhere. I'd sure give it to you," Pudge offered.

Not wanting the conversation about his daughter to dampen the evening, Gus lightened the mood. "Maybe I'll win the lotto or something."

"I buy a Powerball ticket every week. If I win, the money's yours," Pudge said quietly.

"What if it's ten million?" Gus shot back.

The room shook from Pudge's laughter. "Yeah… yeah, it could be ten million, you're right. Then you get two hundred thousand and I keep the rest!"

"Fair enough!" They all laughed together. Gus was deeply touched by the generosity and heartfelt concern shown him by his quirky landlords.

Pleasant conversation filled the room for the remainder of the evening, with Ginny making five more trips to refill the bean bowl—much to Pudge's delight. Gus ate three pieces of Ginny's wonderful pie so as not to make Pudge feel self-conscious about his multiple helpings. Ginny smiled and batted her eyes each time Gus requested another piece of her pie. At six o'clock sharp, Gus excused himself, ran upstairs to put on his red plaid dealer's vest and got ready to go to work.

Chapter 33

Gus loved the atmosphere in the casino. He found the bright lights and noisy slots intoxicating. As he made his way to his blackjack table in the VIP room, located near the back of the boat, he spoke to many of his co-workers along the way. All of them seemed happy to see the immensely likeable Gus. He stopped outside the VIP room at the money cage.

"Howdy, stranger."

"Oh, hi Gus." A tiny lady in a blue business suit smiled warmly. She had dark hair, blue eyes and a pretty face.

"How are you, Trudy?'

"Good, thanks."

"Is everything okay? Haven't seen you for awhile."

"I've been at my mom's. She broke her hip and I had to help take care of her for awhile. My sister is taking over now, so I was able to come home." She shoved a pile of chips across the counter.

"Thank you," she said to the customer.

"Why didn't you tell me you were going home? I've missed you."

Her eyes turned shiny, "You hadn't called me for some time, so I didn't think you cared."

Gus moved closer to the counter and laid his hand gently on her forearm. "I'm so sorry, Trudy. I went to visit Darcy, I should have told you."

Trudy's lip started to quiver.

Gus spoke quickly, "How about dinner tomorrow night at the Spa?" he asked, eyes wide with anticipation.

"Oh…uh I love the Spa." A single tear rolled down her cheek, she managed a weak smile.

Gus leaned over and gave her a peck on the cheek. "I'll pick you up at six o'clock sharp."

She nodded, fighting back more tears. "Thank you, Gus."

"I'm sorry I didn't call you. I was worried about Darcy. It won't happen again."

"Same here." Trudy managed a full smile as a customer approached the cage. "Better go now," she murmured.

Gus squeezed her arm and then made the short journey to his cushy gaming room for the night. He spoke briefly to the departing dealer and then carefully lifted two new dealing trays from beneath the table. He pushed the cards tight and started the first deal.

Gus glanced out of the corner of his eye at a rather thick man who had moved into an open slot at the end of the table.

"Pay twenty-one!" Gus barked to the dismay of the unhappy gamblers. He carefully drug in the lost bets from the across the broad table.

"How ya doing, Doc?"

The greeting stunned the surprised dealer; he hadn't heard the name Doc for over ten years. He pushed the cards tight in the tray and glanced at the new arrival. "Butch, I can't believe it's you."

"How are you, Doc?"

"Fine, Butch. Good to see you."

"Vito told me you were dealin' down here at the Blue Chip—said he ran into you awhile back."

"Yeah, he did."

"You look good!"

"Thanks, Butch."

One of the players cleared his throat. "How about a card, dealer!"

Butch glared at the man.

"It's okay Butch, I better get to work. I get off at midnight."

"How about we have a drink then?" Butch suggested.

Gus hesitated, "Okay, I'll meet you in the lounge up front at midnight."

"See you then."

Still angry, a red-faced Butch glared at the gambler as he backed away from the table and entered the main room. Butch found an open craps table and settled in for a few hours of gambling.

Chapter 34

Butch waved a swizzle stick at his old friend, signaling him to come join him at a rather isolated table in the corner of the smoky lounge. Gus smiled and hurried across the room to Butch's table. He shared a vigorous handshake with the aging mobster and fell into the cushy leather chair across from him.

"Still drinking Scotch?"

A smiling Gus nodded.

"A glass of your finest Scotch for my friend here and I'll have another martini," Butch said to the just arriving waiter.

"Yes sir." The young waiter hustled back to the bar.

There was a brief, uncomfortable silence as each man sat looking at the other. Gus was wondering why his old friend had shown up so suddenly and seemed so intent upon talking to him. Ferinni broke the silence.

"How do you like the boat?" Butch's dark eyes peered toward the outside gaming area.

"I like it fine, thanks."

"Do you live here in Michigan City?"

"Yeah, I got an apartment in town that's not too far from here. Sometimes I even walk to work. How about you, Butch? How are you and Maria?"

"Oh, fine. I'm doing okay and she does a lot of shopping and so forth. The girl thing, you know."

Gus's smile faded quickly as the waiter arrived with their drinks.

Butch, sensing the uneasiness of his old friend, leaned back in his chair, drink in hand. "I've been worried about you, Gus. You just kind of disappeared."

"Well, it was Roxy and that Chief in Elmwood Park, ya know."

"Yeah, I heard about that. Bet you felt like blowing him away," Butch grinned nervously, not sure if Gus would appreciate the blowing him away reference.

Gus's face went blank. He stared menacingly at Butch, looking away at the last minute to break the tension. "I was very hurt by Roxy. I just wanted to get away from her and that town, so I packed up and hopped on the first train to Indiana. The train made a stop here. I saw the lake from the depot and decided to get off—been here ever since."

"Well…uh, looks like everything is working out okay."

"Yeah, I'm happy here."

Tired of the small talk, Butch got to the point. "I came here today because our friend, Ed Moretti, is in trouble."

Gus had also grown up with Moretti in Elmwood Park and was very proud of him. "Sorry to hear that."

Butch leaned forward and laid his forearms on the table. "There are some people trying to bring the President down. They've hatched an elaborate scheme to discredit him and his administration. If their plan goes down, his bid for reelection will be finished. And, no one wants that to happen."

Gus knew what was coming; he felt dismayed and angry. He stirred his drink hastily. "Hell Butch, why'd you come lookin' for me? I left that all behind me. Why don't you just leave me alone?"

Butch leaned even closer, almost whispering, "You're the best, Doc. You know that. That's why I'm here."

Memories of his years as a brutal hit man in the Chicago mob came rushing back to him. Known for his vicious, take no prisoners style, Gus, in his heyday, had been sought after by many of the mob bosses on the tough West Side. He was nicknamed "Doc", because of his resemblance to the slender frontier killer, Doc Holiday. Gus was fearless and a deadly shot, but with mob violence on the wane, and his departure from the Chicago scene some ten years earlier, Gus was certain that his days as a "hit man" were over. That was—until today.

Gus's brow pushed tight. "You're right, Butch. I was the best. I was a heartless killer. I was capable of anything back then. I gunned down a man once for a hundred bucks—a hundred damned dollars!" Shaken by his own revelations, Gus paused momentarily, composed himself and continued. "All of that—it still haunts me today. I can still see their faces: Benny, Paul Paul, Choir Boy, and other guys I whacked. I still dream about them at night and wake up in a cold sweat. There's something about killing someone; it gets inside of you and it never leaves."

"Vito told me that your daughter Darcy is very ill. He said it would take a lot of cash to get her well."

Gus shot up in his chair, his face white with rage. "Listen to me, Butch! I know your tricks! I know how you guys work! Don't bring my daughter into this!"

A stoic Butch ignored his pleas. "I've got approval to go a quarter million on this one. Just one hit, a quarter mil!"

His chest heaving in anger, Gus's eyes clouded over thinking about the awful dilemma he was now facing. That kind of money could pay for Darcy's heart operation. He wanted desperately for his daughter to have her surgery, but not with blood money. Yet, he knew that he could never save enough money to pay for the operation and with each passing day, her chances for survival grew less. But the old Doc Clemente was gone—dead and buried long ago. Could he be resurrected? Could he kill again? The thought of it sickened him.

"This is all about what history will say about our friend, Eddie. He may go down as one of the greatest presidents of all time—a man to be looked up to and admired for years to come. Or he may go down as a shamed man, a forgotten man, like those other nameless presidents like Franklin Pierce of Chester Arthur or one of those guys. That's why it's a quarter mil, it's very important."

Gus winced at the mention of the quarter million; he needed it so badly. He could tell Butch had done his homework. No way would he know the names of Pierce and Arthur otherwise.

He fell back against his chair and exhaled. He didn't really give a damn about Ed Moretti. Oh, he was happy he was President, but he had always been the rich kid on the block. Born of privilege, he drove a new Camaro and wore designer clothes in high school. Gus was not so lucky. The son of a truck driver, he was considered a "hurt" or "loser" as a kid. Ed Moretti wouldn't have given Gus the time of day when he was growing up.

But Gus cared deeply about his Darcy and wanted desperately to make her well. He found the huge offer hard to resist. He could pay for her surgery and have money left over. Maybe, he and Trudy could use some of the money, get married and buy a house. He felt like he was being ripped apart inside.

He gave Butch a hard stare and continued, "What you're doing is bullshit, Butch, and you know it. But I want more than anything for my daughter to live a rich and full life. I would gladly give up my own life for that. So I will consider this on two conditions."

Butch's eyes went wide, "Yes, yes go ahead."

"First, I want paid in cash—cold cash."

"No problem, I was planning on it."

"Secondly, I've got a good life here and I want to keep it that way. I don't want it ruined by this. I don't want anyone to know about this, so I have a question for you."

"Certainly, go ahead."

Gus's eyes darkened and narrowed. "If you bullshit me on this Butch, I will come after you—I promise."

Butch grimaced. A man among men, he was not used to such threats. His anger flared and then subsided, knowing that the man he was facing would not make an idle threat, even to him. "Go ahead," he said quietly.

"Does anyone, besides you, know that you have come here today?"

"No, no one."

"What about Vito?"

"He doesn't know I came here today, but he did offer up your name as a possible trigger man, along with several others."

"Okay then. It's the same for that coward Vito. You can tell him it's me, but if he tells anyone and I find out, I will take him out also. You tell him that."

"I will tell him." Butch's eyes softened. "You have my word of honor. No one else will know. Your life here in this small community will not be affected and if we ever meet again, it will be only to break bread and talk about old times."

Gus fell back against his chair and lifted his drink, "Dio vi benedica il mio amico." Gus blessed Butch in Italian to alleviate the tension and reinforce the close bond that had developed between them over the years.

"Dio vi benedica il mio amico," Butch replied.

"You always get your way, don't you?"

"Not always—just ask Maria!"

Gus smiled. "What do we do next?"

"I have a room at the Holiday Plaza on the edge of town. We can meet in my room tomorrow morning at ten and begin planning. I will give you the details then. I am in Room 127."

Gus looked away. There was an agonizing pause before he turned and spoke, "Ten, it is," he said softly.

Butch downed the remainder of his martini. "I have to go. It's getting late," he said briskly. The two men shook hands. Butch stopped at the bar, paid the tab and then hurried from the lounge.

A shaken Gus was left alone with his thoughts. Just a few hours earlier he was enjoying another day of dealing on his beloved gambling boat. Now, without warning, his entire life had been turned upside down. The agony of it all was almost overwhelming. After years of struggling, he was just now starting to feel like a 'real' human being again. He was angry—angry at Butch and angry at all of the made-men he had thrown in with so many years ago. Always trying to compensate for his small stature, he risked everything to prove to them that he was the deadliest and toughest hit man on the West Side. And whether it be for good or bad, he had accomplished just that. Feared by even the most sinister of the thugs in the dark menacing world of the mob, nobody messed with Gus "Doc" Clemente. Over twenty men had found an early grave at the end of the hot, smoking barrel of Gus's trusty thirty-eight. But what disturbed him most, as he sat alone and shaking, was the realization that deep inside, he knew that he still possessed the ability to kill. Those demons that had driven him to the top of the "hit-man" hierarchy of the Chicago mob were still there, waiting to be called upon. Sure, he needed the money for his beloved Darcy, but how many people could agree to take the life of a person they didn't even know? He downed his Scotch and stood to leave. He felt a gentle touch on his neck.

"Everything okay, Gus?"

He turned to see the worried eyes of his girl, Trudy. "Uh…yes, everything is fine." He mustered a weak smile.

"You poor thing—your shirt is soaked and your face is white."

"I think I'm getting a touch of the flu or something." Gus move rapidly to change the subject. "What are you doing here? Your shift should have ended at seven."

"One of the girls in the cage up front couldn't make it. They asked me to do a double, so I took it. One of the boys stopped on his way out and told me you were back here having a drink with another guy."

"Yeah…uh he was an old friend from Chicago. We were catching up on old times. Can I walk you to your car?"

"Oh sure, thank you." The two reunited lovers navigated their way through the sparsely populated casino.

"I saw a man walk past a little while ago. He looked familiar—like I had seen him on TV, or something. He was a big man. Was that your friend?" Trudy asked as she stepped through the open door and into the parking lot.

"Don't think so. Alonzo's just a construction guy; he builds houses and does remodeling jobs up around Chicago."

"That's nice." Trudy poked around in her purse and found her key and pushed the unlock button.

Gus hurried ahead and politely opened the car door.

She paused, "I'm looking forward to tomorrow night. I've missed you, Gus."

All the feelings that had been coming alive in Gus over the past several years rushed through him as he stood looking at his lovely Trudy. "And, I've missed you."

"Bye Gus."She climbed into her seat and tossed her purse on the passenger seat. Gus slowly closed the door and stood staring at her. The sweet scent of her perfume aroused his senses. He didn't want her to leave.

The electric window shuddered down. "You sure you're okay?"

Gus forced a reassuring smile. "I'm wonderful," he said. He leaned down and planted a warm kiss on her cheek. "Drive carefully," he ordered.

She blushed. "See you tomorrow." The engine's

tappets rattled as the old car pulled away.

A smiling Gus watched as she left the lot and merged slowly into the light traffic on Casino Boulevard. His broad smile suddenly vanished, his brow tightened. "Damn them! Damn those wise-guys!" he wailed. Spinning around, he violently kicked a huge tire on a nearby truck over and over again until his foot was aching in pain. "Damn them!" he shouted once more, waving his clenched fist defiantly in the air. Finally exhausted, his arm fell to his side. He breathed deeply and slowly exhaled. Shoulders slumped, eyes to the ground, he turned and limped slowly toward his car.

Chapter 35

"Good morning, Alex. Please have a chair." A serious looking Josh Dulin pointed to the chair next to him at the end of the large table in his conference room.

"Thank you, Josh." Alex hastily approached the chair and sat down. The CPA tossed a folder in front of him.

"I appreciate your coming to my office; it makes things a lot easier to have all the supporting files and documentation readily at hand. I hope you understand."

"I certainly do." Alex opened the folder.

Josh leaned forward and carefully scanned one of the spread sheets. "Take a look at the sheet labeled "summary". It should be the first one in your folder."

"Yes, I see it. Go ahead."

Josh went on. "We busted our butts all weekend to reach these totals. It took a lot of time."

Alex nodded.

"Look at the bottom of your sheet."

"Okay."

"See the total of the third column?"

Alex moved his finger across the bottom of the page. "Sixty-three million, six hundred and seventy-four thousand!" His eyes wide, Alex glanced at Josh. "That's the total they have embezzled?"

"Yes, I'm afraid it is."

"What in the world?"

"Go on to spread, 1-2."

A stunned Alex flipped to the next spread sheet.

"See the amount I have circled about two thirds of the way down?"

"Yes, just over thirty million."

"That's the amount that has been paid back to the IRA accounts; they still have approximately thirty-three million to go."

Dulin paused and stared at Alex. "I'm glad you ordered the audit when you did. A few months from now the paybacks on the IRAs would have been complete and I really don't think we would have ever caught this. This scheme was very well thought out."

Alex lowered his head and spoke quietly, "And Barnes did this right under my nose."

Dulin leaned forward and laid his hand gently on Alex's shoulder. "Don't beat yourself up on this one Alex. I audit over twenty banks and your management style is one of the best I've seen. The other banks just don't have a corrupt Chairman and Controller. As I explained earlier, this was a very elaborate scheme. There's no way a CEO could know this."

Alex smiled. "I appreciate that, Josh, But I still..."

Josh quickly interrupted his lamenting colleague and pressed on. "Now the question is, why would they do this? Any ideas?"

Back on game, Alex shot back. "Yes, since the discovery of the problem during your Chicago audit, I have been giving this a lot of thought."

"And?"

"I believe it's political. I believe that Barnes and Montrose were skimming the money to help fund the Moretti Presidential Campaign. I think it was part of an aggressive effort by Barnes to gain political equity with the administration. He wants very badly to become the Ambassador to Ireland."

"What about the election laws concerning donations? The amount each individual can give is limited and this is such a huge amount."

"I know, I thought about that. They probably got a list of homeless people, or possibly even dead people, from some activist organization. Reports say there are several federally funded neighborhood organizations in Chicago that amassed thousands of phony registrations during the election. I'm sure they would have been happy to provide the necessary names and addresses."

"Hmm....I see. It's obvious that Barnes and company did their homework. They probably have been replenishing those accounts with the bailout money. Montrose, more than likely, figured out a way to divert funds from the bailout to the accounts. That could be one of the reasons they don't want me to pay back the money; they still need part of it to replenish those accounts."

"And, hopefully, avoid detection."

"Exactly."

"I wonder how much Moretti knows," Dulin mused.

"Probably not a lot. Like most politicians, he more than likely turns a blind-eye toward the facts when it comes to donations—even when he is receiving an unusually large amount from one locale. But something tells me that Ramsey might know. He and Vito Taglioni are old friends and Vito and Barnes have both been profiting mightily from this scam. I'm almost certain they've talked to Ramsey about it, but it will be hard to prove. The powerful have a way of insulating themselves from prosecution."

"It's disgusting." Josh grimaced.

"I know."

"What do you think Vito's roll is in all of this?"

"Vito and Ramsey are old friends. Barnes needed Vito's relationship with Ramsey to pull this thing off. He may have asked Vito to feel Ramsey out to see what he thought about the scam, and at some point, Ramsey bought into it. Such things are commonplace in the windy city."

"Couldn't he have done it without Ramsey's knowledge?"

"Yes, but Barnes wanted Ramsey's approval on the plan for two reasons. It gave him cover from the Feds if something went wrong and more importantly, he wanted Ramsey to know the great risks he was willing to take on the President's behalf."

"To gain that equity you talked about."

"Of course."

"What's in it for Vito?'"

"Probably all those branch approvals. Vito's firm has opened several branches in the Midwest over the past year. Such quick approvals are unheard of."

Dulin interjected, "Unless you know somebody at the top."

"Exactly. It appears that Ramsey probably went to work on the SEC on behalf of Vito as payback for the possible huge donations the campaign would get from the embezzlement scheme. As I said earlier, Vito has enjoyed several amazingly fast branch approvals. And, by the way, these branches are all located in the same cities where Midwest Consolidated Bank has a location. At the same time, Barnes went behind my back to get the board to relax our underwriting guidelines on mortgages which opened the floodgates. A torrent of subprime mortgages was then originated over the next several months. Vito eventually bundled the flaky loans into securities and sold them on the bond market."

"How convenient."

"Yes, and Barnes just happens to have a law office in all of the same cities."

"So they both got rich."

"Yes."

The accountant shook his head in disgust. "Barnes is a rich man, but I guess you never have enough money. It seems like it would have been enough for him just to achieve his political goals, but it appears he couldn't pass up the chance to make millions in the meantime.

"True, but Barnes is very shrewd. I think he got something a whole lot more important than money out of this. I believe Barnes was well aware that subprime mortgages are junk loans. He wanted our Midwest originators doing as many subprime mortgages as possible."

"So Vito could package them into bonds, sell them on the secondary market and then watch them fail. Then Midwest would qualify for the bailout money needed to pay back the embezzled funds."

"Right on."

Dulin paused and leaned back in his chair. He took a deep breath. "The scope of this thing is incredible. The plan these men have put into action is breathtaking."

"I know." Alex glanced at his watch. "Sorry, but I

only have a few more minutes; I have a staff meeting at nine. Tell me Josh, do you feel comfortable with the information you've gathered?"

"Absolutely. I have everything I need. I have documented all the transactions and secured them in my safe. I will have someone bring you a copy later today. When the light finally shines on this rat hole, they won't have anywhere to hide."

"Good. And, as you advised me in Chicago, let's keep a lid on this thing until the right time."

"Definitely."

Alex rose to leave. "I'll be in touch."

The men shared a handshake and Alex quickly left the office.

Chapter 36

"The li...li....little d...d...d...dog rah...ran..." A huge pile of unruly blond curls sat precariously atop her freckled face. Her big blue eyes looked up from the page in frustration, "This one's too hard Mr. Gus."

Gus gently ruffled her thick curls, "I know honey, but let's give it another try. "

"Okay."

Gus enjoyed volunteering at St. Mary's Elementary School in Michigan City.   After a late night at the gambling boat, he crawled out of bed every Tuesday morning at 6:30 sharp and hustled over to the school. He was always the first volunteer to arrive. Gus loved the little six year-olds, who referred to him as Mr. Gus because they had trouble pronouncing his last name. He started volunteering at the school soon after arriving in town ten years ago. Over the years, he had become a well-liked and respected figure at the little elementary school. The ivy-covered red brick building, surrounded by large oak trees, reminded him of his own childhood school, St. Celestine Elementary in Elmwood Park.

"The l...little dog ran a...fter S...Sam."

"That's better Sarah, much better."

Gus heard the classroom door open behind him.

"Excuse me, Mr. Clemente, but Sarah has to take a reading test now with the other children so that will be all for today. Thank you so much for coming. See you next week."

Gus smiled at the pretty, young teacher. "Okay, Mrs. Owen."

"Byé, Mr. Gus."

"Good-bye, Sarah."

"Oh....and Mr. Gus, you can leave the desks in the hall. We will need them for this afternoon.

"Sure, Mrs. Owen." Gus stood and watched as the heavy door banged shut and the hall fell silent. This had been a different kind of day for Gus and the kids—it had been a difficult one. The recent visit from Butch Ferinni was weighing heavily on him. He was terribly conflicted. Working with the children over the years and sharing a close relationship with Trudy had softened the hardened gunman. For the first time in his adult life, he was starting to feel like a human being. It had been a wonderful and unexpected metamorphosis for someone with such a violent past.

Gus's soft tennis shoes glided gently over the cement floor as he walked quietly down the hall toward the front door. Inside the glassed-in office area, the busy principal looked up from her work and smiled at Gus as he walked past. He lifted his hand nervously in response. The friendly administrator had no idea of the battle that was raging inside of her popular volunteer as he walked nervously past the office area.

Gus hurried over and pushed through the front doors; tears were streaming down his face. He dropped his head to hide his red eyes from passer-bys and started down the wide front walkway toward the visitor parking

lot. Sarah and the other children's faces kept flashing
through his mind. He loved them and they trusted him
completely. How could he possibly kill again? How
could he betray the trust of those children? But his
daughter, Darcy, needed that money desperately for her
operation and Ferinni's offer would pay for it. He
thought his head was going to explode as he crawled
into his car and drove away.

. . . .

The sun felt warm on Gus's protruding elbow as he
turned down the alley toward his apartment. He loved
the sound of the gravel crunching beneath the car's
tires—it reminded him of his childhood days in
Elmwood Park where all of the alleys were gravel. He
could hear the birds chirping in the quiet neighborhood
as he pulled into the back parking area. The calming
scene was quickly interrupted by the sound of his
phone ringing. He slid the cell from his pocket and
flipped it open.

"Hello, honey."

"Hi, Dad."

"How are you?"

There was a hesitation; he could tell she was fighting
back the tears. "Not so good, Dad."

Gus killed the engine. "What's the matter, honey?
Has something happened?"

"I've been getting weaker and weaker lately. I missed
a couple of days of work last week. I don't have any
energy. I called the doctor a few days ago and he got me
into the hospital for tests today."

"And?"

"I'm getting worse Dad, my disease is progressing. The doctor says I will have to have surgery soon." She began sobbing. "I d...don't have any insurance and I don't have the money. I'm gonna die, Dad!"

"No, no you won't. You're not going to die. I have the money for the surgery. You're going to be fine."

"Dad! It's two hundred thousand dollars! You don't have that kind of money."

"You're not going to believe what happened, Darcy—I was just about to call you."

"What Dad? What happened?"

"Last night, at the casino, I felt lucky. So I started playing the ten dollar slots after my shift was over. I hit it big, honey! It was the second biggest payoff in the boat's history! Two hundred and twenty thousand dollars!"

"Oh, my gosh! Just last night? Dad, that's wonderful!" The phone went silent for a second, "But that's your money Dad, you should keep it."

"No honey, don't be silly. That why I was playing the slots, to try and win the money for your surgery. I have all I want here, I don't need any money."

"Thank you, Dad, thank you so much."

"You're welcome, honey. Now call that doctor and tell him to schedule that operation. Your old man will pay for it."

"Are you sure, Dad?"

"Darcy!"

"Okay, okay. God bless you, Dad. I love you!"

"I love you too, baby."

"Bye, Dad."

"Bye, honey."

Gus quickly punched in another number.

"Hello, Doc."

"Butch, I want to do the hit now—right away!

"Alright. Let me check out a few things and get back with you."

"Okay Butch, but don't waste any time. I want to get this thing over with."

"I'll call you back yet today."

"You better."

"I will."

"Good-bye."

Chapter 37

Butch stumbled down the cobblestone walkway that led to a little cedar-sided building that was tucked neatly into the side of the hill next to his mansion. His hip was killing him. He pushed open the door to the small house and swiped away the thick cobwebs. He rubbed the inside wall in the darkened room, searching for the light switch. Bumping into the elusive switch, he flipped it on. The old bulb barely illuminated the musty room.

Back in his glory days, this had been the home of Butch's head gardener. Unfortunately, after years of pressure from law enforcement and increasing competition from the Black and Latino gangs, the lucrative drug business had more or less been taken over and he could no longer afford such a luxury. He looked around the room. There was an old black phone covered with dust sitting on a small table next to a worn out sofa. Butch had used the phone back to take calls that he didn't want traced back to him. The phone was still registered to the former gardener, Claude Evans. Since the bill was only nineteen dollars a month, Butch had kept the phone active over the years just in case he needed it. Or, as Maria so delicately put it, "You loved that old fart so much, you can't bring yourself to disonnect his phone."

Butch slid a handkerchief from his trouser pocket, bent over and carefully lifted the receiver, wiping off the thick dust. He then wrapped the handkerchief around the receiver and pressed it to his ear. His broad face broke into a smile at the distinct sound of a dial tone. He punched in the number.

"Hello?"

"Yeah Vito, it's me—Butch, and I got good news."

"Yeah, what is it?"

"Gus is in; he's going to do the job."

"That's good, he's the best." He grunted out a laugh. "He must really love that kid of his."

"Guess so. Gus said he wants to do it right away."

"How about this weekend?"

"That's good, but why this weekend?"

"I've been thinking about this and I have a plan."

"Oh yeah."

Butch waited while Vito blew his nose into the receiver. "Damn it, Vito, turn the receiver away when you blow your nose."

"If you gotta blow, you gotta blow!"

Annoyed, Butch continued, "So what's this plan?"

"My uncle has a small cottage on Lake Wawasee—the same lake Alex and Nicky go to every weekend in the summer. When I was a kid growing up in the Chicago area, we used to go to the lake and spend the whole summer with my uncle, fishing and swimming and goofing around—it's only a two hour drive from Chicago. My uncle is almost ninety now, but he still has that place up at the lake. We still go up there once in awhile. He lets everybody in the family use his cottage. Also, over the years, Alex has invited my wife and me up to his place several times."

"Okay, good, but so what?"

"Alex has a habit—one he seldom breaks. They arrive at the lake on Friday evening and Alex gets up the next morning at the crack of dawn and takes target practice at a nearby shooting range. It's in the Tri-County Game Preserve. He says he gets his aggressions out by blasting away at that target."

Dust plumed as Butch's full backside fell against the arm of the old sofa. "And?"

"Well, like I said, I've spent a lot of time up there. I know that area very well. That game preserve is huge and the shooting range is right in the middle of it and far away from everything. And there's a back way to the range. I found it when I was a kid."

"Go ahead."

"Think about it, Butch. Gus and I can come in the back way to the preserve. It's very rural, very isolated and Alex should be alone that early in the morning. There's a high bluff behind the range near a stand of evergreens. Gus could sit up on that bluff and have a clear shot. Alex would have his back to us—he would never know what hit him. And better yet, the sound of a rifle going off would be very normal—it's squirrel season in Indiana."

Butch's forefinger scraped across stubble on his chin, "Sounds like you might be on to something there."

"But there's one thing, Butch."

"What?"

"Can Gus shoot a rifle?"

Butch grunted, "Gus can shoot anything. He's got a gun cabinet like you wouldn't believe. He took out Jo Jo Marcella up in Wisconsin with a rifle from three hundred yards. He prefers his .38 revolver, but he can shoot anything."

"Great."

Butch shook his head. "Don't you feel a little funny about this, Vito? This guy Alex, is a friend of yours."

"Hey, you gotta do what you gotta do," Vito laughed crudely.

"Maybe *you* ought to shoot Crane and take Gus off the hook."

"I could never do that."

Butch placed his hand over the phone and whispered, "Weasel."

"Did you say something, Butch?"

"No. no."

"I can't think of anything else. Can you?" Vito queried.

"Yes, be sure you have the money with you because Gus wants paid in cash."

"I'll have the cash with me—a quarter mil."

"I know. Where are you getting that kind of cash?"

"Ramsey told me once that the Feds have all kinds of money lying around in a well-secured building near the FBI office in Chicago. It's the money that they confiscate from drug runners."

Butch paused briefly and then spoke, "Alright, but there's one more thing."

"Yeah?"

"You haven't told a soul about this, right? 'Cause if Gus finds out that you have, he says he's going to take you out."

"I'm a businessman, Butch. Do you really think I'm going to tell anybody? Who does Gus think I would tell? My wife? The President of the Chamber of Commerce?

Come on!"

"Alright, alright. Listen, I'll give you Gus's cell number, better give him a call and get everything worked out."

"Okay."

Chapter 38

"Mission accomplished, Mr. Ramsey." Hawk tossed a wadded-up expense voucher at the nearby wastebasket.

"Good. Did everything go according to plan?"

"Yes, exactly as planned. We had a couple of handsome young gentlemen dressed in Century Link uniforms pull up to Crane's house this morning in a green van with the Century Link logo on the side. The men told Mrs. Crane that they were installing a new fiber optic line that would replace her existing phone line and provide her with better service. She gladly let the men in and then hurried off to do her grocery shopping. Once inside, the men installed a bug on Mr. Crane's phone in the den and on the wall phone in the kitchen. She asked the men to lock up when they left. She's the trusting sort."

"Amazing. Now let's hope Alex uses one of those phones. He has an iPhone you know."

"I know, but according to our information, he uses his den phone almost exclusively for business calls."

"Good Barger, good job." There was a pause on the line. "Just curious Barger—how are you going to get those bugs out of there after we're finished?"

"No problem, we will just send the same two guys

out and explain to her that our very sensitive equipment at our electronics center is noticing a slight glitch on the recent installation and we just need to take a quick look at it. The job will only take a minute."

Ramsey laughed out loud. "You guys are diabolical!"

"That's our job."

"I'll be in touch."

"Good day, Mr. Ramsey."

. . . .

Alex stepped through the half-open door from the garage and ducked into the kitchen. He yawned and dropped his leather briefcase on the counter. He scanned the counter for any notes from Nicky. Seeing none, he pulled open the cabinet door above the sink and searched the cluttered shelf for a bottle of Tylenol. Pushing several other meds aside, he grabbed the small bottle and popped the lid off. He poured a glass of water, shook a couple of tabs into his hand and quickly washed then down. "This one's a doozy," he mumbled, rubbing his forehead.

As usual, Alex and Nicky were planning to spend the weekend at their lake home. After the vote at the board meeting earlier in the week, it would be a good place for a quiet celebration by the Cranes. But he also knew that he was now more of a target than ever. He had been extra cautious all week. And since the vote, Barnes had almost vanished from sight—no phone calls, no visits to the office. He was worried; things were too quiet. He knew that Barnes and company would not take this latest defeat lying down. He also knew that they had some suspicions about Josh Dulin's surprise audit at

Louie's office last week. He set the glass on the counter and hurried to his den to dial up Josh.

"Hello?"

"Josh, I'm glad I caught you. I thought you might have already left for the day."

Josh muttered a chuckle "Hardly, we've been short-handed all week. The flu went through this office like the plague. I'll probably be here until after nine."

Alex began to perspire; Nicky always set the air at 78 to save on utilities. "Listen Josh, I'm a little concerned. Things have been too quiet around the office the past several days. It doesn't seem right to me. I'm worried about the audit at Louie's. With all the resources they have at their disposal, I'm afraid they might try to break into your office and confiscate that file. I think it would be advisable for you to take the file out of your office and put it in your safety deposit box at my bank. I will instruct the tellers not to let anyone into your box unless I personally approve. The file will be safe at the bank."

"I agree, Alex. I'll take the file with me tonight and drop it by your office first thing in the morning."

"Thanks, Josh."

"No problem."

Chapter 39

There was a knock on the door. Louie, happily reminiscing about the pretty lady he met at the annual Kiwanis Fish Fry the night before, was shaken out of his trance. He quickly shoved the empty Payday wrapper into his desk drawer and shouted "Come in!"

The door swung open. "Louie, how good to see you!"

"Good morning, Butch. Have a seat." Louie gestured toward one of the two leather chairs in front of his desk.

"Thank you so much, Louie, for coming in early on Saturday."

"No problem. Ava typed all the docs last evening and we're all ready to go."

Butch slowly dropped in the seat, grimacing in pain.

"Hip bothering you?" Louie looked concerned.

"A little bit."

Louie flipped open the file and spread the papers on his desk. "Ready to sign?"

Butch leaned up in the chair. "Ready as I'll ever be."

"Let me go over the documents with you."

"Cut the crap, Louie. I trust you with my life. Where do I sign?"

Louie's face broke into a smile, "Next to the big red X's."

Butch laughed, "Ava knows me—she made it easy."

"I have a voice mail message from my friend Alex Crane. Mind if I listen to it while you're signing?"

A stunned Butch glanced at a smiling Louie. "W…who did you say you're friend was?"

"My boss—Alex Crane. Do you mind?"

"Why…uh no, go right ahead."

A short time later, Louie hung up the phone. The signing completed, Butch tossed the pen on the desk and fell back in his chair. "You say this Crane fellow is a friend of yours?"

"Oh yes, Alex is the best. I'm afraid old Louie wouldn't be around if it weren't for Alex. He's saved my bacon time and again. The big guys in the bank think I'm a buffoon. They want me fired, but Alex won't have any part of it—I love the guy. He called to invite me over to his lake home this weekend for a little get-together with his family."

Butch felt like someone had punched him in the gut. It bothered Butch to think that somewhere, near a lake in Indiana, right at this very moment, that Alex Crane was being stalked by Gus Clemente, who was trying to put a bullet in his head. Midwest has hundreds of branches and branch managers. What are the odds that Crane and Louie would be such good friends? Butch was a hard man, a man who had ordered several killings in his career, but those "hits" were always against bad men—men who would kill at the drop of a hat. Not against a good man, a decent man, like Louie had just described. He was angry at Vito Taglioni for drawing him into this mess. He wished now he had never agreed to this killing. Butch's face drained white and he struggled for words. "Is…uh this all we have to sign."

"I think we've covered everything. Here's your check." Louie handed him a check for $200,000. "Are you alright, Butch?"

Butch smiled wryly, "Oh yeah, must have been something I ate. I best be going. Thanks for everything, Louie."

"Sure you're okay?"

"Oh yeah, thanks again. See ya, Louie."

"See ya, Butch."

Butch stood slowly and exited the room.

Chapter 40

Vito and Gus had agreed to meet at an old, abandoned service station at the edge of the Tri-County Game Preserve. From there, Vito would drive them to the trail that led past the pistol range. It was very early and Gus found himself yawning over and over again as he followed the curvy, tree-lined road that wound its way through rural Indiana. The trip seemed to be taking longer than expected. Finally, he rounded a sharp curve and there it was—the old abandoned convenience center. A variety of weeds and even some small trees had started growing up around the rusted gas pumps. It was apparent that this former stop-off for area hunters had not been used for years. He pulled slowly off the country road, onto the weed covered lot and pulled in behind the gray, rotting building toward the back of the lot. He saw the open hatch of Vito's SUV ahead. A nervous looking Vito stood next to the driver's side door of the large vehicle. He was wearing blue jeans, a white t-shirt, and a bright orange vest and cap.

Gus pulled in behind the SUV and stopped. Both vehicles were hidden from the road. He calmly opened the glove box, and pushed the black button to open the trunk. He lifted a bright, orange hunting cap from the passenger's seat and placed it on his head. Both men had agreed to look the part of hunters as to not draw attention to themselves. He checked in the rearview mirror to be sure his cap was on straight and then rubbed the front of his vest. He could feel the three shells he had placed in the vest pocket the night before. He opened the door and got out of his car.

Vito walked toward him. "Good morning, Gus."

"Morning, Vito." the two shared a quick handshake. "This is really woodsy around here."

"Yeah, it's the middle of nowhere alright."

"Will my car be safe here?"

"Oh yeah, nobody pulls into this old station during the day, too much broken glass." Vito pointed at the shiny chips of broken brown and white glass partially embedded in the surface of the abandoned lot.

"Hope we don't get a flat."

"They tell me local teenagers come back here and neck at night. They can't afford to get a flat, so it must be all right." Vito laughed nervously.

"Got the cash?" Gus asked matter-of-factly.

"Yes." Vito hurried back to the open hatch on his SUV and lifted out a heavy suitcase. He walked over and handed it to Gus.

Gus listened for approaching vehicles. Hearing nothing, he dropped down on one knee beside his car and opened the suitcase. The inside was completely filled with one hundred dollar bills wrapped neatly into stacks.

"Each stack is ten thousand," Vito advised.

An experienced dealer and accustomed to counting money, Gus rapidly spun the edge of several stacks to insure their contents and then gave careful accounting of the number of stacks. "It's okay," he grunted. He lifted the case without ever making eye contact with Vito and walked to the rear of his car. Gus set the suitcase on the ground, opened the trunk and reached inside. He pulled out his .44 magnum rifle with the scope attached. He carefully set the powerful rifle against the rear bumper and then leaned inside the trunk and unscrewed the cover on the spare-tire well. He lifted the cover off and stuck the heavy case in the empty well. He then replaced the cover and screwed the cover tight again. He looked around to be absolutely certain that no one was watching—even at this remote spot. He carefully lifted his rifle and walked to the front of the car.

"Put your rifle in here." Vito pointed under the hatch.

Gus hurried over and laid his rifle next to an old .22 caliber rifle that Vito had brought for the occasion.

"Let's go," Vito ordered. The hatch began to close as the two men walked around either side of the large vehicle and climbed aboard.

"It's not far now—less than a mile," Vito explained.

Dust bellowed up like a giant cloud behind Vito's SUV as he left the old station and negotiated the curvy, gravel road. Gus felt calm inside; he and Vito had hatched a plan, a good plan. Through their discussions, Vito had convinced him that Crane was an arrogant, self-serving SOB who deserved killing. Darcy could have her surgery and get on with her life and he would go back to his new life in Michigan City. It was as simple as that. Like he had done so many times before during his killing days, Gus convinced himself that what he was doing was justified and necessary.

Suddenly, Vito veered to the left and came to a sudden stop in a small indention for parking next to the road. The only vehicle Gus had seen along the way was an old pick-up truck pulled off to the side a few hundred yards back—probably early morning squirrel hunters.

Vito got out and anxiously surveyed the area.

Gus climbed out and walked calmly over to Vito. "Are you sure Crane's in town?" he asked.

"Yes. Two FBI agents have been watching him for sometime. They said Crane and his wife packed up and left for the lake last evening. They arrived here at approximately 9:30 P.M. It's 6:22 A.M. now, Crane should be arriving at the range anytime. He's very punctual and he told me he always starts shooting at 6:30 sharp."

"Are the FBI guys still around?"

"No, they were called off last night and returned to Chicago."

Vito lifted the hatch open. The two men reached inside and removed their respective rifles.

Gus hooked the rifle over his right arm and lifted it slightly in the direction of Vito. His eyes went dark, his brow tightened. "Did you tell anybody about this?"

Caught off guard, Vito took a step back and scanned the face of the legendary killer. "No, hell no! It's like I told Butch, who would I tell, Gus? I'm a respected businessman."

Gus lifted the gun a little higher. "Are you sure?"

"Yes, yes I'm sure."

Gus's brow relaxed a little. He nodded toward the nearby trail. "Okay, then lead the way."

Shaken, Vito reluctantly turned his back to Gus and

headed for the nearby path.

. . . .

The turn signal chimed as Alex pulled down the long lane. The entrance to the Tri-County Game Preserve shooting range was bordered on each side by a tall stand of blue spruce. Alex loved his time alone at the range each Saturday morning. It was so peaceful and serene— a welcome change from the big city.

He pulled to a stop in the empty parking lot, lifted his handgun out from under the seat and stepped out of the SUV. He inhaled the fresh country air and strolled over to the voluntary sign-in shack for the shooting range and quickly scribbled his name. Then, he headed for the range.

The large wooden placard ahead read. Pistol Range, no shotguns allowed. The vacant rifle range was to the left and at right angles from the pistol range. Alex stepped behind the backless stall and pulled a box of shells from his shooting vest. He quickly loaded the .357 magnum pistol and then pulled two ear plugs from his vest and stuffed one carefully in each ear. He leaned on the window shelf and placed both hands firmly on the gun. He took careful aim and opened fire. The barrel jerked upward over and over again as Alex fired several rounds and then paused to check out the target. Satisfied, he took aim and fired again.

. . . .

Twigs snapped beneath their feet as the two men walked aggressively along the seldom used trail. Hearing pistol shots off in the distance, Vito raised his hand and paused on the trail.

"Hear that?"

Gus stopped and listened, "Yeah, someone shooting, think it's Crane?"

"It's him," Vito reassured.

The two men continued along the winding path through the dense woods; soon a clearing was in sight. Vito stopped once again.

"See that rise up there next to that stand of ever-greens?"

"Yeah, I see it."

"That's your spot. There's an opening there between that big spruce and those hard maples that gives you a clear view of the pistol range. Alex will have his back to you. He'll never know what hit him." The corner of Vito's mouth lifted in a nasty grin.

The callous remark gave Gus pause. He studied the face of the heartless stockbroker and then replied, "Why don't you wait here. I'll go on up by myself."

Vito seem relieved. "Sure thing, Gus."

Gus continued along the trail and up the modest rise to the spot that Vito had pointed out to him. And Vito was right—there was an opening between the stand of spruces and a thick wooded area of mainly maple and oak trees. He could see the back of a man, approximately a hundred yards away, leaning through the shooting stall and firing at the target.

Gus carefully took three cartridges from his vest and loaded them into the port of his rifle. From this range with a scope, one shot should be plenty, but he dropped in two extra shells, just in case. Gus got down and laid flat on his belly. He pointed the powerful rifle in the direction of the range. He scooted around a little to get comfortable, pushed his cheek against the stock and took careful aim through the scope. As he adjusted the lens, the man turned around for a moment to reload. Gus focused in on him; it was Alex Crane alright. Vito had e-mailed him a picture the night before. Gus was taken aback by the friendly, kind face on the muscular middle-aged man. He had looked serious and business-like in the photos provided by Vito. Somehow, in jeans and a t-shirt, he looked very human. He reminded Gus of his boss at the gambling vote, Jim Demotte. Jim was one of Gus's favorite people. Gus lowered the scope away from Alex's face to his chest area for a possible body shot. The lettering on the front of his shirt read "WORLD'S GREATEST GRANDPA!"

Beads of perspiration broke out on Gus's forehead. He felt sick inside. This man, by his very appearance, was a good and decent man and a grandpa on top of that. Not in any way did he appear to be the pompous, arrogant ass that Vito had described. The kids at the elementary school raced through Gus's mind. Gus could never kill the grandpa of one of those kids. But in essence, that's what he was about to do. Gus's hand started to shake, the perspiration poured down his face. He tried desperately to get control himself. He had to go ahead with this—his daughter Darcy's life and happiness depended on it.

Down below, in the clearing, Vito paced anxiously back and forth on the trail waiting for the shot to go off. He occasionally glanced up the hill in the direction of Gus.

Back at the range, Alex reloaded and turned around once again and began firing at the target area, his back to Gus.

Steadying himself as best he could, Gus put his forefinger firmly on the trigger. He now had a dead bead on the middle of Alex's back. It would only take a second; all he had to do was squeeze that trigger and it would be over. But as hard as he tried, he couldn't bring himself to squeeze hard enough to fire the rifle.

Suddenly, Gus spun around. His nerves calmed, his hands went steady. He took dead aim through the scope and fired. There was a loud blast. Vito's head jerked violently sideways and his body crashed to the ground. His body was instantly still. Gus rolled over quickly into the tall grass growing next to him. He frantically pulled the grass apart and looked down at Alex. Alex removed one of his ear plugs, looked around briefly and then replaced the plug and went back to shooting.

Gus jumped to his feet with his rifle in hand. He bent down and picked up the empty shell casing and stuffed it in his vest pocket; the casing felt warm against his chest. His mind buzzing as he ran down the hill toward Vito's body. Stumbling several times along the way, he finally stopped next to the financial czar's motionless body. He knelt down and felt his jugular— there was no sign of a pulse. Distraught, and with tears streaming down his face, Gus climbed to his feet and staggered along the trail knocking the protruding branches aside. He paused near the edge of the forest, looked both ways, and then staggered out of the forest. His mind was racing as he ran along the road toward the abandoned service center. His leather boots were not made for running and his arthritic leg started to hurt causing him to limp.

At the sound of an approaching vehicle, he abruptly

dove inside the thick wooded area bordering the road. He leaned back against a large oak tree and waited—his chest heaving. The old truck whizzed by. Gus scrambled back to the road through the cloud of dust left by the passing vehicle and continued his agonizing race back to his car. As he approached the old station, he ducked into a thicket at the intersection across from the station and listened for approaching vehicles. Sweat was pouring down his face; his shirt was stained black. Certain no one was around; he struggled across the narrow intersection and found his way behind the old building to his car. He poked frantically around in his pocket for his keys, opened the trunk, tossed the rifle inside and quietly shut the trunk. Shaking, he struggled to unlock the car door and then fell inside.

As he sat inside his car looking around at the tall trees that bordered his temporary hiding place, Gus felt nauseated. He had made a last minute decision not to kill Alex Crane. His only other option was to take out Vito—the only man other than Butch who knew about the plan. He hated what he had done but Vito was a weasel. He had no children and his wife would probably only grieve briefly at the death of her womanizing husband. He felt he had made the right decision.

He would have to tell Butch Ferinni, but not until the money had been given to his daughter's hospital in Des Moines. Darcy had called him yesterday to inform him that her surgery would take place on Tuesday. With the only person who could implicate him dead, Gus was home free. And, the exact whereabouts of the quarter mil that the FBI guys had given to Vito would never be known.

Gus rolled down the window and listened once again

for approaching vehicles. His eyes twitched as another pick-up drove past and turned toward the preserve. Once the truck had passed, the road fell quiet again. Gus straightened his orange hat, started the engine and quickly pulled out from behind the decaying building and onto the country road. He drove well under the speed limit so as not to draw attention. He gave a modest nod, as Hoosiers always do, to any autos that he passed along the way. Soon he was safely back on U. S. Highway 6 and heading home to Michigan City. He would leave for Des Moines in the morning. The hospital in Iowa said they would accept cash payment, so he would pay the estimated amount on Monday and then take care of any loose ends later.

Unexpectedly, a few miles down the road, Gus began sobbing uncontrollably. He pulled off to the side of the road and buried his hands in his face, continuing to wail for several minutes. Then he dried his eyes with a left-over napkin from a recent visit to MacDonald's and continued on his trip.

. . . .

Alex removed his ear plugs, put the gun back in the leather case and threw the empty cartridge box into the trash can next to the shooting range. Feeling good and wearing a broad grin, he started back toward the parking area. Walking casually, the only sounds he heard were the birds chirping and an occasional muffled rifle shot from somewhere in the expansive preserve. Nearing his vehicle, he felt a vibration at his waist; he reached down and slid out his iPhone.

"Yes, dear?"

Nicky was sobbing almost uncontrollably, "Alex! The most awful thing happened!"

Alex stopped and dropped down on a nearby wooden bench, "What Nicky, what is it?"

"It's J…Josh, Josh Dulin."

"Yes, yes, what about Josh?"

"Oh my God, honey—he's been murdered!"

"Murdered? What are you talking about?"

"Strom just called. They found Josh this morning. He was murdered and robbed late last evening after leaving work. Someone surprised him in the alley behind his office. It's awful! Oh, poor Andrea."

Alex stood and walked toward his SUV, his mind was racing, "Are they sure it was robbery?"

"I guess so; the TV news said they took his money clip and jewelry. They said the robbers did a g…good job, the only thing left in that alley was Josh's body. How could someone do this?" Nicky began sobbing again.

"I'm getting in my car now, honey. I'll be right there." Alex turned off his phone. He knew the robbery was a ruse; the killers were after that file. The first casualty of this deadly game with the powerbrokers in Washington had been his young accountant. He felt horrible inside—Josh would have never been involved in this if it hadn't been for him. He backed quickly around in the empty lot and drove back to the cottage to console Nicky and decide on a plan of action.

Chapter 41

Alex's arms felt heavy as he lifted the two five-gallon gas cans from the back of the Escalade, but not as heavy as his heart. It was now late morning and Alex was now even more sickened by the death of Josh Dulin. He wished it had been him. He was furious with Barnes and his powerful allies in Washington. He wanted revenge and he wanted it now.

"You okay, honey?" Nicky asked.

"Yes, I'm okay."

"How about that boat ride?" Nicky had asked earlier if they could take a boat ride. Alex, still very suspicious about the death of Josh, had been scanning the area for any signs of his FBI friends all morning and he had seen nothing.

"Okay honey, I think we're alone. It could do us both some good."

Nicky smiled, but the smile soon faded. "It's so awful about Josh."

"I know. He was a good man." Alex wanted very much to explain his suspicions about Josh's death to Nicky, but he dared not. He and Josh were the only two who knew the results of the audit in Elmwood Park and he wanted to keep it that way. Alex closed the tailgate and followed Nicky around the house and down to the lake.

. . . .

Later that afternoon, their cheeks pink and hair going every direction, the two somber sojourners returned to the cottage from their boat ride. Nicky piled life jackets and beach towels over her arm. Alex hopped out of the boat and lifted the empty gas cans that were still sitting on the pier. Nicky climbed out of the boat and headed up the hill with Alex close behind. When they reached the garage, Alex's cell phone rang. He set down the cans and answered it.

"Hello Strom."

"Are you sitting down?"

"No, why?"

"It's Vito."

"Vito?"

"Yes, he was found shot to death in that game preserve near your lake late this afternoon. Barnes just called me."

Alex crumbled against the side of the garage shaking his head. "Are you kidding me, I was at that preserve early this morning shooting my pistol."

"It's so awful—Josh and now Vito."

"What happened? Do they know who did it?" Alex was beside himself at this point. Josh and Vito within twenty-four hours of one another.

Strom continued. "My wife called Anita and she said that Vito told her that he was going to the preserve early this morning and take target practice with his old .22 rifle. She said he was going to take a back trail to the range, the one he used as a kid. She said he had done this once or twice before. She was asleep when he left and wasn't sure of the time."

"How's Anita doing?"

"Surprisingly well, Esther said she was pretty matter-of-fact about things."

"Hmmm, have you heard anything else?"

"Yes, I listened to the news report on Channel 6 and they said that the local authorities are investigating, and at this point, it looks like a terrible accident. They think he could have been hit by an errant rifle shot from someone taking target practice at the nearby rifle range. The DNR officer who was interviewed said that Vito was in a restricted area near the range, but it's not well marked and many hunters unknowingly wander into that area. So it could have also been an accidental shooting by a hunter. They indicated that there are no signs of foul play at this time. And by the way, could that be the range you were at today?"

"Yes, there's only one range."

"They estimated he was shot somewhere between 6:00 A.M. and 10 A.M."

"I was there at 6:30."

"Did you hear anything?"

"No, not really. I was the only one at the range at the time; most people don't shoot until a little later when it's not as damp. I thought I heard something once but its squirrel season—you hear rifle shots all of the time around here."

There was a pause at the other end. "Sorry to bring you such bad news, especially after Josh yesterday."

"Oh no, Strom, please, you did exactly the right thing. I had to know. Thank you for calling. It's just so numbing."

"It certainly is. Well, I'd better run. Let's keep in touch; we have a couple of funerals coming up. I'll call you when I get the details."

"Okay Strom, thanks again."

Nicky stepped out of the back door and saw Alex slumped against the garage. "What's the matter, dear?"

Alex sighed, "That was Strom. Vito was accidentally shot and killed today just a short distance from the practice range at Tri-County."

Nicky stepped off the back porch and fell against her husband, holding him tightly, as much for herself as him. "Oh my!" she sobbed.

"I know. This is all unbelievable."

"What is going on here, honey? Josh and now Vito!"

Alex stood up and grabbed Nicky by her shoulders. "I'm not sure honey, but I'm worried that this whole situation with the TARP money has gotten out of hand—way out of hand. Barnes has connections with the White House and the President wants me to keep the money very badly for political reasons. The cars we've seen are Government goons—they've have been tailing me for some time."

"Oh, my goodness!"

"I know. I didn't want to worry you, but it's getting so intense that I'm worried about your safety. I'm going to call my Uncle Ned and take you there right away. You'll be safe at his place."

. . . .

Alex's uncle, Ned Crane, a retired Green Beret officer, was one of the most decorated soldiers of the

Vietnam era. During one heroic effort, he strapped a machine gun on each shoulder, wrapped several belts of ammo around his waist and single-handedly charged a nest of Viet Cong snipers nestled in a thicket of trees near his beleaguered platoon. There was heavy return fire and he was hit twice in the upper arm and thigh but that didn't stop Sergeant Crane. He continued to charge up the hill and eventually wiped out all twenty-two Viet Cong. Bloodied and exhausted, and with his platoon safe from harm, he led his men, all of them alive and well, back to the large base camp.

The awards ceremony was held several months later in Washington, DC and was attended by President Johnson and his top military brass. Five Star General Edward Stanton said the following at the ceremony: "In a war, where the enemy is often unknown and the battle grounds are mostly undefined, there has always been one constant in this unconventional war. And that is, our enemy fears one thing more than death itself, and that one thing is the man standing next to me. Ladies and Gentlemen I give you a man among men and a soldier among soldiers, the unstoppable, courageous, Sergeant Ned Crane." The televised ceremony went coast to coast making good ole Uncle Ned a national hero—at least for a short while

But as time passed, the harrowing events of that war began to take their toll. Now 70 and still in excellent physical condition, Ned Crane lived alone in an abandoned church in an isolated woods just west of Ft. Wayne, Indiana. Over the years, he had become more and more reclusive. His home was now an armed camp. The old church and its sprawling grounds were surrounded on all sides by thick, barbed-wire fencing.

He also had four well-trained Rottweilers and a huge German Shepherd that roamed the perimeter barking at anything and everything that moved. No one in their right mind would get within a hundred yards of his place.

Inside, Uncle Ned maintained a huge cache of weapons, including several powerful AK-47's and M16's, along with assorted military handguns and bayonets for up close and personal combat. He had created several well-placed lookouts in the large building to give him a clear view of anyone coming or going from the premises. He had sensor operated spotlights placed strategically on the roof and in several of the large trees that surrounded the church. Anybody or anything moving at night would trigger the sensors making the grounds around the fortress bright as day. Alex felt certain that there wasn't a safer place on earth to send his beloved Nicky.

....

Nicky's mouth dropped open. "Uncle Ned's? No way!" She lifted a tissue from her pocket and dabbed her damp eyes.

Alex squeezed her a little tighter, "Listen honey, I know he's a little nutso, but he loves his family and he loves you."

"A little nutso is putting it mildly."

"Please honey."

Nicky shook her head, "I'm getting scared, Alex. First Josh and then Vito and now you're asking me to go live with your crazy Uncle Ned."

"Honey, I'm concerned that these tragedies weren't

random or accidental. I need to get you to a safe place until I can figure out exactly what is going on. Hopefully it will only be for a few days."

Nicky sighed deeply. "What about those dogs? They bark constantly."

"I know." Alex said softly.

Nicky's expression softened as she looked into the tortured eyes of her husband. "I understand honey, I know you're worried. I don't want to go, but I will." She smiled warmly, "Thanks for loving me so much."

Alex gave her a peck on the cheek. He turned and lifted his cell phone to dial Uncle Ned.

Nicky quickly spoke up, "Have you thought about what you're going to say to him? If he thinks the President is after you, he'll attack the White House with guns a-blazing."

"I know. I'm going to tell him that you and I have been threatened by extortionists and we need his help."

"Hmmm...good! Extortionists."

After several missed calls, Alex finally got through to Uncle Ned. Alex was hoping he would be able to help out. Protective by nature, he loved his family and would do anything to protect his "blood" as he liked to call them.

"Hi Uncle Ned, this is your nephew, Alex."

"Alex, so good to hear from you. How's everything?"

"Well, not the greatest. I have a favor to ask of you."

"Anything my boy, you know that."

"I have been threatened by extortionists and I need a safe place for Nicky to stay for a while. Can you help me out?"

"Why sure, you can bring Nicky out here. She'll be safe, I can assure you of that! Anybody that messes with

my blood, messes with old Ned!" he replied enthu-
siastically. "And you tell your lovely Nicky that I'm a
damned good cook on top of it. I ain't goin no where,
bring her out any time. She can stay as long as she likes."

"Thanks Uncle Ned, it may be yet today."

"That's fine."

"Good-bye Uncle Ned."

"Back at ya."

Alex never doubted his eccentric uncle's assessment;
he knew that Nicky would be fine with Uncle Ned. Alex
stuck his iPhone back in the case. "He's happy to have
you dear and he said the food's good. He said you can
come out right away."

"Oh well," she said wryly. "He talks a lot, so there's
never a dull moment."

"Better get packed dear. We need to get you over
there as soon as we can."

Chapter 42

Alex arrived back at the cottage after a longer than planned visit with his voluble Uncle Ned. When he entered the kitchen from the garage, the only sound he heard was the ticking of the old clock above the refrigerator. With Nicky safe, he could now begin to plan his strategy. But first, he had to call Louie Campano about the invitation to the lake he had extended to him earlier in the month. Alex punched in Louie's cell number and glanced over at the family room. Yellow bars of sunlight drifted through the window forming a pattern of squares on the opposing wall. The squares were even and orderly, *So different from my life right now,* he thought.

"Hello, Alex."

"Hi, Louie. How are you?"

"Good, thank you, and how are you doing?"

"Not so good. Listen Louie, it's about tomorrow. I'm afraid I have to cancel the invitation."

"I know, I heard about Vito a little while ago. Word spreads fast in the old neighborhood. You have more important things on your mind than my visit right now with Josh and now Vito."

"Thank you Louie, for being so understanding. It's

all so shocking. Vito was killed just a short distance from where I was target shooting this morning."

The phone suddenly went dead on the other end.

"Louie, are you still there?"

"Yes, sorry. Listen Alex, I think we need to talk in private—right away."

"What are you talking about?"

"I'll tell you when I talk to you."

Alex shook his head, "Okay, but I sure wish…"

Louie interrupted, "I'm sorry Alex, but I'm coming to the lake after all. I'll be there first thing in the morning, if it's okay."

"Yes, of course, Nicky's gone and…"

Louie's phone clicked off. Confused again, Alex fell back against the counter. He watched the thin black hand on the noisy clock jerk forward with each tick. Alex looked away from the clock at the family portrait above the fireplace. He stared lovingly at Nicky, Jarod, Missy and the kids. He walked to the family room, grabbed the remote and turned on the television. He dropped back in his recliner and turned the sound down low. It wasn't long before he was fast asleep.

Chapter 43

The coffee pot groaned, the inviting scent of fresh-brewed coffee drifted throughout the sun-filled kitchen. Alex paused when he heard the sound of a truck engine drifting through the open kitchen window. Louie had arrived. Alex hurried out back to greet him.

Louie's red truck jerked to a stop at the end of the long drive. He smiled at Alex and then struggled past the steering wheel and climbed out of the driver's side. He stepped forward, his big arms opened wide. He engulfed the fast approaching Alex in a giant bear hug.

"Good morning, Alex. How are you?" Louie muttered in the midst of several hard slaps to Alex's back.

"Fine, fine," Alex gurgled. "Come in, come in." Alex waved his arm toward the kitchen door inside the garage.

"You have such a beautiful place," Louie exclaimed as he followed Alex through the garage.

"Thank you."

Once inside the kitchen, Alex hustled over to the coffeemaker. "Coffee?"

"Yes, one Equal please."

"Coming right up." Alex dumped the sweetener in

Louie's coffee. He poured himself a cup and walked over to the kitchen table near where Louie was standing.

"Please, sit down."

"Thank you."

Alex set the cup of coffee in front of Louie and the two men sat down. The smile suddenly drained from Louie's face. He spoke calmly, "Alex, I am a man of few words, so I will get right to the point."

Alex nodded.

"I fear for your life, my friend. I fear for your life very much."

Alex's brow furrowed, "Please explain."

Louie took a sip of coffee. "When I first heard about Josh, I thought, what a tragedy. I was so angry at the thugs who jumped him in that alley. And then when I heard about Vito yesterday, I was stunned. But I still thought it was just a coincidence that two men that I knew well had been tragically killed just a day apart. I didn't put two and two together."

"Then?"

"Then, when you told me last evening that you have been target shooting right next to where Vito was killed, it all started to fall into place for me."

Alex leaned forward on the table. He looked puzzled.

"I know these men you're dealing with Alex. I have known them all my life. Some of them are friends of mine, some are not—but I know them. They are from a different world than you and I and they play by a different set of rules."

Alex sighed, "I'm starting to learn that."

Louie's brown eyes clouded over. "You have been like a brother to me Alex and I am very worried."

"About what, Louie? Please explain."

Louie exhaled slowly. "I have a good friend who is very high up in the mob in Chicago; he's the head of the Elmwood Park gang. The other day I was closing a loan for him in my office. Somehow, during our conversation, your name came up. I proceeded to tell him what a wonderful friend you have been to me and my friend's face turned white. He looked stunned. What I said had struck a cord with him. I was taken aback by his reaction."

Alex shrugged his shoulders, "Maybe he's met me or something."

"No, no. It was much stronger reaction than that. It was something very important to him, I could tell. I have thought about it a lot since then and I think I know what may have been bothering him."

"What do you think?"

"He and I are close, very close. I truly think that he had been asked by one of the big boys in the Moretti administration to arrange a hit on you—probably Ramsey. He knows my friend also. And, I'm sure my friend would try and oblige them—it's the Italian thing to do. But he is much closer with me than the others. We played high school football together and have stayed close over the years. So when I told him how much I thought of you and how much you had helped me, it sickened him. I truly believe that's what happened."

"But if that is true, why wasn't I shot?"

"I'm not sure, but I think Vito may have been in that game preserve to help the shooter, to give the him directions around the area or something. Then at some point, the hit man decided to kill Vito instead of you."

"But why?"

"Maybe they argued or maybe Vito didn't pay him. I don't know why, but I'm almost certain it happened that way. A lot of the mob guys don't like Vito. He was a low level guy in the syndicate for awhile and they think he's a weasel. It wouldn't take much for a mob guy to take out Vito. It makes sense to me."

"But he could have still shot me."

"Yes I know, but after shooting Vito, he may have been anxious to flee the area. I think you got lucky— very lucky."

Alex fell back in his chair and stared at Louie. The thought of his possible murder just the day before was upsetting. "I would have been a sitting duck at that shooting range. I would have never known what hit me."

"Thank God, something went wrong."

Alex shrugged, "Do you have any idea who the hit man may have been?"

"No, there are a hundred guys who would have done this for my mob pal. He's very persuasive. And you can be sure of one thing."

"What's that?"

"He would never divulge the shooter. He would die first."

Alex grimaced, "They'll be coming after me again. I'm sure they know by now that Vito was shot instead of me."

"You are up against a group of men who have un-limited resources at their disposal and I'm sure they're not happy right now."

"What can I do? I'm not going to roll over and let these people run over me or worse yet, kill me."

A wry grin broke out on Louie face. "I think I may

have the answer for you."

Alex looked puzzled.

Louie reached inside his jacket pocket and pulled out an envelope. He opened it and carefully spread several pictures on the table in front of Alex. "Recognize anyone?"

Alex studied the pictures, his eyes went wide. He glanced back at Louie. "That's Ben Ramsey and he appears to be snorting coke!"

Louie's brow lifted. "This was taken a little over a week ago at a party on Chicago's North Side. I have a standing invitation to a weekly party in a very trendy condo just off Rush Street. Many of Chicago's finest are in attendance at these parties, so it didn't surprise me when I ran into Ben Ramsey there that night. Later on, I was standing in a dark little corridor by the bathroom and I decided to click a few pictures with my cell; it's just a nervous habit of mine. I'm kind of shy and it gives me something to do. When I developed the pictures a few days later I was shocked. I had no idea that I had captured Ramsey in such a vulnerable situation. I was shocked and decided to destroy the photos to protect Ramsey. But for some reason—I'm not sure why—I decided at the last minute not to destroy them."

Alex shook his head. "Unbelievable! We have Moretti's Chief of Staff and right hand man snorting coke at a party. If the media gets ahold of this, it will explode like a time bomb!"

The big Italian's eyes narrowed, "Eddie Moretti's popularity has been slipping lately due to the economic crisis. A scandal this size, involving Ramsey, would kill his chances of ever being re-elected."

"Can I hold on to these photos?"

"They're all yours, Alex and here's the memory card." Louie handed him the small card. "I would suggest you make duplicate copies and put them and the card in a secure location—somewhere Ramsey and his gang would never suspect."

"I have an uncle who was a Green Beret in Nam. He lives way out in the country and his house is like an armed camp."

"Sounds like a good place."

"But what about you, Louie? Won't Ramsey suspect you? After all, he saw you at the party. I don't want to put you in any danger."

Louie grunted a couple of sarcastic chuckles. "Are you kidding? They think I'm stupid, a dufus. There's no way those guys would ever believe that a big dummy like me would understand how to take pictures with my cell phone. And besides, there were probably over a hundred people at that party and anyone of them could have taken these pictures."

Alex stood and walked over to warm his coffee. "You know, I just heard on television the other day that President Moretti is coming to Chicago next week for an international economic summit; over eighty countries will be there."

"I know, it's been all over the local media. Do you have Ramsey's cell number?" Louie queried.

"Yes, he gave it to me at our recent meeting. He wanted me to be able to reach him right away if I changed my mind on the TARP situation."

"Good, then I would suggest that you call him right away before he has a chance to send another assassin after you." Louie pushed back his chair and stood up. "I must be going back to Elmwood Park so I can attend the noon mass at Saint Celestine."

Alex turned. "How can I ever repay you?"

"You already have, Alex—a thousand times over. My job is everything to me and after the buyout, my head was on the chopping block, but you wouldn't let it happen. You stood up for me and saved my job. I'm forever in your debt. Bless you, mio amico."

The two men shared a quick embrace. Louie smiled warmly and hurried out the back door and though the garage to his truck. Alex watched him guide the old truck onto Vawter Park Road and slowly disappear.

Chapter 44

Clad only in his housecoat and slippers, Ben Ramsey pushed his arms to the sky and yawned mightily. The cool summer breeze felt good on his face on this Sunday morning as he walked down the stone pavers in front of his three story home in Arlington, Virginia. He paused at the end of the walk, leaned over and pulled the Washington Times out of the narrow cylinder. Ben liked living in Arlington. It was just over the Potomac from DC and close enough to the White House so he could be there in fifteen minutes, but far enough to give him and his wife the feeling of being outside the hustle and bustle of the nation's capitol.

He turned and walked back toward his house, pausing briefly to take a look at the front page. The main headline read: Economic Woes Continue for Administration. He frowned and then scanned the rest of the first page. His eyes froze on a smaller heading at the bottom right of the page. Second Indy business leader killed. "Hot damn, they got him," he murmured. He hurried to his front porch and sat down on the edge of a cast iron chair to read the rest of the article. He felt a vibration on his side and quickly slid his phone from the terrycloth pocket. The secure line to the President was flashing, he quickly answered.

"Good morning, Mr. President."

"Good morning, Ramsey."

"Well, we've got one problem out of the way."

"What are you talking about?"

"Crane's gone; I just read the headline in the *Times*."

"Read the article dummy, Crane has not been killed."

Ramsey quickly searched the article. "Oh my God!"

"Good job, Ramsey."

"Listen Ed, this is shocking to me. Vito's mob buddy said this hit man was one of the best."

"He must not be too good. He got the wrong man. This is devastating, Ben. We took a terrible chance here and got nothing."

Ben was shaking. "I just don't understand. I can't imagine what went wrong and how Vito got killed."

"The paper says it was an accident, but we both know better than that. I want you at the White House first thing in the morning so we can try and figure out what to do about this mess. I'm leaving for Chicago later in the morning, so don't be late." The phone went dead.

Ramsey fell back against the iron chair, his chest heaving. Shaken and disoriented, his phone rang again. He checked the unfamiliar number and answered. "Hello."

"Morning Ben, Alex Crane calling. Are you surprised?"

"S...surprised, why would I be surprised?"

"Cut the crap, Ramsey!" Alex wasn't a hundred percent certain he had been the target of a murder plot when he dialed Ramsey, but the nervousness in the top aide's voice took away any doubt. "We need to talk, Ben.

Now!"

"Listen Crane, you've got your nerve calling me at my home on Sunday. I have nothing to talk to you about."

"Oh, I think you do. It seems as though I came across some pictures of a man who looks exactly like you and he happens to be doing a little blow at a party on Rush Street."

"What are you talking about? I...I don't do blow, you're reaching here, Crane." Ramsey was beside himself; he stood and paced back and forth on the small porch, running his fingers through his hair.

"The pictures are very clear. There's no mistake about it—it's you!"

Ramsey slipped a handkerchief from his robe and wiped his brow. He felt weak and vulnerable. He knew he was taking an awful chance when he snorted coke at those parties. There would always be someone trying to make political hay off such a situation. His actions that night were reckless and foolish and now he was apparently going to pay for it. Crane had delivered him a couple of hard body blows. He felt he had to punch back. "You're bluffing, Crane; I want to see those pictures."

"Any time Ben, you name the place."

Ramsey was now certain that Crane had the pictures. He spoke almost inaudibly in response to Crane's open-ended invitation, "What do you want out of me, Crane?"

Smelling blood, Alex moved in for the kill. "Listen close, Ramsey. Here's what we are going to do. As you know, President Moretti is coming to Chicago this week for the economic summit and I want you to arrange a…"

. . . .

"Now here are the latest pickings from the Political Grapevine." It was the bottom of the six o'clock hour and Fox News Anchor, Bret Baier, was starting his daily segment on politics. He continued, "It seems as though President Moretti has decided, at the last moment, to take a break from the International Economic Summit in Chicago on Tuesday afternoon and enjoy a game of golf with an old friend, as he so aptly put it at a briefing this morning. The President will travel to nearby Indiana and play a round of golf with Alex Crane, the Chief Executive Officer of Midwest Consolidated Bank, the largest banking conglomerate in the Midwest. Crane, a political moderate, has donated to both parties over the years. No one is certain of the reason for the sudden change in plans, but as Moretti's top aide, Ben Ramsey, joked this morning, 'The President never passes up the chance for a game of golf.' This will be the thirty-first time the President has played golf in less than a year in office. President Bush by contrast, played twenty-four times in over eight years in office" Baier paused and shuffled some papers, "In other news…."

Chapter 45

It was almost noon on Tuesday and Alex was making final preparations for his outing with the President at 1 P.M. Strom Winslow had informed him, through an e-mail earlier that morning, that Josh's funeral would be on Wednesday in his hometown of South Bend and Vito's would be on Thursday in Elmwood Park, Illinois.

Monday had been a very busy day for Alex. He had called his secretary, Erica, early in the morning to tell her that he would be staying at the lake to attend Josh and Vito's funerals. Later in the morning, he had gone to the local CVS Drug Store to make duplicate copies of the Ramsey pictures. After leaving CVS, he made a stop at the local bank where he maintained a checking account and a small safety deposit box. Alex placed a set of the radio-active pictures in the secured box and then headed to Uncle Ned's to give him another copy of the pictures, along with the memory card, for safe keeping.

Upon arriving at Uncle Ned's, Alex was pleased to find that Nicky seemed to be tolerating her stay with his eccentric uncle very well. Ned reassured him that he was taking good care of Nicky and that he would hide the sealed envelope Alex had given him in a safe in his basement. The safe was in a small room hidden behind a fake cabinet. Then, with an AK47 dangling from his shoulder, he led Alex to the basement, showed him the safe and gave him a copy of the combination. Alex winced as he watched a big wad of chewing tobacco splash on the cement floor. "Ain't nobody ever gonna get near that envelope, I guarantee you that," Ned grunted as he swiped his shirtsleeve across his frothy mouth. Alex thanked his indelicate uncle, hurried upstairs and reassured Nicky he would come for her soon. Then he climbed into his SUV and drove the hour back to his lake home.

Tuesday morning, Alex received a final e-mail, followed by a reaffirming cell phone call at 9:00 A.M. from Hal Withers, an aide to the President. Withers instructed Alex that the President planned to arrive at South Shore Golf Course at approximately 12:15 P.M. that day. Then, after hitting a bucket of balls and chipping and putting for ten or fifteen minutes, he would be ready to tee off at 1:00 P.M. sharp. Withers indicated that the President would not have time for a luncheon and would eat something on the way there. He said the President was very much looking forward to this opportunity to spend a little time on the golf course and out in the fresh air. The lack of any mention of Alex's name during the entire planning process of the impromptu outing was telling. It was obvious to Alex that the President did not want to meet with him and resented the intrusion into his busy schedule. But the very fact that he was coming screamed at Alex that he had the most powerful man in the world back on his heels. He grinned a wry grin as he tossed his golf shoes and bag in the back of the Escalade and closed the hatch.

Chapter 46

The surroundings were almost surrealistic as Alex followed the Sheriff Deputy's car into the parking lot at nearby South Shore Golf Club. He was stunned by the total lack of activity around the popular course. The parking lot was empty except for several law enforcement vehicles: sheriff's cars, local city police cars, and several unmarked FBI vehicles. The local media in the resort area had been going crazy with this story for the past day and a half. The greater Lake Wawasee area was buzzing with excitement at the very thought of the charismatic President of the United States playing a round of golf right here in their backyard. But when the County Sheriff announced early Monday morning that the area for five miles around the golf course would be cordoned off, he meant business. Accept for an occasional official vehicle coming or going, even the always busy State Road 13, was dead quiet.

The Sheriff's Deputy led Alex to a predetermined parking spot near the clubhouse and signaled to Alex to pull in. Alex pulled in the spot as ordered, turned off his engine and just sat in his vehicle for a moment reflecting on what was about to happen. It was 12:10 and the President would be arriving in about five minutes. Never in his wildest dreams did Alex think he would ever be in a situation like this one. He was about to play a game of golf with the President of the United States alone, with only the Secret Service men there to guard the President. It was almost overwhelming; he wished Nicky were there to give him a hug or a word of encouragement. It was so difficult to face this awesome situation totally alone—no one to talk to, no one to bounce things off of. The President, on the other hand, would be surrounded by all of his usual support personnel and large security force. He would be in his element and confident. But Alex's life experiences had prepared him well for such a situation. Raised on a farm by a stern father, he was taught at an early age to be tough and independent. He knew what he had to do today and he would do it. He didn't doubt that.

Alex was shaken from his thoughts by a tap on the driver's side window. He turned to see one of his golfing buddies smiling through the window. It was Hank Zimmerman, a Colonel at the nearby State Police Post. He had evidently been assigned as security for the big event. It made Alex feel good to see a familiar face. He quickly got out of the car and shook hands aggressively with his old friend.

"You ready for this, buddy?" Hank barked.

"I guess so."

"I hear Moretti's a pretty good stick. He's gonna kick your butt."

Alex laughed. He loved hearing the friendly jostling from Hank. It made him feel normal, if only for a moment. "That could be," he replied.

"Don't give him any shots, okay?"

"Okay."

"Well, I'd better go. It looks like the big guy is here." Hank nodded at the long procession of black vehicles moving south on State Road 13. Alex watched as they started to filter into the mostly vacant parking lot at South Shore. Hank gave him a high five and hurried away.

Alex walked calmly to the back of his vehicle and opened the rear hatch while still watching the vehicles navigate their way into the parking lot. It was, indeed, an impressive sight. Suddenly, a long black limo appeared and pulled to a stop near Alex. He watched with rapt attention, waiting for the President to step out of the impressive limo at any moment and greet him. Alex lifted his bag out of his trunk and stood watching, but still, the President didn't appear. After what seemed an eternity, the limo pulled away and a nondescript black security vehicle pulled forward. The back door swung open and a smiling Ed Moretti jumped out and pushed his hand toward Alex.

"You must be Alex. Hello, I'm Ed Moretti."

"Why…uh hello Mr. President; how nice to meet you." The two shared a quick handshake. Alex thought he was much taller in person than he appeared on television and there was an aura about him—he exuded charm and charisma.

"It's Ed, please call me Ed."

"Okay, Ed."

While the two were sharing their greeting, another man got out of the car on the far side and hurried around to greet Alex.

"Hello Alex, I'm Hal Withers. We've talked a few times over the past couple of days." He smiled and extended his hand and the two men shook.

"Nice to meet you, Hal." Alex turned toward the President. "I was expecting you to be in that big limo."

The President chuckled, "Can't be too careful these days. We do things like this quite often." He leaned down, looked in at the driver and raised his thumb in the air. The trunk flipped open and the President walked behind the car to change his shoes.

Withers quickly took over. "The President is going to the range. He likes to hit balls for awhile and then practice his chipping and putting. And he likes to practice alone." The aide paused, as if gathering himself. "And, as you requested, the two of you will be riding in an electric cart, no caddies. And he wants you to drive since he doesn't know the course."

Accustomed to calling all the shots, the deference to Alex's request for a cart seemed difficult for the arrogant aide to spit out. The President preferred a caddy, but Alex wanted them alone with no one else around. "The President will see you on the first tee at 1:00 sharp."

"That's fine, Mr. Withers. I will do a little putting and then go to the range when the President is finished."

Alex was stunned by the brevity of the exchange. The media had reported that the President was having "a golf game with an old friend". *What a joke!* he thought. The cold shoulder by the President was numbing, but in a way, it was appropriate. This was a difficult situation for the President. This was no time for unnecessary niceties.

"See you at one." Withers smiled.

Alex forced a grin and nodded. He lifted his bag and headed for the practice green for some chipping and putting.

When Alex arrived at the vacant putting green, he glanced back at the parking lot. The President was leaning on his bag and surrounded by members of the traveling media group who had just arrived. They were pushing and shoving one another, trying to get closer to the President. Alex almost felt a little sympathy for the man. A few seconds later, John, the course owner, pulled up in golf cart and strapped the Chief Executive's bag on the back. The President jumped aboard. The owner gunned the cart and headed for the practice range, much to the dismay of a long-faced press corps. Three carts full of Secret Service were in close pursuit, with each man scanning the nearby landscape looking for potential problems.

. . . .

Alex left the practice range and arrived at the first tee a little before 1:00. It was a hot, muggy August day with the temperature nearing 90. The course owner had provided the golfers with his fancy Club Cart for the occasion. Alex locked the foot brake and stepped out of the cart. He lifted a handkerchief from his pocket and wiped his forehead dry and squinted into the bright sun. The President was near the clubhouse talking with reporters one last time before he teed off.

At Alex's request, there would be no reporters near the men while they were golfing. The President excused himself from the pesky reporters and walked briskly toward the first tee. Withers hurried ahead of him and strapped his large bag, embossed on the back with a large American Flag, on Alex's cart. The President arrived shortly thereafter. Withers nodded and hurried back toward the clubhouse.

Several tall, athletic looking young men wearing gray slacks and white golf shirts surrounded the first tee. They were close enough to protect their leader, but far enough away so the Alex and the President could talk privately.

"Looks like we've got a hot one on our hands, Crane." The two men once again exchanged a quick handshake.

"Typical August weather in Indiana," Alex mused.

The President wasted no time in taking his driver from the bag and strolling over to the first tee for a few practice swings. It was as if he couldn't wait to get this round of golf over.

"I hear you're a good stick," he quipped without ever looking directly at Alex.

"Looks like somebody's been spreading lies again." Alex couldn't help but be impressed by the athletic looking, handsome man on the tee. His practice swings were smooth and powerful. He was obviously an accomplished golfer.

"You're no poor boy, Crane. How about $50.00 a hole and double for birds?" For the first time, the President gave Alex a quick stare—like a hustler on the move.

"Sounds good." Alex was surprised that the President, who was obviously aware of the circumstances of this situation, would throw a wager in the middle of things. It seemed out of place to Alex.

The President strolled to the front of the tee, bent over and teed up his ball. He took his stance and after a couple of quick wiggles, his body went still. He lifted the club slowly and took a hard swing at the ball. The metal-headed driver blasted into the little white ball. The ball carried high and long down the fairway and landed in the left rough just thirty yards away from the green on the three hundred yard hole.

"Nice drive, Mr. President."

"Thank you, Crane," The President laughed nervously, "Thought I might reach it in one. It's a little longer than it looks."

"Yes, I think it is." Alex approached the first tee, bent down and teed his ball up. He took his stance and knocked the ball right down the middle, just twenty yards from the green."

"Impressive drive, Crane, I better keep my checkbook handy." The President dropped his driver in his bag and climbed on the cart, crossing his legs and leaning away from Alex. The body language was telling.

Alex stuffed his driver in the bag, hopped aboard and accelerated away from the tee. He wasted no time getting down to business.

"I hope you don't mind the cart. Caddies have to stand very close to the golfer. I thought we needed some privacy."

Moretti replied coolly, "No problem, a cart is fine."

Alex stopped the cart midway between the two balls. The President's demeanor seemed to be getting more and more agitated. He got out of the cart, snatched his pitching wedge from his bag and walked over to his ball. He took his stance and knocked the ball on the green some twenty feet from the hole.

As he walked back toward the cart, he spoke to Alex. "You've made some serious allegations, Crane. This is the big leagues; I hope you know what you're doing."

Alex's eyes narrowed, "Two men are dead, Moretti, I

think I understand the gravity of the situation here in the big leagues." Alex knocked his ball a foot from the hole for a tap-in birdie. The President two putted for a par.

Both men climbed aboard the cart and headed for the second tee. The tension in the cart was growing. Upon arriving at the tee, President Moretti called one of the muscular Secret Service men over to talk to him. It was the one Alex had seen him huddle with several times before. He was probably telling him to keep the men at a distance, fearing that the men might hear something they shouldn't about their wonderful boss. Then the President grabbed his driver from the bag and approached the tee. Not having honors, he stopped and waited on Alex with his hands draped over the top of this driver. Alex lifted his driver from the bag and approached the tee. He paused just a few feet from the President. "After we hit, I have some pictures I want to show you."

Alex drove his ball straight down the fairway and very long. The President wiped his brow quickly with his handkerchief. Alex knew that Ramsey had undoubtedly told him about the pictures, but the mention of the photos seemed to unnerve him. The President took his stance and hit a bouncing shot about a hundred yards off the tee. "Damn!" he muttered.

Both men returned to the cart. Alex reached in his front pocket and pulled out an envelope. He slowly opened it and took out several pictures and handed them to the Chief Executive.

A scowling Moretti reluctantly took the pictures from Alex. His expression soon changed; his eyes twitched as he examined the damning pictures of his most trusted aide, Ben Ramsey, surrounded by beautiful women, snorting cocaine in a lavishly decorated room. Now fully appreciating the gravity of the situation, his face broke into a big smile. He patted Alex on the back and pointed at the pictures as if they were snapshots of Alex's grandson at a little league game. Then he quickly stacked the pictures back together to protect them from being seen by one of the Secret Service agents nearby and handed them back to Alex, who quickly stuffed them back in his pant pocket.

Still smiling broadly, the shaken President spoke quietly, "What's your game, Crane?"

Emboldened by the pictures, a confident Alex pushed down on the pedal and pulled steadily away from the tee. The Secret Service agents hustled to keep up while staying a safe distance. Alex felt anxious, but it was also intoxicating to have the most powerful man in the universe in the palm of his hand.

He spoke calmly to the Chief Executive, "Listen closely, Mr. President. I want to assure you that I have copies of these photos secured in several locations. If anything happens to me, any member of my family or any of my close associates, or if I ever see any of your goons anywhere near my family or friends again, I have instructed the holders of the photos to deliver them immediately to the national media. I have given them the phone numbers and contacts in the media they will need. Also…."

The President quietly interrupted, "Do any of them know the contents of the pictures?"

"No, absolutely not. They are in sealed containers and I have asked them not to open them and I'm sure they will not. These are people I would trust with my life."

The President seemed satisfied, so Alex went on. "I want you to make Barnes O'Brien the new Ambassador to Ireland immediately. I want him out of my organization as soon as possible and that's the best way to do it."

Moretti nodded in the affirmative. "I'll appoint him later this week."

Alex pulled the cart to a stop next to the President's ball. The shaken leader grabbed his fairway wood and quickly topped the ball down the fairway. He climbed back in the cart.

"And, I want absolutely no more communications from your administration in regard to my policy on repayment of the TARP monies."

Once again the President nodded.

Alex took a deep breath and continued. "The rest of the money that your operatives have embezzled from my branch office in Elmwood Park must be paid back in full—every single dime. Right now there is still approximately thirty million dollars owing."

There was a slight hesitation and then a quick nod from the President. This didn't surprise Alex—he wasn't sure if the President even knew of the embezzlement, but the President could inquire about it and find out soon enough. The money may be paid back anyway, but Alex wanted to make sure every dime of it was repaid. By challenging the President, he was sure that it would be.

Alex drove on. The cart bounced along the bumpy ground in the rough and back onto the much smoother fairway. He stopped next to his ball, jumped out and selected a club. He took his stance and knocked the ball on the green. He climbed back in the cart and peered sideways at the President. The usually jovial Chief Executive appeared solemn and stoic.

Alex went on, "In return for the above, I will promise to never release the contents of the photos or the findings of the audit conducted by Josh Dulin at our Chicago office just before his untimely murder late last week. Josh and I are the only two people on earth who knew of that audit."

The cart jerked to a stop next to the President's ball. He got out of the cart and stood still for a moment; his long face staring at Alex. "You're one tough SOB, Crane. I underestimated you."

Alex spoke softly, "I don't feel so tough right now, Mr. President. I feel I'm giving up more than I'm getting. But I'm smart enough to know that I could never win in a fight with the most powerful man in the world. You're lucky, Mr. President, very lucky. If I were single and alone in this world, I would have destroyed you."

Moretti smiled. "Of that I'm certain, Mr. Crane." The President paused. "There's one more thing. I truly hope you don't think that I had anything to do with the death of your friend, Josh Dulin. I knew nothing of that embezzlement scheme until just now."

"I guess that's something I'll never know for sure, Mr. President."

The President paused, staring directly at Alex. After what seemed an eternity, he finally spoke, "How about some golf?" he smiled wryly.

"I believe you're a hundred down."

The corner of Ed Moretti's eyes turned up at the friendly comment. "I know," he replied. "Let's double the bet."

"Double it is, Mr. President."

Chapter 47

Two Months Later

The waitress laid down a coaster and then set a glass of Riesling on the table next to Nicky.

"I love this place Alex; we should come here more often."

"I know," a smiling Alex replied.

Nicky poked him playfully on his arm. "What's with you? You've had that smile plastered on your face all day."

"I guess I'm just happy, that's all. We've been through so much over the past few months. This little getaway is just what the doctor ordered."

"It's good practice for you with your retirement starting first of the year. You have to start learning how to have some fun."

"I know."

"Do you think Louie will make a good president?" Nicky asked.

"Yes, I think the board made a wonderful choice."

She grinned slyly. "The board?"

"Well, I did have some input, I guess."

Nicky beamed. She loved Louie. "It wouldn't have

happened if Barnes was still on the board."

Alex shook his head. "That's for sure. We have a good board now."

Not wanting to dwell on the negative, Alex quickly changed the subject away from his nemesis Barnes. "You know, I reviewed Louie's college transcripts during the interviewing process and his I.Q. is 132."

"You're kidding! Not good ole Louie?"

"Yeah, I knew he was a really a smart guy. But he's still just Louie, if you know what I mean."

"Yes, I do." She scooted up in her chair and laid her hand on her purse. "Want to circulate for awhile?"

"Sounds good."

"Can I take my wine with me?"

"Why not?"

. . . .

"Pardon me dealer, but I've been meaning to ask about your white carnation. What's the special occasion?"

"My girl and I just got married; her name's Trudy."

"And you're working on your wedding day?"

"Yeah, I took a shift for a sick friend. We'll be leaving on our honeymoon as soon as I get off work. We're going to Niagara Falls." The friendly dealer stared at Alex for a second. "You come here often?"

"I've been here once or twice with my golfing buddies."

"I thought so," Gus grinned. "Your face looked a little familiar."

He flipped over a card. "Pay eighteen."

Alex lifted his whole card and then tossed it on the

table. "Seventeen!" he said shaking his head.

"Twenty!" a nearby player announced.

The dealer immediately shoved a stack of chips in front of the happy winner. After paying the winner, he dragged the dead cards from around the table and prepared for the next deal. A pretty young lady in a white taffeta dress with dark curly hair and rosy cheeks casually pushed in next to him. He gave her a quick peck on the cheek. He looked at her with pride, "This is my daughter, Darcy everybody. I just got married today and my daughter has come home to stay. I'm a lucky guy."

Alex joined a chorus of congratulations from the other players. A few seconds later he felt Nicky squeeze in next to him. "I'm hungry and I hear they've got a pretty good restaurant here on the boat. Ready for dinner?"

"Sure." A card bounced in front of the player next to Alex. "Deal me out," he said quickly to the dealer.

"Will do, mister. Pleasure talking to you."

"Likewise."

Alex collected his remaining chips, turned and extended his arm to Nicky. The two walked arm in arm toward the restaurant by the front entrance.

"The blackjack dealer just got married."

"He looked like such a sweet man."

"The young lady next to him was his daughter. She just moved back to town."

"She's pretty."

"Not as pretty as you, my dear."

Nicky laid her head on her husband's shoulder, "Flattery will get you everywhere."

Alex glanced at his wife's slightly squinted, empathetic eyes—there was a tired, pained look in them. He knew the past several months had been overwhelming for his sensitive mate. Not a complainer, he knew it must have been terribly difficult for her with mysterious men following them around, late night phone calls, and the tragic deaths of two men she knew well. He wanted to make this a fun and special night for her.

"You deserve all the flattery I can give you, my lovely. And if you don't object, I would like to invite you to my room after dinner; I'm in 236 at the Holiday Plaza."

Nicky faked a blush and replied coyly. "Why, how could I? We've just met."

Alex paused and turned toward his wife, his hands gently caressing her shoulders. "That's true, but in the short time we've been together, I've grown to love you more than anything in the world. It's as though we've been together all of our lives."

"Well, if we had been together all of our lives, Mr. Crane," her voice began to break up and she spoke softly, "I would consider myself the luckiest girl in the world." Her eyes clouded over, her hands slid gently around his waist. She pulled him close and whispered, "I've been so worried about you, Alex. Why if something would have happened to you, I don't know what I would have done."

Alex smiled at his tearful wife. "Is that a yes, my dear?"

Nicky collected herself and poked around in her purse. She lifted out a small computer card. "Why isn't this something, I'm in Room 236 at the Holiday Plaza also."

"Let's get room ser...." They replied in unison. Neither of them finished the quick retort. They laughed as they stood facing one another—two sets of loving eyes scanning the other's face and saying I love you over and over again without ever speaking a word. For the first time, in as long as he could remember, Alex felt a tear roll down his cheek. He smiled as he wiped the tear away and kissed his wife tenderly on the forehead. After a warm hug, the two lovers hurried, hand in hand, from the noisy boat to the parking lot and then to their car for their short drive to the Holiday Plaza Motel.

About the Author

R B Conroy resides in Leesburg, Indiana with his wife Cheryl. A native Hoosier, R B takes a page from his third book and once again writes about his home state in his most recent effort *Deadly Game*. This fast-paced thriller begins in Indianapolis and ends with an unforgettable scene near the shores of beautiful Lake Wawasee in northern Indiana. As we speak, Conroy is hard at work on his next project.

R B Conroy's other novels are:

Devil Rising

Return of the Gun

In My Father's Image

They are available from:

Amazon.com
and
Barnes & Noble

LaVergne, TN USA
28 February 2011
218151LV00001B/18/P